BRICK

COOPER CONSTRUCTION SERIES
BOOK 1

By Jen Davis

BRICK

Limitless Publishing, LLC
Kailua, HI 96734
www.limitlesspublishing.com

Formatting: Limitless Publishing

ISBN-13: 978-1-64034-520-1
ISBN-10: 1-64034-520-5

Dedication

David, Catie, Michael, and Mom: Your love and support mean everything. I am so blessed to have you all in my life.

CHAPTER ONE

Brick

Brick slammed his fist into the side of Pete's head, knocking the sniveling junkie into a heap on the floor.

"I'll get the money for you. I swear. Please, God." Pete climbed to his knees, his dark hands laced together like he was praying. But prayer couldn't help him now. Brick had a job to do.

With an unforgiving backhand, he laid Pete flat. The guy lay, unmoving, on the filthy carpet of his cheap-ass apartment, surrounded by cigarette butts, empty beer cans, and the carcass of a giant cockroach.

They always thought if they could fake unconsciousness, the beating would stop. They were wrong.

"Get up." He sounded bored. "If I have to come down there, it's going to get worse for you." He didn't have to try to be intimidating anymore. Being a big motherfucker had its perks. No one wanted to fight a guy over six feet tall, carrying the kind of muscles you'd see on a pro-wrestler. Even worse for the punks who got in his way, he'd lost his soul a lifetime ago.

He wouldn't think twice about crushing Pete's body or spirit. He wouldn't kill him—not yet, not while the piece of shit owed Sucre money—but he'd make him wish he were dead. The years Brick spent cultivating his status as a legend in this neighborhood guaranteed one thing: everyone knew if he paid you a visit, there was no escape from the punishment you were due.

"I'm getting up, man." Pete groaned as he climbed to his feet, clutching his head.

He delivered a hard punch to the guy's stomach. Pete's breath left his body with a pained exhale.

"The money was due yesterday, Pete." A powerful right hook followed next. Blood dribbled from the corner of the gaunt man's mouth. And now he was crying, for fuck's sake.

"I'll do anything, Brick," Pete blubbered. "You want a blow job? I'll suck your dick, man."

He wrinkled his nose. This was always the worst part.

Panic flaring in his eyes, Pete held out his hands. "No. No. You want a girl? Yeah, you do. I've got a daughter. She—"

His fist shut down the offer more effectively than words ever could. He welcomed the sting in his knuckles as he knocked out a couple of the guy's teeth in the process. Pete clawed at his own neck, wheezing as he choked.

The little girl with light brown skin and braids,

whom Pete had shoved into the bathroom when he got here, couldn't have been more than ten years old. Sick bastard.

He didn't hurt kids. Ever. It was the only line he refused to cross. Nobody knew it, and they never would. The second he revealed a weakness for anything, someone would use it against him. He learned that lesson the hard way. It paid not to care about much of anything—or anyone—which wasn't too hard, since nobody gave a shit about him, either.

The unmistakable scent of piss wafted to his nose, though it was a miracle he could smell anything over the stench of rotting garbage overflowing from the can near the kitchen sink. At least Pete hadn't shit himself.

"You'll deliver Sucre's money tomorrow. With interest. Or I'm going to have to come back here." He wrapped his hand around Pete's jaw and squeezed. "You don't want me to come back here."

Pete shook his head, but he only moved a fraction of an inch in the vise of Brick's fingers.

Satisfied he'd made his point, he dropped Pete to the floor and turned his back on the pathetic excuse for a man left crying in a soggy heap. Despite his warning, he knew how all of this would end. Pete didn't have the money today, and he wouldn't have it tomorrow.

So, Brick would return in less than twenty-four hours to do this all again. Tomorrow it would be worse. Tomorrow, he'd leave Pete nursing broken bones. The next night, he'd leave Pete dead on the floor. There would be no deals, no pardons. None of Pete's prayers would make a difference. God didn't listen to prayers in this neighborhood, and even if He did, the Savior himself couldn't stop what Pete had coming to him.

The smell outside the tenement apartment wasn't much better than inside. It still stank of piss, although it was fainter and cut with the heartier scents coming from the dumpsters, and a whiff of marijuana. In one deep breath, anyone could pick up the stench of his world.

A dozen guys stood on the blacktop between the buildings, most of them smoking or shooting the shit. One ran a dark cloth over his Glock, as though he expected to see his reflection in the damn thing. But he shoved his weapon into the waistband of his jeans when he saw Brick coming.

The crowd parted as he made his way to his second-hand half-ton Chevy pick-up truck.

The reason you build a hard-core reputation is for moments like this. Where everyone's eyes turn away as you walk past. Where no one dares lift a hand against you because they know you would cut it off.

Even the scariest fuckers kept their distance. Because he was the thing that went bump in the night.

He held his stony expression as he cranked the engine and drove to his apartment. He rarely had to fake the Boogeyman routine these days…except when it involved kids. This life had scooped out whatever humanity he'd been born with a long time ago.

Still, he sighed when he made it inside his apartment and locked the door. His little one-bedroom wasn't much bigger than Pete's place, but it was clean. And it was his.

Nothing about the apartment made it special. A drab, grey paint shadowed the walls, barely a shade darker than the low-grade, bristly carpet. Threadbare fabric covered the couch cushions—green—or it had been, before age leeched all the color away years ago. The sofa could seat two, but he wasn't even sure why he had it. He always sat in the recliner when he was home, and he didn't invite company. Home was the only place he could relax his guard, or at least stop looking over his shoulder.

No photos. No decorations. Nothing anyone could use to get to know him or use against him. He didn't even own a TV. The only nods to the life he once had hid beneath the false bottom of a drawer in his nightstand. Even if someone ever found the broken toy race car, they wouldn't know why it mattered to him—he wasn't sure himself. The picture of him with his grandmother couldn't cause trouble, either. Sucre worked tirelessly, exploiting that weakness for all it was worth. But he kept them hidden. The last tiny vestiges of his humanity.

Bone tired, he shuffled to the bathroom to wash his hands and face. As he dried his skin with a hand towel, frayed and ragged from years of use, he avoided the mirror over the sink.

He didn't need his reflection to tell him what an ugly bastard he was. *A face only a mother could love.*

Too bad his mother was dead. His father too. Sucre had seen to it. And now he worked for the son-of-a-bitch loan shark and drug dealer who ran

Atlanta's underbelly. He was the number one enforcer in a stable of muscle growing larger and more brutal every day.

He used to dream of getting out, but he didn't dream anymore. All dreaming ever did was leave you hurt and disappointed. He bashed heads, he earned his money, and he squirreled it away so one day he'd have enough to move his grandmother far out of Sucre's reach. Then, his very last known weakness would be off the table, and God have mercy on any man who tried to control him again.

Because Brick would have none.

***

Liv

Liv shivered against the chill seeping into her bones as she surveyed the packed interior of the plane. About two dozen people lined the edges, their gear strapped on, ready as they'd ever be to jump into the great beyond.

The guy across from her, a ginger, probably in his thirties, gripped his crossed arms so tightly, he had to be hurting himself. She wasn't sure if seeing her own fear reflected in another person's face made things better or worse. The guy's Adam's apple bobbed as he swallowed, and the decidedly undignified squeak he made answered her question.

It was worse. Definitely worse.

Unsticking her dry tongue from the roof of her mouth, she forced a deep breath and pushed her gaze away from Mr. Squeaky. The expression on the forty-something African American woman beside him told a very different story. Her brown eyes gleamed with anticipation, but otherwise, her face looked as serene as a summer's day. Then she winked.

"You look like you're about to puke, kiddo." Carol nudged her with her foot. "You've got to stop thinking so hard. You're borrowing trouble. Live in the moment."

Sage advice from a woman who knew better than most how to live for the now. Carol was her best friend, her rock. And the reason she stood ten thousand feet off the ground, strapped to a stranger, and putting her life in his hands. Liv only knew two things about her jump-partner: his name was Louie, and he said he'd been jumping out of planes almost every day for the past eight years. Either Louie was completely certifiable or proof skydiving wasn't as suicidal as her hindbrain insisted.

Or maybe it was a bit of both.

Louie's barrel chest rumbled behind her with a whoop she felt more than heard as the door opened. He'd warned her before they took off how loud it would be, but the words couldn't have prepared her. The wind roared like the gates of hell had opened wide.

Still, Carol's smile never wavered.

Not even as she and her partner moved toward the exit. Not even as she stepped out into the nothing and disappeared from sight.

Carol could do anything.

She'd survived breast cancer, not once, but twice. Her wisdom, her laughter, and her generosity of spirit kept Liv sane through her own battle with the Big-C. Through every chemo session. Through every moment of pain, of nausea, of despair, Carol was there, showing her it wasn't enough just to survive. They both deserved to live.

This jump celebrated their victory. The golden ticket. Remission.

No more days and nights kneeling in front of the toilet, heaving, even when she had nothing left to throw up. No more losing the thick blonde hair that reminded her of her mom. And no more weakness.

Liv was strong now, or at least getting there, and she was done playing it safe. What good had it ever done her? Every choice she'd ever made for her life, she'd based on what she thought she was supposed to do, and when the possibility of death came calling, she had virtually nothing to show for it. Her boyfriend dumped her, she had no friends to turn to, and she'd never really *done* anything.

If she wanted a different kind of future, she had to leave the mistakes of her past behind. So what if she didn't know how? Fear had no place in this new reality. And if she couldn't trust herself to make the kind of choices to change her life, at least now she had a friend who could push her in the right direction.

Carol's face flashed before her eyes as Louie prodded her toward the open door.

Live for the moment.

The sky in front of her beckoned clear and blue and stretched out into forever.

She took a deep breath, stepped out of the plane, and flew.

CHAPTER TWO

Brick

The lukewarm spray of the shower did shit to ease the tightness in Brick's shoulders, but it served well enough to help the soap erase the grime of the city from his skin. He washed his body in quick, efficient movements, then used the bar of Dial to lather the top of his head. He kept his dark hair too short to bother with shampoo. Hair long enough for someone to grab created a liability.

His internal clock warned him to move faster. Xander expected the crew at the site by six-thirty, and the foreman was one of the few people in this world he didn't want to disappoint. They weren't tight or anything, but the man gave him a chance to be something other than a thug every day.

It felt good to build something rather than destroy it.

He threw on clothes, then made a final check of his tiny apartment. Windows, secure. Hidden weapons, in place. Money? Nestled safely in the fat, hollow legs of his coffee table.

No one he knew would have the balls to break into his home, but he didn't take any chances. Only a few more thousand dollars and he'd finally have enough to get out of Sucre's trap.

He pulled up to the site next to a Cooper Construction pickup with minutes to spare. Their latest gig had them building a three-bedroom house in the suburbs.

It was the closest he would ever get to a place like this, but it didn't matter. One day, a family would live here. Kids would make happy memories and shit, and he'd have something to do with it. It was good work. Clean work. And on this job, he could pretend to be a regular guy instead of the bone-crusher who made crackheads like Pete piss their pants. No one seemed scared of him here. A welcome change from the other side of his life.

"Brick."

Xander's assistant, Robby, wasn't even cautious around him. On the street, a skinny guy like him would be running away from Brick, not toward him. The kid looked downright happy to see him when he stepped up with his clipboard in his hand.

"Did you hear? The house we wrapped up in Dunwoody last month is going to be a model home. I knew the place looked amazing. You guys did some great work. I was just telling Xander—"

Robby prattled on, barely taking a breath. How he'd become the assistant's favorite person to gossip with, he'd never fucking know.

"—you know what I mean?"

He really didn't, but he nodded anyway. "Who

am I working with today, kid?"

Robby startled a little at his voice before glancing down at his clipboard. "You're with Kane and Will."

He checked over his shoulder and saw both the guys in question already headed his way. When he looked back, the tips of Robby's ears and his cheeks were turning pink. He followed the assistant's gaze to Matt and Cyrus, the last two members of the five-man crew, strapping on their hardhats and tool belts near the curb.

Robby averted his eyes back to the papers on his clipboard. "I'm, uh, going to go give Xander a call and let him know you guys are getting underway." The kid almost tripped over his feet, scrambling to get away.

Weird.

Brick tilted his head at the men on his team, and they followed him toward the area where they'd be working. Kane was the closest thing he had to a friend on the crew. Hell, anywhere, come to think of it. They were both big men used to others giving them a wide berth. The dude might have been part of a local biker gang, but he had never asked. The same way Kane never asked him about what he did for Sucre. Both predators respected each other's strength without feeling the need to make a challenge.

Will, well, he would fit right in with those All-American football types the girls loved. He'd only joined the crew recently, but he seemed all right for someone who looked like he hung out at the mall. He got the job done; nothing else mattered.

They worked in a steady rhythm, assembling the floor frame quickly. Kane and Will didn't waste time running their mouths. They had all the horizontal supports in by lunchtime. The two other men on the crew hefted over the lumber.

A breeze ruffled the plans Robby had left rolled up on the ground, but it didn't give any relief from the midday heat and humidity. Even though it wasn't quite summertime yet, the Georgia sun could already fry an egg on the sidewalk.

His phone pinged, and as he swiped into the text, a photo of his grandma filled the screen. She slept in her bed at the nursing home, her thin frame draped with a white sheet.

He fought the urge to growl against the near-daily reminder of Sucre's hold over him.

At least she's safe.

Forcing a measured breath, he returned the phone to his back pocket. Less than a minute later, Robby called everyone outside for pizza.

The guys trudged toward the food, their shoulders hunched from bending over for the last five hours. A couple of them walked on the plywood stretched between the slab and the side of the street, but most tromped through the overturned dirt where crews had laid the sewer lines a few days ago.

One by one, each man grabbed a couple of slices before fanning out for a few minutes' R&R. As Brick chomped down on a slice of pepperoni, an unfamiliar car pulled up to the curb.

He watched intently as a petite woman climbed out of the driver's seat, then he sucked in a breath.

Pretty girls were a dime a dozen, but there was something special about this one. He tried to drink in everything about her at once, from her fair skin, to the freckles on the bridge of her nose, to the golden hair draped over her shoulders. Her light eyes sparkled, and a smile lit her face. With her pristine white sundress and strappy sandals, she looked like a goddamned angel, as out of place at the dirty work site as he would be sitting in a church.

Somebody on the crew was a lucky bastard.

The girl made her way straight to Will. She kissed his cheek before handing him the giant cookie cake she'd carried over from the car.

"Happy birthday, big brother." She grinned.

His breath sped up when he realized this wasn't Will's girl. Maybe he should've known better, but it's not as though he was tight enough with anyone here to recognize their families.

He moved closer to them without meaning to. Now only six feet away, he could tell her eyes were more blue than green; her teeth were straight and shiny, and he could pick up the faint scent of vanilla over the sawdust in the air.

Will shook his head as he admired the cake. "You didn't have to do this, Liv. Aren't you supposed to be at work? Who's watching your class?"

She laughed, a light, tinkling sound, like the princess in a cartoon he saw when he was a kid. "My students are at lunch. Don't worry. I'm not here to cramp your style." She pinched his cheek. "Well, I don't mind cramping it a little. But mostly,

I wanted to invite your buddies out here to come have a drink Friday night to help celebrate your birthday."

Her gaze passed over the guys in the crew. "Y'all hear?" As if they all hadn't been staring at her since she'd stepped out of her car. "Friday night. Seven o'clock at Moe's. First round is on me. If you need some extra motivation, I might be able to dig up some adorable photos of Baby Will in the bathtub."

Kane chuckled. "Make it a picture of *you* in the bathtub and you've got yourself a deal."

Brick elbowed the smart-ass in the stomach.

"Shut the fuck up, man." Will growled. "You're talking shit about my sister."

The woman didn't seem upset, though. She wasn't even looking at Kane.

Her gaze locked squarely on *him*, and he stood frozen under the weight of those baby blues. He didn't even breathe.

But for a second, neither did she.

At least, that's what his overactive imagination said.

He dragged in a breath of air, and in a flash, the spell was broken.

She gave him her back as she kissed Will's scruffy cheek again. "Oh, hush. Don't get mad at your friend. He probably hasn't seen a naked woman in years." Grinning, she winked at Kane, who had the decency to take his lumps in silence. "Friday at seven. Don't be late."

With one last wave, Will's sister made her way to her little Toyota. Though he had no idea why, he couldn't resist watching her every move, until she disappeared.

Friday night.

For the first time in God knows how long, he had something to look forward to.

***

Liv

Liv slipped back into her classroom moments before the bell rang, and kids poured in behind her. Desks were packed closely together in the small room. The school had been around since the 1950s, and the evidence surrounded her, from the green linoleum floor to the metal doors and the sagging ceiling. The window unit air conditioner hummed loudly as it struggled to cool the stifling space.

Most of her students made it clear they considered her English class a necessary evil they had to endure to graduate, but a special few—like the one approaching her now—showed they appreciated the power of language and the nuances of the written word.

Devon flashed her a toothy smile as he took his seat in the second row, next to his best friend, Justin. "Nice hair, Miss T."

She ran her palm over the new extensions, the weight unfamiliar after so long without it. Dipping her head, she acknowledged the compliment.

"Are we gonna watch the movie today or what?"

She didn't recognize the voice from the back of the room, but she knew what he was asking about.

They'd been reading *The Outsiders* and waiting impatiently for the day they could watch the movie as a reward for getting through the book.

"Tomorrow," she promised, sparking an equal number of cheers and groans. "We have one more day of discussion first. We've all finished the reading, right?" She glanced around the room. "Who can tell me what Johnny tried to say in his last message to Ponyboy?"

After a few seconds, Devon spoke. She had to strain to make out his soft words. "He wants him to stay innocent. Something better than the guys in his hood. He wanted him to have a future."

She nodded and was about to turn away when he added, "But the poem says it's impossible. None of us can stay untouched by the world. It's a fantasy." He shrugged and stared down at the open notebook on his desk.

"Even if no one can stay innocent entirely, it doesn't mean we don't try to rise above." She resisted the urge to put her hand on his shoulder and kept walking the aisles between the desks. "What do you guys think?"

A handful of kids jumped in with an answer, but the more his classmates debated each other, the deeper Devon sank in his chair. Inexplicably, his normally smiling face grew stonier with every passing minute.

His quiet words had raised the hair on her arms, but once the bell rang, he scooted out of the classroom too quickly for her to ask him about it. He couldn't avoid her forever, though. She'd follow up the first chance she got.

The rest of the day passed in a blur, and she ended the night alone in her cozy one-bedroom apartment. Curled up on her overstuffed blue sofa, papers covering the coffee table, she sipped a glass of wine and tried to focus on the pages in front of her. For some reason, she couldn't shake Devon's words or his withdrawal from the class discussion.

She tried distracting herself with plans for Will's birthday party. His first since he'd gotten out of prison, she'd been planning the celebration for weeks.

Skipping lunch to visit his work site had been totally worth it. The delight in his eyes when she presented his cake mirrored the joy she remembered from his birthdays as a kid. She missed seeing a smile on her brother's face, and if she could, she'd put one there every day. She loved making him happy almost as much as embarrassing him with her open party invitation to his friends.

Her thoughts flitted to the big man who'd caught her eye during her announcement. Now, *he* was something she could focus on.

He had something about him that drew her like a magnet. Something in the eyes. Something she couldn't put into words.

He wasn't handsome. His face was broad, his features were wide-set, and his nose had clearly suffered a break or two in his lifetime. He was— compelling. Raw. Powerful. His brown skin had a golden undertone, indicative of an ethnicity she couldn't quite place. She pictured it warm to the touch, like the sun's rays had soaked its very essence into his flesh.

He'd watched every move she made so intensely, he looked as though he would've lifted a car out of his way if it got between the two of them.

She shivered.

He made Ryan, her ex from *before*, seem like a boy by comparison. Yeah, he'd been in his late twenties, but he was *pretty*, not *compelling*. At the time, she'd thought she wanted a pretty man. He fit the pattern of the other guys she dated. They went to museums and plays. He talked about literature and…carbs.

He talked a lot about carbs.

Dinner always required reservations, and last year they'd summered in the Hamptons. Actually, they'd spent two weeks there last August, but Ryan said things like "summered." He came from money, and while their financial disparity didn't exactly cause their problems, something between them didn't quite click.

At least not for her. She hadn't seen it at the time, but it had been a blessing he left when she got sick. He fit all these check-boxes she'd had about what a man should be: successful, articulate, manicured—but looking back, he'd left her cold.

The guy at the work site gave off nothing but heat. She set down her glass and closed her eyes at the memory of those thick, muscled forearms, his intense stare.

A man like him might burn her alive.

And for the first time in her life, Liv Turner was ready to burn.

CHAPTER THREE

Brick

A one-two punch to the gut almost took Brick to his knees. The man facing him in the ring had to be close to three hundred pounds and within an inch of his own six foot, four inches in height. The guy hit like a battering ram, but he moved slowly, and his eyes telegraphed his plan of attack. Brick only let him score the hits to his midsection to stretch the clock on the fight.

Sucre wanted it to last twelve minutes to make maximum bank, and he called the shots.

Three minutes left.

His opponent's short black dreads swayed as he circled the ring. The guy had a lot to learn, because one day someone would grab his hair and use it against him. Not tonight, though. Brick had other plans to put him down.

Two minutes.

He threw out a punch to the guy's solar plexus, but at half his regular force. It paid to keep his boss happy in more ways than one. Not only would it keep him at the top of the heap, but Sucre would throw a few hundred bucks his way for the trouble, a bonus on top of the cash he made fighting in one of these bare-knuckled matches.

One minute to go.

The cheers and jeers of nearly two hundred people crammed into the small gym echoed like thunder in his ears. The weak fluorescent lights flickered, but no one gave any sign they noticed. The crowd paid well for the pleasure of watching him bleed, and they were getting what they paid for.

He could live with a couple of bruises and broken ribs if it got him closer to his goal. Plus, these kinds of fights added to the legend of his strength. The better fighter he was in the ring, the less he had to fight on the street.

Sucre tugged on his right ear, giving the signal to end the match.

He balled his left fist and plowed it into his opponent's bare midsection. As the guy's head and shoulders jerked forward with the impact, he punched him in the back of the skull, dropping him to the mat like a bag of concrete. The crowd roared its approval, and Sucre gave him a short nod.

Brick stayed stone-faced. No one wanted to see him smile.

Monsters don't have emotions.

The so-called referee grabbed him by the wrist and lifted his hand into the air in victory. The signal meant eight hundred dollars in the bank. Or in the legs of his coffee table.

He climbed out of the ring, breathing through his mouth to avoid the scents of body odor and cheap beer coming from the crowd. For the hundredth time, he wished he had a decent hot shower waiting for him to wash away the blood and the stink of this place, but hot water was a luxury other people had.

"Need a ride home, Big Man?" One of the girls who worked the corner down the way pursed her blood red lips into the semblance of a kiss. He didn't know her name, but he couldn't mistake her invitation.

He shook his head and kept walking straight toward the door. He used to take the whores up on their offers when the loneliness got to him, until he realized he left their beds even emptier inside than before he touched them.

Those women didn't want him. Some wanted the dubious prestige of being an enforcer's girl. Others thought they could use him to pay off a debt to Sucre. And in a few cases—those he didn't want to think about—someone coerced the girls into his bed to further their own agenda.

He had no problem with whores, but the transaction had to be fair, his money for their sex. It was only to give his body release. It would never be more.

His apartment was less than a block from the gym, so he had no need to get dressed. Pulling the key out of his sock, he unlocked the door and ran an eagle eye over his space. Nothing looked disturbed. He allowed his shoulders to droop as he trudged to the bathroom.

The soap and water stung cuts and scrapes he didn't even know he had, but he didn't mind the burn. He stood under the spray until the water went from warm to downright cold. Teeth chattering, he climbed out and fell into the bed, wrapped only in a towel.

Six hours later, the chimes on his phone had him jumping up with his gun in his hand. One day, he might find an alarm that didn't wake him ready to put holes in someone, but not today.

His muscles protested as he dragged on his clothes for work, but he couldn't deny a tingle of anticipation as he buckled his belt. The party at the bar would be tonight, and Will's sister would be there.

The angel in the white dress. He'd get to see her again.

He'd keep his distance—he had to. She was light and everything soft and good. He was a stain on the darkest part of humanity.

Still. It didn't hurt to look.

***

Moe's was a lot closer to the worksite than the downtown scene where Brick usually spent his nights, which meant it was cleaner. The lights shined brighter, and instead of giving him a whiff of beer or decades-old nicotine, it smelled of nothing at all. Wait. He caught the distant scent of a chicken-tenders basket a waitress placed at the center of a table near the front door. It made his mouth water.

The guys from the crew bunched around the pool tables in the back. He arrived last, since he'd run home to shower after sweating it out in the sun all day. He didn't expect to get close to her, but he didn't want to offend Will's sister with the stench of B.O.

As usual, Robby made a beeline straight for him. The kid damn near bounced on the balls of his feet. "You made it. The guys said you wouldn't come, but I knew you wouldn't ditch us." Robby linked a lanky arm in his and dragged him toward the group. "Told you he would come."

He barely stopped himself from shuffling his feet at Robby's proud pronouncement. Not because the guys all looked at him, but because *she* did too.

Will's sister wore jeans and a light blue T-shirt. Even in her casual clothes, she still carried the same ethereal beauty she had wearing her white dress two days before. A high ponytail made her neck look long and graceful. It also gave him a better view of her face. She wore hardly any makeup, and with her natural beauty, she didn't need it. Everything about her fucking glowed.

She'd been playing pool one-on-one with Cyrus.

He resisted the urge to try and spook the good-looking Iranian bastard right out of the bar. Cy was an okay guy, ex-military, and he did good work. He always got it right the first time. He just didn't do well with loud noises. The guys learned their lesson when Kane used the nail gun without warning and Cyrus tried to tackle him for his trouble. It was no small thing, since even *he* would think twice before throwing down with that tattooed motherfucker.

So, it probably wasn't fair to call Cy a bastard, but the man needed to find someone else to play pool with. Cy cleared his throat and pulled Will's sister's attention back to the game. Brick turned his body away entirely to make himself stop staring.

Kane waited two tables down. He lifted his pool cue in greeting, his smile showing he didn't hold a grudge from the elbow thing on Wednesday. "Brick. Get over here. I need someone else on my team. Robby can't play for shit."

Robby's smile faltered for a moment. Then, he brought it back, even if it didn't shine quite as bright as before. "Kane's right. Pool's not really my game."

Brick pressed a twenty into the kid's palm and spoke softly. "Why don't you get us some beers? My treat."

Nodding, the kid scampered away to the bar.

Kane rolled up the sleeves on the red and black checked flannel he wore, revealing the intricate skull tats on his left forearm and the array of female devils and angels inked on his right. "You missed the free booze, brother. Will's sister bought us all shots."

He would not think of—*fuck, she's bent halfway over the table trying to hit the shot. Those jeans are hugging her ass in all the right places. Stop. Looking.*

Cursing under his breath, he squeezed his eyes shut briefly, then grabbed a stick from the rack on the wall. "Stripes or solids?"

"Solids," Kane growled. "The kid didn't sink a single shot."

Brick shrugged as he knocked the two-ball in the side pocket. As much time as he spent in Sucre's bar, he had plenty of practice at pool. "He only wants to belong. The kid's got a lot of heart." Did he sound like a fucking Boy Scout or what? He shook his head at the drivel coming out of his mouth, then banked the four into the corner pocket.

He waited for Kane to call him on it, but instead the guy nodded in agreement. "I know. Anyone else talk as much as him, I'd tell 'em to shut the fuck up, but with Robby, it'd be like kicking a puppy, you know? I don't get why he wants to latch on to us. There's not a soul in this crew who's not fucked up in one way or another. We're going to corrupt him, brother."

The one-ball sank, and he chuckled, the sound of his own laughter foreign to his ears. "I can't believe it hasn't happened already."

Will grumbled from the other side of the table. "You ladies going to keep giggling over there, or are we going to move this game along?"

Brick raised his eyebrow, which in his neighborhood would usually leave a man shaking in his boots. Here, it went ignored. Will snarled and stood next to his teammate, Matt, folding his arms like a pouting child.

For the second time in as many minutes, he wanted to laugh, but this time, he stifled the urge and focused on the table. As he moved to sink the five, Robby returned, jostling his arm.

"Got the beer."

The shot went wild, and the cue ball scratched. Kane sighed deeply and raked his hand through his long dark hair.

Robby looked totally clueless. "I hope Bud's okay. The bartender gave me two pitchers. Who's thirsty?" He held up the beer, one pitcher in each hand.

No glasses in sight.

He could tell the moment Robby realized his mistake, that proud smile starting to slip. "I'll grab us some cups, kid." It would be a while before his turn again anyway. He stepped over to the bar, then froze. The hair stood up on the back of his neck, a sure sign someone watched him. He turned his head a fraction and caught sight of *her*, barely two feet away.

She looked dead at him. Her bottom lip caught between her teeth before sliding free.

As his stomach did a slow flip, he tried to center himself. Maybe she was looking at someone else. He faced her full-on, and her gaze didn't waver.

Instead of turning away, she tilted her chin and offered a friendly smile. "You work with my brother." She stuck out her hand. "My name's Olivia. But everyone calls me Liv."

Her hand stayed outstretched. Did she want him to touch her? He moved slowly, giving her plenty of time to retreat, before wrapping his big hand around her delicate one. He squeezed gently—carefully— noting the softness of her palm and the warmth of her skin before letting go.

"I'm Brick," he rumbled.

Her brow furrowed. "Rick?"

"Brick."

Liv's forehead relaxed as she gave a slow nod.

"Oh, I get it. Cause you're built like a brick shithouse."

He gaped. Most people thought it had something to do with him hitting like a ton of bricks. Only he knew it was because his dad used to call him "thick as a brick."

She covered her mouth with her hand. "Sorry. My mouth gets away from me sometimes when I start drinking. I swear it sounds downright charming in my head and when it comes out of my mouth...blech." Her hand dropped dramatically to the bar.

His head spun. Words failed him. Why would she care what she sounded like? Why was she even talking to him? Maybe she was only being friendly.

He could be friendly...or at least pretend to be. A half smile lifted one corner of his mouth. It felt weird. "You sound charming enough to me."

"Yeah?" Her eyes lit, and she leaned her body against the bar. "What's your pleasure tonight?"

He blinked. She couldn't be asking what it sounded like.

"From the bar, Dirty Mind." She smirked. "What are you *drinking* tonight?"

"Beer."

"I've always been partial to wine, myself."

He scowled. "Nasty."

"Hush. The only thing better is champagne. Though I love an Asti too. The bubbles put it over the top." She smiled so easily, he could almost forget a girl like her would probably cross a crowded street if she saw him coming.

Olivia raised her hand to the bartender and

ordered two glasses of Asti. "C'mon. Try a glass with me."

The twenty-something college guy served them with a smile, and Olivia pushed one of the glasses toward Brick.

He eyed it suspiciously. It looked like wine.

"Sip it." She took a small drink, and pleasure lit her face. "Let it roll over your tongue."

He followed her lead. "Not bad." Not at all like the shit he'd tried the one and only time he took a date to Olive Garden. The only thing good about that night had been the breadsticks.

"In high school, I had a friend who managed to score us bottles of this stuff from her big sister. We'd go up in her old tree house and drink while we listened to The Killers and My Chemical Romance." She chuckled. "We thought we were so badass."

He grunted. "The Killers are still badass."

"Damn right. What else do you listen to?"

He shrugged. No one had ever cared what kind of music he liked. "Some of the older Linkin Park stuff. Avenged Sevenfold."

She wiggled onto a barstool. "'Bat Country' is my favorite."

"No way," he deadpanned. "You seem more like a Top Forty kind of girl."

She tapped him lightly on the shoulder. "See what you get for judging a book by its cover? I shudder to think what else you thought when you first saw me."

He didn't skip a beat. "I thought you were beautiful. I couldn't take my eyes off you." Fuck.

28

Was he writing a high school love letter?

She ran her finger around the rim of her glass. A pink blush stained her cheeks. "I couldn't take mine off you either. I've been thinking about you ever since." Her eyes widened at her own words.

Every molecule of oxygen left the room. For one second, he allowed himself to imagine how it would be to have a woman like this one as his own. Someone clean. Unexpected. Lovely. His heart raced.

How it would feel to touch her and not have her turn away. To taste her lips.

No.

Reality came barreling back into his brain. He'd only come here to look, to be close to her. He had no business talking to this woman...laughing with her...flirting with her. His hands were damn-near stained with blood. He was broken.

Beneath her.

And if Sucre ever got wind she had caught his eye, it could be a death sentence.

Only her ignorance about his real life allowed her to look at him as though he might be a normal guy. A mistake he needed to correct quickly.

Why the hell would she be thinking about me?

"You shouldn't." He pushed his empty glass away and swallowed against the gravel in his throat. "You shouldn't think about me at all. I'm not a good man, Olivia. Probably the worst you'll ever meet." He dropped a ten-dollar-bill on the bar, then snagged a handful of plastic cups. "You're better off staying far away from me."

He allowed himself one last look into her wide

blue eyes, then returned to his crew. One more drink, then he would leave. And he would not look at Olivia again.

Of course, he knew he wouldn't be able to keep the promise. The image of her face had burned in his brain whether he liked it or not.

Fuck it. I'm leaving now.

CHAPTER FOUR

Liv

Liv sat frozen on her stool at the bar, replaying her conversation with Brick.

What had just happened?

He made it clear the attraction she felt toward him wasn't one-sided. His eyes drank her in when he walked in the door like she was water in the desert. She hadn't imagined it. There had been a spark when they talked, and when she showed him her interest, his pupils had dilated, and his breathing had sped up. He'd looked as though he wanted to kiss her, then he'd shut down, and less than a minute after rejoining his friends by the pool tables, he'd marched out the door.

Why?

No matter what he said about himself, she'd pegged him as a nice guy. Not only had he stuck up for her, with the elbow jab at the work-site, but he'd been kind to the foreman's assistant, even if he'd been subtle about it. First, when his biker buddy slammed Robby's skill at playing pool, then when the guy forgot to bring cups for the beer. A lot of the guys she knew would have made fun of his mistakes. Ryan would have.

Were those small tells enough to judge Brick better than he judged himself? She trusted her own judgment about men as far as she could throw one. She'd thought Ryan had loved her, and wasn't he a colossal miscalculation?

Her brother stepped into her line of sight. His blue eyes flashed. "Why were you talking to Brick?"

Great. Will had kicked into Protector Mode. "Hello to you too, big brother. Yes, I *am* having a nice time at this birthday party I threw for you." Her voice climbed. "Oh, no need to thank me for this. It's what any sister would do."

"I'm serious, Liv." He looked at the ceiling, then modulated his voice. "You need to stay away from him. He's no good for you. Besides, you should be focusing on yourself. Taking it easy." He pulled on her ponytail like he had when she was fifteen.

Annoyance prickled beneath her skin. Will had been gone for years, and it was far too late for him to try to resume his role as her older-sibling savior. Besides, she finished her chemo months ago. She was in complete remission, and Will knew it. It grated for him to bring it up now, especially when she was still reeling a little from Brick's bizarre brush-off. "I've had about enough of men telling me what's good for me tonight," she warned. "I know you were gone for a while, but I am twenty-six years old, Will. A grown-ass woman. Don't treat

32

me like a child."

"Then don't act like a child." He sounded reasonable, which grated more.

She narrowed her eyes, and he scowled in response.

"You don't know the first thing about Brick Barlow, and you're making eyes at him like a lovesick schoolgirl."

Her irritation went up another notch. She growled as she got to her feet. "I haven't had a daddy in almost seventeen years. I don't need you to come back in my life and try to act like one now. Brick and I only talked at the bar for a few minutes, which you clearly saw. But if I wanted to fuck a rodeo clown and post it to PornHub, it would still be none of your business."

"All grown up, huh? Too many drinks could be clouding your judgment." He swiped her driver's license from the bar and held it in the air with a smirk. "I'm officially cutting you off."

She resisted the urge to fight him for it, like she did when he'd swipe one of her toys as a kid. Back then, he'd laugh, holding the prize over her head, while she jumped and tried to reach. He wanted her to do it now, be the same kid he remembered. She would *not* give him the satisfaction.

She didn't drive tonight, anyway.

Instead, she clipped his shoulder with hers as she headed toward the door. "Happy birthday. Dick."

It wasn't until her Lyft driver dropped her home, she allowed herself to think more about what happened. As she searched her memories, she grew surer and surer Brick had a thing for her. Still, she couldn't ignore the puffy, purple black eye he had tonight and the scabbed-over knuckles on his hand.

He was obviously into some rough stuff but trying to keep her away from it. Perhaps she should listen to him and keep her distance.

The way he'd looked at her, though…no one had ever looked at her that way. Sure, she'd had boyfriends over the years and a fair amount of sex, so she'd seen desire. But never anything this intense.

Brick's eyes consumed her. It was a stark, naked, needful thing, and it burned her from the inside out.

He made her feel *alive*. Wasn't that what she was looking for?

When he'd grasped her fingers, his touch echoed in every part of her body. She could still feel the thick callouses on his skin, the roughness completely at odds with the careful way he touched her hand.

She dreamed of those calloused hands as she slept, wrapped in the sheets of her bed. The way they scratched against the tender skin of her nipples. How they ghosted down her body, attending her between her legs.

His features were hazy, but Brick's eyes were unmistakable; his fierce stare locked on her face as he gave her pleasure.

It had never been like this with Ryan.

She woke up as she came, her own fingers moving beneath her panties. Sweat drenched her body, but her limbs felt languid. Loose. Satisfied. Groaning, she pulled the pillow over her head.

If she was going to forget Brick Barlow, she had

her work cut out for her.

***

"This may be a little harder than I thought," Liv mumbled as she curled up into a ball on the mat.

When she'd taken the plunge and accepted her sister's invitation to try a Krav Maga class, she'd expected to feel strong and empowered, not like roadkill.

She and Izzy were the last two people remaining in the mid-sized room. Designed for basic workouts and sparring, it was bare, except for the padding on the floor. Nowhere to hide. A large window took up one wall, filling the open space with sunlight.

Izzy held out her hand and laughed as Liv slowly pulled herself up. "Don't be such a baby. You should've signed up for one of these classes years ago."

"Easy for you to say," she grumbled. "You work out in your sleep."

Iz wasn't taking the class with her. She was teaching it, and her big sister showed no mercy.

"Hey, you said you wanted to do this. It's not enough to talk the talk, Nugget, you've got to walk the walk." Ignoring her grimace at the family nickname, Iz continued, "You don't work in the best part of town. You live alone. You need to be able to protect yourself. It won't do you any good if I go easy on you." Her sister cracked open a bottle of water and handed it over.

At least Iz didn't doubt her ability to put herself through the physical challenge, though this would

35

be tougher than she expected. Her arm shook as she lifted the water bottle to her lips. "I know." She trudged toward the door. "I don't want you to take it easy on me. I can do this."

Izzy's hearty laugh boomed behind her. "I might believe it if you weren't hobbling around like an old lady. C'mon. Get showered. We're going to be late for lunch with Carol."

The hot water soothed her quivering muscles. Izzy had worked her like a dog. Running. Cardio. Punching. Kicking. She had no illusions of becoming the same kind of badass as her sister. For one thing, Izzy's life revolved around the gym. Nothing about Liv was hard. She was a nurturer. She fought for people, not against them.

Still, this class provided a chance to prove something to herself—and to her brother and everyone else who considered her a fragile flower.

Pride swelled in her chest. No fragile flowers here.

And check me out, stepping out of my safety zone.

Now that she was healthy—and single—she needed to try new things, expand her world. Skydiving was only the tip of the iceberg.

Looking back on her time with Ryan, she'd been a cardboard cut-out of the woman she wanted to be. She did her work, but she hadn't been connecting with the kids. Thanks to students like Devon, teaching had become more than simply a job.

She had pleasant acquaintances, but no real friends other than Carol. Ryan's world had been her world before she got sick, and it all went away when their relationship ended. It really hadn't been much of a loss, but realizing that took time.

It would be easy to blame her ex for washing the vibrancy from her life. But had it ever really been there? Probably not. Celebrating her new lease on life meant living it differently.

She smiled as she toweled off. Jumping out of the plane rocked as a follow-up to the cliff diving trip at Lake Hartwell. She still couldn't believe she'd done it. Carol had written several other items they still needed to mark off on their Dare to Dream list. Scuba diving. Racecar driving.

Her cheeks warmed. Maybe she needed to add *a forbidden romance* to the list or at least add it to the unwritten pile of crazy shit she'd been trying. Like karaoke. The old Liv—the one who played it safe— she would have never dragged Carol to Kings of Karaoke to face her fear of singing in public with a rousing rendition of "Moves Like Jagger." The old Liv would have never gone to Mardi Gras and flashed her boobs on Bourbon Street. And she never would have ridden the mechanical bull at PBR Atlanta.

Every one of those things scared the crap out of her, but she didn't regret any of them. She *liked* being the kind of woman who pushed the envelope. It was liberating to turn her back on being afraid.

Izzy drove her to the sushi bar down the street. Liv would have preferred Chipotle, but her sister offered to pay, and she had a weird thing about what she would eat.

Carol stood right inside the front door and greeted her with a warm hug. She had laughter in her eyes as she pulled away. "You look rode hard and put up wet, girlfriend."

"Fuck you." She meant it, but only a little, and Carol took it in stride, linking their arms together as they followed the hostess to the table.

Iz ordered a plate of raw stuff, while Liv opted for a shrimp tempura roll in a Bento Box. She'd earned her carbs, dammit.

Carol ordered lo mein.

The restaurant had a trendy and an upscale look with fancy light fixtures and a huge water feature at the center of the dining room. White linen cloths covered the tables, while chrome and black lacquered accents popped throughout the room.

As she sipped her Miso soup, she eyed her sister. Izzy sat straight in her chair, her face watchful and alert. They shared the same blonde hair and blue eyes, but beyond their genetics, they couldn't be more different. Iz was all hard lines and sharp edges. She wore her hair pulled into a tight French braid. Even her clothes were crisp and defined, with an ironed Oxford shirt and dark jeans. At least she rolled up her sleeves in deference to the heat.

Liv liked soft fabrics and flowing material—dresses mostly, like the one she wore today—but even her jeans were supple and worn. The only rough thing she'd ever wanted against her skin had turned her away in the bar last night. And wow, look how well she was doing in her efforts not to think of him.

She forced the image of his face out of her head. "I wish you could have made it to Moe's last night. It would've been great to have you there for Will's birthday."

Izzy poked the lettuce in her salad around with her chopsticks. "I'm sorry. You know I'm not big on a crowded bar scene."

She did but had no idea why. As much as she knew her sister loved her, she suspected Iz kept a lot of things to herself.

"Besides," Iz continued briskly, "we're having dinner together tonight. You're welcome to come if you want."

Normally, she would jump at the chance for a night with her entire family, but the idea of seeing Will right now made her blood boil. Even if she did need to retrieve her license, she hadn't quite forgiven him for the way he'd behaved the night before.

"Nah." She struggled to keep her voice even. "We'll all get together for the Sunday dinner I've got planned next weekend. You guys can go ahead and have some quality time together now. I've got a ton of papers to grade, but make him give you my driver's license. I need it to drive to work Monday."

Izzy's eyebrows flew up, and it appeared she planned to press for more, but the waitress returned with their next course before she could speak. Iz could always see right through her bullshit. Ever since their parents had died more than a decade ago, they'd been more than sisters—more than friends. Especially while Will had been in prison, they were the only family each other had.

Still, she did *not* want to retread what happened last night.

Carol snickered. "Sounds like the same excuse

you gave me when I tried to get you to have dinner with Rosita and me last Saturday night."

A crinkle formed between Izzy's brow as she frowned at Liv. "I thought you liked Rosita."

True. Carol's girlfriend was awesome. She'd been a total rock throughout the chemo treatments, everything Carol's now ex-husband hadn't been the first time she got sick. A loud and boisterous spitfire, Rosita clearly loved Carol with her whole heart. And she would have ripped Liv a new one without a moment's hesitation for jumping out—

Oh, shit.

Carol swallowed a spoonful of broth. "She didn't want to face the music…"

Liv shook her head frantically.

"…for our skydiving trip."

Thunderclouds passed over Izzy's eyes. "Your. What?"

A grin teased the corner of Carol's lips. Wily bitch. She'd done it on purpose.

"Skydiving," Liv murmured. "It was on the list."

Jaw locked, Iz pushed away the plate, half her food untouched. "You know how I feel about your damn list." Her sister glared at her, then Carol, and back again, as if she couldn't decide where to lay the blame. "There's got to be a better way to celebrate your survival."

"You don't understand."

Izzy stood abruptly, her napkin falling off her lap onto the floor. "No. *You* don't understand. I just got my family back together."

"And I'm not going anywhere. You're going to see me more than ever now since I'm coming to your gym." She placed her hand on Izzy's arm. "Don't be mad."

Iz stood still for a moment before nodding once and dropping four twenties on the table. "I'll text you the class schedule." She left without saying goodbye.

Liv glared at Carol, who casually moved the noodles around in her bowl. "Why did you *do* that?"

"She needs to stop babying you. And *you* need to stop tiptoeing around her. She's your blood. You need someone you can share your secrets with."

"I've got you, don't I?" She shook off her irritation and stuffed a piece of her shrimp tempura roll into her mouth.

Carol's face took on a look she couldn't read. Her friend opened her mouth, then closed it with a small shake of her head. She probably planned to give her another lecture on the importance of family, but thankfully, changed her mind.

"You know she flipped out when I showed her the pictures from cliff diving." Izzy gave her a verbal beat down and epic shaming, all rolled into one. A lecture about how Iz thought remission meant she could finally stop worrying about planning her own sister's funeral. Lots of yelling. Tears.

"Some secrets are better kept undercover, but I've got one begging to be shared." She leaned closer to Carol. "I met a guy."

"Forgive me if I withhold my enthusiasm. Your taste in men leans a bit toward the stuffy asshat end of the spectrum." Carol had never met Ryan, but Liv had showed her some pictures, and more

41

importantly, told her a few stories. "Let me guess. A pasty-white investment banker who wears a custom suit to work every day. No. A politician. Phony and full of himself."

"Hey, not fair." At least not entirely. "He works with my brother. In construction, thank you."

Carol sat up straighter. "A man who works with his hands. I like it. Go on."

"Will hates him. Or at least he hates the idea of me anywhere near him." She sipped her iced tea, watching Carol practically vibrating in her chair. "He's not even remotely pasty. Plus, he's big as a fucking house, and he thinks I'm beautiful."

"Damn straight. You are."

Now she took a turn playing with her food. "The only problem is he thinks he'd be trouble for me." She deflated at the memory. "He said I'd be better off staying away."

Carol eyed her speculatively. "But what do *you* think?"

She wrinkled her nose. She had zero faith in her decision-making ability at this point. Rarely had she ever put herself out there, and when she did, she ended up with douchebags like Ryan in her life. "I don't know," she mumbled.

"We've talked about this," Carol soothed. "You need to figure out who you want to be and live your life to support your choice. All those times we sat together in the treatment room, you told me you wanted to take your life in a different direction. Do you want to be the old Liv or the new one?" Leaning over, her friend tugged on her extensions. "Stop waffling about this guy and tell me. What.

Do. You. Think?"

Her heart sped up, and the tingling in her chest came back with a vengeance. "I think," she drawled as she opened her eyes, "I need a little more trouble in my life."

"You're damn right, you do."

CHAPTER FIVE

Liv

A cop was going to pull her over.

Liv eased her foot off the accelerator, slowing the car down. Surely ten miles an hour under the speed limit was better than five. She hit her blinker half a block before her turn, gritting her teeth as some dickhead honked and passed on the left.

It didn't matter if there were no police in sight. Driving without a license could get her a ticket she couldn't afford, and for what felt like the hundredth time since Friday night, she cursed her brother under her breath.

Izzy had done her part and had asked Will to hand over her ID at dinner the night before, but he'd conveniently left it at home.

A terse text exchange later and he promised to drop it off this morning. But then he didn't show up, and she'd had to go to work without it. Now she was back at his construction site to get the damn thing herself.

She jumped out of her car and stalked toward the trailer set up on the side of the property. Robby stood right outside the door, scribbling on his clipboard.

He looked up when her foot crunched into an empty water bottle. "Hey." The grin spreading across his face quickly died when he caught her expression. He advanced down the three wooden stairs to meet her. "Is everything okay?"

"Is my brother here?" She winced at the hard edge to her voice. It wasn't Robby's fault her brother had pissed her off.

"I'm sorry." He toed over some sawdust on the ground with his suede work-boot. "I sent him to go pick up some supplies. Can I give him a message?"

She squeezed her eyes shut and counted to ten in her head. "Ask him to drop my license off in my mailbox before he goes home." She breathed deep. "Please."

"Sure." He backed up the steps without turning around. "I'll go write up a note for him now."

Great. She'd chased away a perfectly nice guy who had only been trying to help her out. Spinning on her heel, she considered a dozen ways to get her brother back for being a pain in her ass. Putting sugar in his salt shaker. Signing him up to Hair Club for Men. Filling his shampoo bottle with Nair.

Plotting her ideas for her revenge, she didn't even look right in front of her. Until she stepped into a wall of broad chest and black cotton. The impact almost knocked her back, but two expansive hands wrapped around her upper arms and steadied her.

She recognized Brick without even seeing his face. She had an awareness of him she couldn't quantify.

Her body softened in his grip.

Those hands. She wanted them everywhere.

Her knees threatened to give out from the nearness of him.

"You're better off staying far away from me."

She locked her legs and steeled her spine at the memory of his rebuke at the bar. "You can let me go now."

The cords of his neck tensed. Then, he released her and stepped back, giving her a full look at the man who'd been plaguing her thoughts for days now. A dusting of stubble shadowed his jaw. His brown eyes searched hers and tightened as if he had found something he didn't like. "What's wrong? Are you okay?"

He gave every indication of genuine concern. His hand even reached toward her—for a second, anyway—before he clenched his fist and dropped it to his side.

Here comes trouble.

Because, oh yeah, he wanted to touch her.

A tickle of excitement swept up her spine, and all the irritation she'd carried a moment before dissipated like a flash summer storm giving way to gentle breezes and blue skies. She ran her tongue over her bottom lip before flashing a wicked smile. "I am now."

Bold as brass, she swept her gaze over his powerful arms and muscular chest. "I didn't find what I was looking for, but I definitely like what I see."

Brick's jaw dropped, and it would have been downright funny if she wasn't so busy basking in her sass.

Something kept this guy from pursuing her, but it sure as hell wasn't a lack of chemistry. More convinced than ever, she decided her first read on Brick Barlow had hit the bullseye. The attraction tugging her toward him went both ways.

She winked—WINKED—before gliding past him, her arm brushing his on the way to the car. She had no guarantee he would watch her leave, but she put an extra sway in her step just in case.

Let him see what he was missing.

She didn't think about her brother or her missing license again the entire drive home.

***

Brick

Brick pushed thoughts of Olivia and her surprise appearance at the site out of his mind as he pulled his truck to a red light. Robby said she'd been there looking for her brother. It had nothing to do with him. Even in his head, she had no place in this sewer he called a life. Especially when he was on the job.

His *other* job.

He had to break in one of Sucre's newer thugs tonight.

Tre had been roughing up guys for the boss about a year now, but this would be his first kill. He looked a little too excited about the idea.

"What's your favorite way to do it?" The recruit asked the question for a second time, and Brick didn't plan to give him any more of an answer now than he did before.

The first time he'd ever taken a life, he'd thrown up on the floor right next to the body. No one knew, but the truth didn't need any witnesses. Marty Zimmerman's dead eyes still haunted him to this day. Marty had only been sixteen years old, but at the time, so was he. Sucre had given him no choice. It was kill or be killed.

He'd spent half his life as a killer, and he didn't enjoy the job any more now than he did then. His body grew bigger, and with practice, he'd become more efficient. He definitely didn't throw up anymore, but he had no *favorite way* to kill somebody. It was simply what he had to do to keep his grandmother alive.

Sucre's crew grew with each passing year, and with it, so did his reach. He also had back-up plans and schemes in place designed to survive even if someone ever took him out. Knowing the consequences of the man's wrath gave Brick all the motivation he needed to do his job.

Somehow, he thought it would be different for Tre. He'd bet a hundred bucks the kid had a boner right now.

They headed back to Pete's place. The junkie had come up with a little cash to buy himself a few days, but now the clock had run out. If he had any kind of sense, he'd be nowhere near his apartment.

Then again, no one with sense borrowed money

from Sucre.

Tre practically vibrated in the passenger seat of Brick's truck. "Maybe I'll slit his throat. Whataya think? Or maybe slice open his gut and pull out his intestines. Send a message."

He ground his teeth. There was no one to send a message to; everyone in the neighborhood already knew what would happen if they crossed the boss. This was simply the required follow-through. It didn't matter if it got messy or not because no one would ever see it.

"We've gotta dump the body when we're done, Tre. You understand, right?"

Tre shrugged and glanced out the window. His knee bounced a mile a minute. "Yeah, I know. It's the principle of the thing. A man's got to take pride in his work."

A man. He almost rolled his eyes. Tre couldn't be more than nineteen. Breaking people didn't make you a man. It made you a monster.

He pulled into the parking lot and cut the ignition. "This is your show, Tre. I'm only here to make sure it doesn't go south."

Tre grinned widely, showcasing the shiny gold tooth where his upper left incisor should be. His remaining white teeth were a sharp contrast to his dark brown skin. "I got this, bro. One day they're gonna say my name with the same kind of respect they say yours." He whistled the opening strains of "Time is on My Side." Sounded creepy as fuck.

Tre elbowed him in the side, but with no force behind it. "You like? I heard it in an old Denzel movie once. Thinking about making it my signature

song. People hear me coming, they piss their pants."
He repeated the same notes over and over,
anticipation building on his face.

Fear was not the same thing as respect. Tre
would learn that one day when he realized no one
invited him to their kitchen table. No one wanted to
introduce him to their family. No one wanted him
near their kids.

It was a lesson learned only through experience.

He followed Tre's strutting form across the
blacktop. Tonight, the cracked pavement was
deserted, like something on the wind warned away
even the natural predators who called this place
home.

Tre kicked in the door without even trying the
knob. "Mother fucker!" He swiped at a rickety
lamp, sending it flying across the room. It landed
about two feet from Pete's body, which now
sprawled out on the living room floor. The junkie
lay in his own filth, covered in vomit with a needle
still hanging from his arm.

He thanked the dead man silently for doing the
job himself. It actually happened far more often
than Sucre knew. At least a third of his hits ended
up foiled by suicides or overdoses where he only
had to clean up the mess. Dead was dead. He got
the credit either way.

Tre didn't share his pragmatism. "Goddamn
pussy." He shook his head. "At least we don't have
to deal with the body now."

The kid wasn't thinking this through. "The fuck
we don't. We can't let people think they can escape
Sucre with an O.D. He's got to disappear, like

anyone else would. Otherwise Sucre looks weak. *You* look weak." He didn't explain they'd have to punish Pete's family if word got out he had killed himself. No way would he touch the guy's little girl, who by some small mercy was noticeably absent from the apartment.

Thankfully, Tre didn't have the smarts or experience to figure it out himself. Otherwise, he would've probably been chomping at the bit to find another target. "Shit, man, you're right. Thanks." The kid surveyed the room. "Where do we start?"

"We start with a tarp." He pulled the black, folded, plastic sheet from the backpack he carried on all his jobs. "We roll him up. Get him out. And leave the rest for the rats."

***

Brick didn't realize he'd hoped to catch a glimpse of Olivia at the construction site again the next morning until he recognized his pang of disappointment when he didn't see Will with the crew. In fact, only a handful of the guys were there when he arrived. Even stranger, he saw no sign of Robby, only Kane and Matt.

He didn't know Matt very well. The guy kept to himself, did the work, went home. He was black— clean-cut, twenty-five or so—and he usually wore a nice T-shirt or polo tucked into his khakis. Today, he had on a bright green tee with a pocket over his heart. He appeared to be a much safer man to be around than Kane with the biker's arms sleeved in tattoos and the scar cutting across his cheek. But appearances could be deceiving. Matt could be a church deacon or a serial killer, for all Brick knew.

Kane wandered over as soon as Brick climbed out of his truck. "Crew's split today. The company won a last-minute bid on a big place in Decatur."

"So why didn't they put another team on it? Xander's not the only foreman they've got."

Kane gave a short nod. "True. But he's the best." He lifted one shoulder. "And since we're his crew, *we're* the best, brother. So, they want us."

Hard to argue there. Splitting everyone up would slow down both jobs, but at least everyone had stable work for a while.

They planned to finish up the subflooring so they could get started on the walls. It was his favorite part of any build. It warmed him seeing the bones of the house taking shape.

Matt nodded as they joined him on the slab. They all worked in easy silence until about eleven-thirty when Kane called for a lunch break. "Guess we've got no pizza today. Tell me what you want, and I'll run over to the deli around the corner."

"I'll go," Matt said mildly, the first words Brick had heard from him in months of working together.

Matt took their orders and stuck the cash in his back pocket as he walked to his car.

Kane stroked his beard. "I saw you talking to Will's sister the other night."

Fuck. He carefully blanked his face. "Sure. She seems like a nice girl."

Kane laughed…a rich, full-belly laugh. The man never did anything halfway. "You want to play it low-key? *She's a nice girl?* So you wouldn't mind if I hit that? 'Cause you see, I think a pretty little thing like her would taste like honey between her legs and—" He stopped talking and grinned when Brick started growling.

Fucker. He pushed the noise down in his throat and ground his teeth together.

"I thought it would take a little more work to get you going."

He narrowed his eyes. He didn't like being played. "She's not for me." He held up his hand before Kane could start talking again. "She's not for you, either, man. Olivia deserves someone better than the likes of us. Someone whose hands are clean." His were black as tar.

Kane's mirth disappeared like it had never been there. "I hear you, but the girl couldn't keep her eyes off you, brother. And you can be sure Will noticed."

"So? He'll get over it. There's nothing happening."

"Brick, you need to pay closer attention to the folks around you. I thought you were supposed to be this badass ballbreaker. How do you survive if you don't bother to read the room?"

So much for their silent understanding to pretend their outside lives didn't exist. He poked at a small hole in his jeans. "I didn't think I had to worry about that kind of shit out here. This is my escape, man." He didn't realize the truth until the words came out of his mouth. He wished he could stuff them back in.

But Kane proved far too perceptive. "Yeah. I get it. I'm just saying be careful with Will. Dude's on parole after a ten-year run in Reidsville."

He did a double take. "For what?"

"Don't know, but I doubt it was for jaywalking. I saw him having it out with your girl after you walked away from the bar. Watch out. Whatever is going on with you and his sister, he doesn't like it."

A bead of cold sweat tingled down his spine. He didn't worry about his own safety, but could Olivia be in danger from her brother? Nah, he couldn't miss their easy affection when she brought the cookie cake last week. He shook it off. She'd be fine. She didn't need him sticking his nose into her life and fucking it up.

She *did* need him to keep his distance. "Message received. Will's got nothing to worry about because nothing's going to happen with me and his sister."

Kane nodded sympathetically. "No matter how much you want it to."

No matter how much he wanted it to.

CHAPTER SIX

Liv

Liv's muscles screamed with every step down the school hallway. A few of the kids noticed how she hobbled around and got a good laugh out of it.

Her arms had felt like Jell-O the night before as she'd forced them through another round of mock punches. Her third Krav Maga class had been no easier than the first. If anything, she'd struggled even more because every muscle in her body burned from the last workout.

But she had something to prove, didn't she? Her body couldn't hold her back anymore.

Bright and observant as he was, Devon didn't miss her pitiful movements. He shook his head with a quiet laugh as she shuffled to the smartboard.

She hadn't had a chance to talk to him one-on-one since his unsettling analysis in class last Wednesday. This week, though, he acted more like himself again. He could have been having a bad day. Everyone gets melancholy from time to time.

55

Now he was back to sporting his killer smile, flirting with the girls, and more than ready to discuss the reading of *1984*.

She still had things to talk to him about. He probably didn't know what he wanted to do with his life—he was only a junior—but if he played his cards right, he could get a full scholarship to any school in the state. He was smart, worldly, and quick on his feet. Her mission before the end of next year would be to help him channel his gifts into a stellar ACT score and an unforgettable college application essay. If she could convince him to go to college in the first place.

She stopped him after class before he could make it out the door. "Hey. You got a second?"

He nodded to his friend, Justin, before turning back to her. "What's going on, Miss Turner? Everything okay with my essay?"

She gestured for him to sit down and cocked her hip against her desk right in front of him. "Have you given any thought to the summer ACT prep class I told you about?"

He shrugged lazily. "Nah. Those tests aren't for me." He slouched in the chair, affecting an air of nonchalance she didn't believe for a minute. "You should be talking to Terese about this stuff." The girl who always took a front row seat in class was his only equal in smarts.

"Terese has already taken her ACTs, and she's working on applying for early admission to Mercer University. This isn't about her. We're talking about *you*." She pursed her lips. "Devon, you're one of the brightest students I've ever had. You can do anything with your life. If you do well on your ACTs, you can go to college on a scholarship. You can study whatever you want. *Be* whatever you want."

His shoulders tensed, and he sat up in his chair. "I appreciate what you're trying to do, but my family needs me here. College isn't in the cards."

"There are schools right here in Atlanta—Georgia Tech, Morehouse. I don't know your family situation—"

"It's complicated." He rubbed his forehead.

"Family can definitely be." She knew firsthand, but at least Will and Iz had always put her future first. "They can be infuriating and frustrating, and they can also surprise you sometimes. Have you talked to them about this?"

"No, but—"

"Then you don't really know for sure how they'll react. Maybe there's a way to give everyone what they need. I'd be happy to talk to—"

"No." He smacked his hand on the desk, knocking a pencil to the floor.

She took a step back, and Devon shook his head ruefully.

"Look," he softened his voice. "I know you mean well." He rose to his feet and walked to the door. He stopped without turning to face her. "But give me some space, okay?" He didn't wait for her answer before disappearing into the hallway with his friend.

Damn.

She packed up her things at half-speed, replaying her conversation with Devon. She knew nothing about his family situation, but she *would* find out. Tomorrow, she'd meet with his guidance counselor, see what he knew. The end of the school year was right around the corner.

In the meantime, she wanted a drink.

The minute she stepped into her apartment, she dropped her bag and went straight for the good wine she usually reserved for weekends. Parking her ass in one of the kitchen chairs, she took a generous sip. Any second now, it would do the trick.

She glanced at the empty chair beside her. Took in the silence of the room. Drinking alone—so fucking cliché.

Dumping the rest of the glass in the sink, she ordered a Lyft and waited out front for the driver to arrive. She had her license back—Will had left in the mailbox as she'd demanded—but if she drank, she didn't drive. Within five minutes, she walked through the door at Moe's.

Maybe some part of her hoped she'd see Brick there again, even if it wasn't logical. She'd never seen him there before the night they met. He'd probably only come for the party. Still, she scanned the room for his face.

A fickle emotion like hope rarely made sense. Old Liv only did things if they made sense.

Of course, Brick wasn't there. She took a seat on one of the black leather bar stools and ordered a Jack and Coke. She downed it in five minutes. She ordered another and stared at the highball glass when the bartender—Brent, according to his nametag—set it in front of her with a crooked smile.

Was he flirting or did he feel sorry for her?

A single woman, drinking away her disappointment at the bar. Another fucking cliché.

This was a mistake.

Her legs ached too much to stand, though. She dragged the glass closer and took a gulp before the ice could melt. Her eyes squeezed shut. The second drink definitely tasted stronger than the first.

"It's not safe for you to drink by yourself."

She froze, her hand still wrapped around the glass. She recognized the deep rasp of his voice instantly. Goosebumps broke out on her arms as her body processed his proximity. "Brick," she breathed, opening her eyes to see the man who refused to leave her thoughts.

His black eye had healed, but his hands were still busted up. A dark T-shirt hugged his barrel chest, and the shadow of a beard crept over his jaw.

She ran her fingers over her lips as she wondered how the bristles would scratch her skin if she kissed him.

He sighed deeply as he sat down on the stool to her left. "What are you doing here, Olivia?"

Thinking of you. "Same thing as you, I'd imagine." She pushed her drink toward him and lifted her brow.

He answered her unspoken challenge, fitting his lips over the glass where hers had been seconds earlier. He drained the rest of her whiskey in an instant. Nodding to the bartender, he procured a replacement in seconds, but Brent left off the smile with the delivery. Brick didn't spare him a glance.

He stared at the amber liquid, then swirled the ice around with his finger.

The dozen or so people at the bar had doubled in the past few minutes, but everyone else disappeared into the background. Her focus lasered only on Brick. Inches away from her. Taking up all the air in the room. The sass and confidence she had fueling her at the construction site abandoned her.

When he spoke again, he did it so quietly, the music drifting from the overhead speakers almost drowned it out. "Did you come here to see me?"

Say no. Say no.

"Yes." Her mouth had broken free from her brain.

"Why?" he asked hoarsely, flexing his fingers on the bar.

She turned to him fully and picked up the hand closest to her; he flinched at the contact. "Your hands are hurt."

Finally, he pulled his gaze from the whiskey and stared at his big hand in hers.

What a contrast they made. The pads of his thick fingers were darkened by work, his fingernails jagged and worn. Her nails were short and clean, and a gold ring glinted on her pale thumb.

He tried to pull away. "You don't want to touch them. Trust me. You don't know where they've been." His voice sounded hollow.

She held on tight. "Brick—"

His dark eyes flashed heat as they locked with hers. "What do you want from me?" he growled. "Are you trying to take a walk on the wild side? You looking for a hard fuck? Because that's all I'm good for. And you're better than some cheap quickie. Too good to roll around in the dirt with

60

me."

"You don't even know me." Her temper flared. She was *not* some kind of porcelain figurine.

He finally succeeded in pulling his hand away, and she felt the loss of his touch in an instant.

"No. *You* don't know *me*. It's what I'm trying to tell you."

"Maybe I want to know you. Is the possibility so hard to believe?"

He reared back at the words, and she wished she could stuff them back in her mouth.

She had to quit making a fool of herself. The man couldn't have made himself any clearer. She shook her head at her own stupidity and laughed ruefully. When would she learn she couldn't trust her own instincts when it came to a guy?

"I'm sorry. I don't usually throw myself at men. Especially men who aren't interested." She dug into her purse and dropped a twenty-dollar bill on the bar before striding out.

***

Brick

Brick remained on his stool, staring dumbfounded as Olivia stormed out of the bar.

"Maybe I want to know you." That's what she'd said.

And what did he do? He fucking chased her out of the place.

Why did she want anything to do him? Did she imagine him in her bed? He'd practically offered to fuck her, and she never blinked an eye. Instead, she'd held his hand.

The same hand he'd used to dump Pete's body. The one that put his last boxing opponent in the emergency room. The one that punched the heavy bag until he bled, trying to beat away his ridiculous fantasies...of her.

Their entire exchange only lasted five minutes. Their others hadn't lasted much longer. In all, he'd spent fifteen minutes with her. Twenty, at most. How could he be so obsessed with a woman he'd barely spoken to? How could she feel the same way?

It's simple. She can't.

This whole thing was stupid. *He* was stupid.

He knew shit about this girl except her taste in music and choice of whiskey. *And Asti. She loved the bubbles.*

All this mooning over her was ridiculous. He finished the drink in front of him and set the glass down on the polished wood. This place was way too nice for the likes of him. Even in his nicest jeans, he stood out like a sore thumb. It had been stupid to come here in the first place.

Time to move on, starting at the gym, his salvation whenever he needed escape from his fucked-up life. He made it in fifteen minutes in his truck. Then the familiar, dank smell welcomed him back into the pit.

Binding his hands tightly with tape, he stubbornly pushed aside thoughts of blue eyes and freckles, warm skin, and gentle touches. His eyes narrowed on the heavy bag as he rammed his fists into the leather. Each hit slammed harder than the last, and the force shook his target from the chain where it hung.

For ten minutes—twenty—thirty—he pummeled the damn thing, until a crowd formed around him to watch his punishment. And it *was* punishment. For seeking her out. For allowing himself to know her touch. For letting her leave with a wounded expression on her face.

"Fuck," he roared as he delivered one more punishing blow. Suddenly, he had no fire left. Exhausted, he forced himself to put one foot in front of the other, ignoring the spectators on his way out the door.

At least he was too tired to dream of her now.

***

He did dream about her, obviously, the kind of dream a lesser man might blush about. But Brick promised himself on the way to his work site he would spend his waking moments focused on the job. He did his damnedest, but the sunshine was the same color as her fucking hair, and twice he had to walk past the spot where she'd flirted with him days ago.

He kicked a chunk of wood-scrap in the yard, sending it flying to the curb. A man should be able to control his own thoughts, and he was…failing.

Despite the constant specter of Olivia hovering over him, late in the afternoon, he stopped mooning over her long enough to pick up on something strange going on with Robby. The guy kept circling around him like a shark in blood-infested water.

Brick snorted.

Robby was as far from a shark as any human being could be. Maybe a dolphin or a baby otter, but not a shark.

What do baby otters circle?

Robby gave him the side eye, and Brick schooled his features. He had no desire to invite a conversation. He came here to work, not to socialize.

His knees ached as he hunched over the partially constructed wall lying on the slab.

"Can I help?" Robby's voice pulled his attention back.

He glanced up, lifting his eyebrow in a way Robby never seemed to find as badass as other people did. "You know how to inlet hurricane bracing into the studs?"

"I don't mean if I can help you with the house." Robby waved the question away as if the answer were obvious. His job involved scheduling the crew, ordering supplies, and reporting back to Xander. "I'm asking if I can help with what's bothering you."

He stopped working, leaned back on his heels, and took in the guy's earnest expression. "What makes you think something is bothering me, kid?"

"Because I have eyes." Robby wrinkled his nose. "And why do you always call me *kid*? I'm twenty-three years old, Brick."

Maybe, but he looked closer to twenty, and a naive twenty at that. Had he ever been so innocent? Lifting his hands in surrender, he shook his head. "I didn't know it bothered you."

"It doesn't really," Robby sighed, settling on the floor beside him. "Not from you, anyway. Sometimes, though, there are people I wish would see me as more." He lowered his voice, almost speaking more to himself than Brick. "As if wishing would make a difference."

Aw hell. It bugged the hell out him for Robby to sound so small.

He made himself comfortable next to the kid—man, whatever—and uncapped his water bottle. "You talking about someone special?"

"I'm talking about a guy. A completely unattainable, completely straight, completely perfect…guy." Robby let his pronouncement hang in the air defiantly, then he deflated a little. "Does it bother you?"

He chugged down about half the bottle before wiping his mouth with the back of his arm. "You being gay? I hate to break it to you, but it's not exactly a secret."

"Who told you?" Robby's eyes held the panic of a rabbit trapped in a snare.

When an animal got scared, it needed soothing, or else it could break its own neck fighting its fear. He modulated his voice to speak as gently as he could. "Nobody had to tell me. And I don't give a shit, Robby. You don't judge me. I don't judge you."

He meant it. Robby was sweet. Kind. He extended genuine friendship to people, which was a rare thing. Who the guy wanted to warm his bed didn't matter in the least.

Robby stared at him like he'd unleashed the secrets of the universe. "Thank you," he said softly.

"Don't sweat it."

Robby gave him a wobbly smile. "You're a good guy, Brick."

He shut down whatever softness must be showing on his face. "I'm really not. You should believe me when I tell you. You don't know me. You don't know what I'm really like." He returned to his knees, bending back over the wall he'd been working on.

The dismissal worked as intended. When he looked up again, Robby had moved on. The kid didn't talk to him for the rest of the day, but he smiled and waved when Brick headed toward his truck at quitting time.

For the life of him, he couldn't understand what was happening. No one had ever looked at him through rose-colored glasses before. Now, twice in the same week, he had to shut down the crazy-ass idea he was someone safe to be around, someone worth knowing.

The envelope on his passenger seat told a very different story. It had been waiting under the windshield wiper when he left for work this morning. A five-inch lock of grey hair rested inside, no doubt his grandmother's. Sucre always delivered his message crystal clear; no one was out of his reach.

He scratched his head as he pulled his beat-up blue truck to a stop, waiting out the red light. The windows were down, the smell of freshly cut grass reminding him how far he was from home. He could cover the distance from the work site to his apartment in a half hour, but this neighborhood might as well have sat on another planet, it functioned so differently from his own.

Maybe the environment tricked Robby and Olivia into thinking he was a regular guy. They'd only ever seen him in places like this, where people could walk around without checking over their shoulder. Where a stray dog posed the biggest threat, and guys like Sucre only existed in the movies.

He took one more deep breath as the light turned green before hitting the accelerator. It would be awesome to belong here, to have a dog and a kid and someone like Olivia in his bed every night, but those kinds of fantasies were dangerous. Sucre would never let him go. The best he could hope for was to save his grandma, then disappear to somewhere his sick fuck of a boss could never find him.

CHAPTER SEVEN

Brick

The king of Brick's corner of the underworld was a fifty-year-old Mexican with a bald head and an expensive purple suit that would have looked ridiculous on anyone else. Anyone who might hesitate to order the skin flayed from your body.

Sucre proved daily he had no qualms about such things. Still, Brick knew the man refused to think of himself as a thug. He took pride in those over-priced suits and the sparkling rings he wore on every finger. Even his name was an attempt to sound like something other than he was. He'd told Brick once after too many tequila shots it meant *sugar* in French, and he thought it sounded slick.

Brick didn't know his real name, and it didn't really matter. The Sucre persona was firmly in place long before they ever met.

Sucre waited for him on the plush throne in the back of El Cabron, the dark bar where he held court. An actual fucking throne with gold trim and blue velvet seat cushions. No one else dared touch it unless they wanted their fingers broken. Brick knew the bitter lesson better than anyone, since he'd be the one to break those fingers.

No less than four women ever sat at Sucre's feet. He showed off an assortment of girls, black, white, Hispanic. They were different every day, but they all had the same things in common; they were young, barely dressed, and they wanted either the power or the drugs Sucre could provide. They'd all end up in the man's bed tonight.

"Brick." Sucre smiled and swung out his arm, palm up, in a royal gesture of greeting.

He ducked his head in deference, then took a seat in the chair always kept empty for him to the left of the throne. He said nothing. Sucre would let him know when he wanted him to talk.

The bar smelled like stale beer and weed. Everyone here smoked freely. Sucre owned the place, and no cop had ever dared step foot inside. Not if he wanted to step out again.

Sucre stretched lazily in his seat, his body undulating like the serpent living under his skin. He nudged one of the girls with his shiny black wingtip shoe. "We've got company, *hermosa*. Why don't you greet Brick properly?"

The blonde nodded her head without hesitation and walked on her knees the short distance to Brick's feet. She barely looked eighteen, but her eyes were old and her spirit, broken. The heavy make-up she wore barely covered the purple bruise on her left cheekbone. He'd seen this kind of girl too many times to count, and he wanted no part of what she had to offer.

The girl would probably fuck him right here if Sucre said the word. She put her hands on his knees and fitted her body between his legs. "What's your pleasure, baby?"

"Get me a beer," he growled, fighting the revulsion from her touch. This girl was every bit as damaged and dirty as him. It should have been a match made in heaven, but he wanted out of this cesspool. Not to mention, an eighteen year old struck him as more of a child than anyone old enough to be in his bed. Like the groupies at the gym, the girls Sucre commanded didn't turn him on; they made him sad. There was no room for feeling anything in a place like this.

The tiny girl sauntered off toward the bar, her high heels clicking on the floor and her short skirt barely covering the cheeks of her ass. Sucre shot him a knowing look. "Only a beer, huh? One day, I'm going to find a girl you can't resist, *hijo*."

He dug his nails into his palms as he forced an easy smile. "You know I like to find my own pussy, sir, but I appreciate the offer."

"*Por supuesto*. Nothing but the best for you, Brick. How's your grandmother doing? I hear she got herself a haircut this week." The man never missed an opportunity to rub salt in a wound.

He shrugged. It was futile to pretend like he didn't care, but they played the game. Sucre's men sent him a picture of his grandmother almost every day. While she slept, while she had lunch, even once during a sponge bath. He swallowed his rage and forced his words to sound bland. "I appreciate you asking about her."

Sucre answered with a sly smile, and he imagined a mouthful of sharpened teeth beneath his lips. "Anything for family." Their dance complete, it was time to move on to business. "So, tell me how things are progressing with Tre."

He struggled to find an answer his boss would find acceptable. "He has a lot of enthusiasm for the job."

Sucre tilted his head. "You say it like it's a bad thing. I want my boys to enjoy their work."

"Whatever you say." The slight narrowing of Sucre's eyes kept him talking. "I only want to make sure he maintains some discipline. He hasn't crossed any lines. I—*We* want 'em to be afraid to cross you, but not afraid to do business with you. I don't want anything to mess with the operation."

The blonde returned with his beer, but he kept his attention firmly on his boss. Sucre steepled his hands in front of his chin, considering Brick's words. "You're right. This is why you're my guy, Brick. Big man like you, people might underestimate your intelligence, but not me. You're always thinking." He tapped at his temple. "And you can rest assured, I know it."

Why did those words feel like a warning?

"I'm feeling a bit...unsettled. Why don't you come to my office for a few minutes, so we can finish talking?"

Fuck.

Brick finally accepted the beer and took a deep pull from the bottle. He hated it when Sucre dragged him to the back room. It wasn't so much an office as a room dominated by a king-sized bed with red satin sheets and chairs lining the walls on either side. Sucre intended to fuck his girls and give Brick a front-row seat. It was one of a thousand ways his boss flexed his dominance. The only small blessing was Sucre no longer asked him to join in.

Sucre led the way, the girls and Brick at his heels. As soon as the door closed, two of the girls scurried to Sucre's feet, removing his shoes. The third carefully removed his jacket and hung it on the back of one of the chairs. There would be hell to pay if Sucre found any wrinkles.

He sat down and faced the show. He knew better than to avert his eyes, but he let the scene in front of him drift slightly out of focus.

One layer at a time, the girls peeled away Sucre's clothes, leaving him naked at the foot of the bed. The scars of hard living marked his light brown skin, but his body was firm and packed with wiry muscle. The only visible hair was a trim patch surrounding his hardening dick.

The girls efficiently stripped their own clothes, and a gaunt brunette dropped to her knees to start sucking him off. Sucre grinned and widened his stance as the blonde who brought Brick his beer kneeled behind him to start licking his ass. The black girl sprawled out on the bed as the redhead climbed up and dropped her head between her legs.

The girl-on-girl show was for Sucre, but he knew Sucre's blow job was what *he* was meant to see. His boss turned a fraction every couple of minutes, to make sure Brick could see his servicing from every angle.

He kept his eyes open, watching Brick watch him.

A classic Sucre power-move to remind him of his place. To remind him he could as easily been the one forced to his knees, and he only sat in this chair because Sucre wanted him there.

It had been years since Sucre had used his body for entertainment, but time didn't dull the memories. The humiliation burned as hot as it did the first time he'd had a dick shoved to the back of his throat, or even worse, one shoved in his ass. The pain had been sharp, and the physical discomfort lasted for days. But the powerlessness, the desolation, those feelings never went away.

He didn't peg Sucre as gay—or even bi. It was all about the control, about domination. It didn't matter if Brick was bigger or stronger. Sucre ruled as the top predator, and anyone would be a fool to forget it.

He was no fool.

So, he sat, and he watched as Sucre ran his hands into the brunette's hair and grabbed hold. As his hips moved faster, her eyes watered, and her throat gagged. Only at the end did his boss close his eyes, and everyone in the room went still as he came with a harsh groan.

When he raised his lids, the girls grabbed their clothes and scurried out, leaving behind the scent of their flowery, cheap perfume. Sucre reclined naked on the bed, his fingers laced behind his head. "Do I need to worry about Tre turning into a loose cannon?"

"No, sir. I'm watching him."

"Excellent. Why don't you take him with you to make house calls tonight?"

House calls. More like shakedowns. "Yes, sir. How many have we got tonight?"

"Only two. I've got the names in my coat pocket."

Brick climbed to his feet and fished the slip of paper from the inside of Sucre's suit coat.

"Oh, and Brick?"

He stopped at the door and turned toward Sucre's voice.

"Grab some video of Tre on the job. It always pays to have insurance."

CHAPTER EIGHT

Liv

Liv hummed along to the old *NSync song playing on Spotify as she bustled around the small kitchenette. She'd mostly set the table before Izzy arrived and now wrapped up the finishing touches while her sister mixed the sweet tea. No less than a cup of sugar would do.

She beamed at the spread of fancy dinnerware and the linen tablecloth. "I'm so glad we're starting Sunday dinners again."

Iz smiled her agreement. They tried to keep the tradition alive when Will went to jail, but it hurt too much without him.

Her irritation with her brother had faded over the course of the week, and now she counted the minutes to his arrival. She squeaked when he knocked once and let himself in, then wrapped his waist in a brief, but probably too-tight, hug.

Will had perfect timing. He showed up right as the rolls came out of the oven.

Placing the basket of bread next to the gravy boat, she gestured to the cooling roast at the center of the table. "You wanna carve, big brother?" It had been Will's job for as long as she could remember.

He took the offered knife with a smile and got to work. When he finished slicing the beef, the three of them sat down and filled their plates.

The silence hung heavy over the table, so she broke the ice. "How's the build going, Will?" She really wanted to ask about Brick, but she wouldn't open such a messy can of worms.

Her brother grunted. "We've got two going on right now, but they're coming along." He shoveled a heaping forkful of meat into his mouth.

"Everything else okay? You seem a little stressed."

He swallowed and bit into his roll, chewing and talking at the same time. "My P.O.'s been riding me a bit. He's being an asshole, making me come in a lot, pushing lots of random drug tests and shit. I'm ready to get my life back, you know?"

Izzy nodded sympathetically. "You've only got six more months of parole. Then you're free of the hassle. You can do this, Will."

He focused on his plate, putting away nearly half of his food in only a minute or two. She had never seen anyone eat so fast. When he noticed her attention, his cheeks—now filled like a chipmunk—colored, and he wiped his mouth with a napkin. "How about you, Iz? Things going well with your kung fu classes?"

"Krav Maga." She rolled her eyes. "And yes, things are going great. Our little sister is one of the newest recruits."

Will's jaw dropped. "Liv?"

"Don't act all surprised," Liv chided. "I'm strong enough."

"You don't have anything to prove, Liv. Just because I worry about you, it doesn't make me a *dick*." He pushed his plate away, then took a healthy gulp of red wine. "I'm your brother. Worry is part of the job description."

"You can worry all you want. It's different from telling me what to do and who I'm allowed to talk to." Despite her best efforts to stay calm, her face grew hot.

Iz waved her white cloth napkin in the air like a flag of surrender. "Anyone want to tell me what's going on?"

"Nothing but our baby sister making time with a thug on my construction crew." He poured himself another glass of Merlot. "He works for a drug dealer, Liv, and you were making doe-eyes at him."

No way. "You know that for sure?"

He scoffed. "What? You're defending him?"

"I don't *know* him, Will, and it's a non-issue. He's not interested in me." Now Liv took a turn finding solace in the wine. Apparently, she'd have to throw out a perfectly good pitcher of tea tonight. It sat untouched on the counter near the sink.

Izzy appeared offended on her behalf. "I don't know this guy from Adam, but I can't believe he's not interested." She waved her forkful of green beans in Liv's direction. "You're the whole package."

"Fine. He's interested, but he shut me down."

She shot a dirty look at her brother. "Satisfied? He told me he was bad news and sent me on my way."

Will narrowed his eyes. "When did this happen?" Over-protective mode: engaged.

"You're missing the point," she ground out. "He said no, Will. Stop beating the horse. It's dead."

"Whatever." He drained his glass, and when he set it down, the base clinked hard against the table. "I've got to get going. Got to get up early tomorrow."

"Two weeks," Izzy piped up. "We'll do lunch at my place."

He lifted his hand in a careless wave as he walked through the small living room and out the front door.

"Okay. Spill." Izzy rubbed her hands together. "Tell me about this guy."

She leaned back in her chair and sighed. "Nothing to tell. He's—" She searched for the right word. "Unavailable."

Izzy smirked. "And apparently, a drug dealer. You know how to pick 'em, Liv. First the cliff diving, then *sky*diving, now this."

Hmm. Either Iz believed he wasn't interested or she didn't take Will's warning at face value, because no way she'd be making cracks if she really thought Liv might hook up with some guy selling smack. This was the same sister who lost her shit when she found out Liv's friends smoked in high school.

"Shut up." Liv said it without heat. "I don't know his story. I just kinda wanted to find it out. There's something about him, Iz." She shook her head. "But it doesn't matter. He really did turn me down."

Grabbing her nearly empty plate, Izzy stood. "Fuck him, then. Come on. This mess isn't going to clean itself. Help me clear the table and tell me how your training is going."

Resisting the urge to sulk, she complied, picking up the remaining dishes and scraping the last of the food into the garbage can. "It's okay. The workouts still kick my ass, but at least I'm regaining the ability to move my arms and legs without agonizing pain." She'd been working with one of the other trainers, Eduardo, the past week.

"I'll take what I can get. Have you done any sparring yet?"

She piled the dishes into the sink. "No. At what point in the training does it usually start?"

Izzy flipped on the water, rinsing the dishes, while Liv loaded them in the dishwasher. They'd always done it the same way when they'd lived together years ago. "It depends. If you want, you can spar with me when you're ready."

She laughed. "I'm not sure if fighting with you is better or worse than fighting with a stranger."

"Better. I promise you." They worked together for a few minutes, finishing up the kitchen. Despite the small space, they had enough room to tag-team the job. Liv had been cleaning up behind herself as she cooked, so they didn't have much to do.

As they wrapped up, Carol let herself in the door. She ambled into the kitchen, swiped a glass, and picked up the wine bottle. Wrinkling her nose, she shook it deliberately. "Tell me this is not your only bottle."

Liv covered her eyes with her hands and peeked through her fingers. "Guilty. I forgot how much we could put away." The last time she and her sister drank together had been before her diagnosis.

"Isn't there a bar around here? It shouldn't be too crowded on a Sunday night, right?"

She cringed inwardly, thinking of the last time she'd been at Moe's, but she pushed the memory away. "Yeah. A few blocks from the McDonald's. I don't have any money, though." The party for Will had wiped her out for the week.

Carol smiled brightly. "Perfect. Let's go. Drinks are on me."

"Sorry, Nugget." Iz swiped her keys from the counter. "I'm headed home. I've reached my limit."

Grabbing her purse, Liv followed Carol to the car. She was being silly. What were the chances? It's not like Brick would be there again.

***

Brick was there again.

Liv wanted to kick herself when she spotted him approaching the bar in the exact same place where they'd spoken twice before. She and Carol polished off their first round of drinks and the bartender brought their second less than a minute before he showed up. She groaned into her glass of Cabernet at the sight of him.

"What?" Carol swiveled her head, following her gaze. "Holy shit. Is he the guy? It's the big dude, isn't it? Girl, he's not pasty at all."

She nodded miserably and forced her eyes to meet her friend's. "Can we please go? I embarrassed myself last time I talked to him."

"Hell no. We were here first. Besides, he's seen you now." Carol glanced quickly to the side and back again. "And…he's headed this way."

Blanking her face, she held her breath until she felt the tingle of his presence beside her.

"Olivia."

She sucked in air and turned her head when he rasped her name. She loved the sound of his voice, deep with a touch of Georgia flavor. "Brick."

He shuffled his feet. "I'm sorry. I shouldn't've—"

"Sit down, buddy." Carol popped to her feet and offered her chair to him.

He studied her, looking unsure whether to follow her command.

"You plan on ditching my friend again?"

He shook his head.

"Then sit down and talk to her." She hefted her purse onto her shoulder. "In fact, you can take her home. I'm out of here."

Brick's gaze followed her as she flounced out the door before he slowly lowered himself to the chair. His black T-shirt strained as he folded and then unfolded his arms.

"I thought you wanted me to stay away from you," she said softly. "Kind of hard to do when you keep showing up in my space."

"Fair enough." He watched his hand as it flexed around his bottle of Bud.

The man always focused anywhere but on her.

"You can't even look at me?"

When his gaze traveled upward, his face betrayed his harsh need. "I can look. The problem is making myself stop."

She had so many questions about who he was. Why he made her brother so sure he was dangerous. Thank God Carol hadn't heard Will's accusations. Otherwise, she'd still be giving the guy the third degree instead of strapping on her seatbelt and heading home.

She frowned. Maybe she should be doing the same…but which scenario? Ask the questions or walk away?

The old Liv would have chosen the latter.

"Are you a drug dealer?" The words popped out of her mouth before she made a conscious decision to ask.

Brick swallowed deeply from the drink he'd carried to the table. "I'm not, but I work for one. I don't sell his product, but I won't lie to you, what I do is no better. It's—" He ground his teeth. "I hate it. I'm trying to get out, but it's complicated. And dangerous. It's why I blew you off. You shouldn't be anywhere near my kind of life."

Okay, he was trying to walk away. He couldn't be all bad.

Brick didn't wait for a response. "I want you to be safe. Do you…have someone to keep you safe, Olivia?"

Keep her safe? Who could've *kept her safe* from the cancer when it appeared out of nowhere last year? No one. She'd fought it and fucking won. She didn't need anyone to keep her safe. What could be a bigger threat than the one she'd already faced?

"I'm safe." Why the hell did her voice sound so breathy?

"No one is safe." It seemed like he said it more to himself than to her.

Tough to argue the same conclusion she'd reached on her own ten seconds ago, but he looked so put out, she couldn't help but grin. "Then why did you ask?"

He ignored the question. "I heard your brother just got out of jail. Is it true?"

She didn't answer at first. Will's nightmare was no one's business but his own. She wouldn't share the details, but she acknowledged the truth with a nod.

Brick leaned toward her, vibrating with intensity. "What did he do?"

"What happened with my brother is not my story to tell." She would never spread her family secrets around. Even annoyed at Will, she'd never even consider betraying him.

"But would he ever hurt you? I know he got angry—"

"Stop right there." Her lips pressed into a hard line. "My brother would *never* hurt me. He and my sister practically raised me, and he has never laid a hand on me in my entire life."

Brick's face softened for a moment before his questioning look returned. "What happened to your parents?"

She didn't talk about them much, but something in the way he asked the question struck a chord. He cared about her answer. "My dad had cancer. He died when I was nine. Five years later, we lost Mom in a car accident. Will was eighteen, so the social workers let us stay together." Even after all these years, the memory of losing her mom cut her wide open. She drained her wine glass and pushed it away.

He didn't take her hand, but he moved his closer, letting the back of it rest against hers. "I'm sorry. I know what it is to lose your parents." For a moment, his hard face looked unguarded. He seemed ten years younger.

Then his jaw firmed. "Whatever Will had to do to take care of you...I have nothing but respect. Obviously, you turned out amazing. Keeping a roof over your head at eighteen, that's some stand-up shit."

Her skin flamed where he touched her. Everything inside her strained for deeper contact. When his words finally registered, her reply came out in a rush. "Mom had life insurance, thank God. It paid off the house and helped us pay the bills for a few years. We sold the place when I graduated from high school. My share paid for college. My sister started her Krav Maga classes."

The money came too late for Will. The familiar feeling of helplessness bubbled in her chest. "I wish we would have sold it sooner. Let Will use his share for a decent lawyer." She buried her face in her hands. Losing Will carved out a hole in her heart she hadn't fully healed.

Brick slid his chair closer and gently wrapped his arm around her shoulder. She turned into his embrace without thinking, seeking more of his comforting warmth. He smelled of Dial soap and a hint of sandalwood. Indulging herself, she breathed in deeply, committing his scent to memory.

"He wouldn't let you sacrifice for him," his deep voice rumbled. "He wanted you to have a home."

Reluctantly, she pulled her head up to face him, but his arm remained at her back. Their faces were so close together, she could see the individual bristles of the five o'clock shadow on his face. She swallowed against the awareness of his touch. "Classic Will. Stubborn ass. When he got out, he used his money to buy a little place of his own. He's still trying to take care of me, though."

Brick's arm fell away. "By warning you away from me."

"He's earned the right to tell me what he thinks, but I make the decisions about my personal life. I've always tried to do the right thing, and while it hasn't always been the most exciting path, it's what brought me to teaching, which is one of the greatest joys in my life. The other stuff—the things I don't like about my life—I'm working to change them. But again, on *my* terms."

Brick tilted his head. "You're a teacher?"

She warmed at the approval in his eyes. "Yeah. High school."

He chuckled. "I'll bet the boys love you."

"Eh. I get a few flirts, but nothing too crazy. I think most kids can tell when they get a teacher who really cares. I think it's instinct. All I know is, helping them inspires me. I want to help them have better lives. Help them find opportunities."

Brick rubbed his finger over the stem of her wine

glass. "School was never really my thing. Maybe if I had someone like you looking out for me back then, my life would be different." He blinked hard and stood abruptly. "Come on. It's getting late. I told your friend I would take you home."

She rose unsteadily to her feet, the effects of her cumulative five glasses of wine buzzing in her ears. She forced one foot in front of the other, following his broad back as he led the way through the small crowd, out the front door.

The hinges groaned as Brick opened the passenger door of his big navy work-truck, and she climbed inside. A moment later, he eased behind the wheel. "Where to?"

She was tempted not to answer. She wanted this night to last, but she murmured her address, and she'd barely closed her eyes before they arrived.

Without missing a beat, Brick climbed out and walked her to her door. She knew she was supposed to go in, but she couldn't bring herself to do it. Instead, she stepped close to his body, breathing in his scent mingled with the sweet smell of night jasmine blooming nearby. He froze, and she ran her fingertips up the side of his arm.

"Do you want to kiss me?" She bit her lip. "Sometimes I think you do. Sometimes, I think you want it as much as I do." She let her hand fall. "Is it all in my head?"

He groaned. "I lie in bed at night, dreaming about what it would be like to kiss you." Moving slowly, he reached for her hand. She closed her eyes, her pulse racing in her ears.

And finally, she felt his lips…feather across her

palm.

Everything within her wanted to throw herself in his arms, but when she opened her eyes, he'd already stepped back.

"Thanks for making my dreams come true, Livie-mine." Then, like a ghost, he disappeared into the night.

***

Five minutes after she locked her door and slid off her shoes, Liv's phone buzzed in her purse.

Carol: I see u made it home OK. I want details.

Liv scowled at Carol's text.

Liv: R U spying on me? #creeper

She set down the phone to unbutton her jeans, but it buzzed again in seconds.

Carol: U think I'd really leave u alone with some strange guy? Of course, I followed u. #dumbass

She should've known. She probably *would* have known if she could've taken her eyes off Brick for five seconds.

She finished stripping down and crawled into bed wearing only her underwear and T-shirt.

Liv: Fine. Will call u l8r.

She fell asleep with the phone in her hand and dreamed of soft, full lips…the rasp of stubble…and the unmistakable want in Brick's eyes as he told her goodnight.

CHAPTER NINE

Liv

More than twenty-four hours of insidious nausea reminded Liv why she didn't often overindulge in alcohol. But by Tuesday evening, the punishing aftermath from her night of drinking had subsided enough for her to return to the gym. Thank God, because Izzy didn't cut her any slack. In fact, she rode her harder than her other instructor ever did.

When she said so, Iz muttered something about Eduardo being a pussy and demanded ten more push-ups. The work-out kicked her ass as much as the hangover did. Almost.

The cardio and strength training were only warm-ups, though. "We're going to spar tonight, Liv. You ready to show me what you've got?"

Like before, the only thing in the room, aside from her and her sister, was a slightly padded mat. There was nowhere to hide from Izzy's enthusiasm, and the single metal door was the only escape from the interior whitewashed brick walls.

Using the back of her wrist, she wiped away the sweat pouring from her forehead. Iz barely appeared ruffled from their thirty minutes of exertion. "Somehow I think I'm going to regret this."

"Hush. The only way to see what you've learned is to put it to the test." Iz waved her forward. "Come at me."

Studying her sister, she searched for an opening. Iz appeared relaxed, but underneath lurked a jungle cat…all lazy-limbed and laid back—until she ripped your face off your fucking head. Still, like an idiot, she took a swing. Iz batted her away like a fly.

"Again."

This time, she stepped in and tried to take Iz with an elbow to the chest, but her sister stepped deftly aside and swept out her leg, knocking her down to all fours. Then for good measure, Iz gave a gentle kick to her sore midsection.

"Again."

As she climbed to her feet, her face heated. This shit was getting old. Gritting her teeth, she launched a kick toward Izzy's knee, but a fast-moving foot blocked her path. She didn't wait before taking her next swing, but her sister countered.

She thought she could move out of the way. She moved into the path of her sister's fist.

The impact made light flash in her eyes.

She couldn't remember anything ever hurting so much. "You fucking hit me!" Her stomach rolled, her lunch threatened to decorate her shoes, and Izzy didn't even have the decency to look sorry about it.

She covered her left eye, tears pouring down her cheeks.

"You stepped into my fist, dummy." Bitch didn't act even a *little bit* sorry, but she did put an arm around her shoulders. "I guess you've suffered enough for tonight."

"I hate you. I'm going over to Carol's tonight, and now I look like a punching bag."

Izzy laughed. "It's only a little red. Wait a few minutes. It will fade, and all you'll have left is a little injured pride." Her sister maneuvered her toward the door. "I'll take you to Carol's, and you can tell her all about how mean I am."

Thank God she didn't have to drive. She only wanted to close her eyes…and maybe whimper a little. In the five minutes it took to get to Carol's apartment, her eye had swollen so much she couldn't open it. This would not go over well at school.

Once they got to the porch and into the light, Iz couldn't hide her wince. "Yeah. That's gonna leave a mark. I'm sorry, Nugget." She rang the bell, and Carol's eyes were wide as saucers when she opened the door.

"Maybe I should be glad I'm an only child."

Izzy lifted her hand in a one-finger salute before heading back to her car.

Carol led her into the living room before continuing to the kitchen. She pulled an ice pack out of the freezer, then tossed it toward the couch. Liv swiped it from the cushion beside her and gently held it to her face.

Carol handed her a bottle of water. "I don't have any booze."

The very thought of alcohol made her groan. "No

booze. No way. No how." She didn't even want the water. She set it on the coffee table.

Carol curled up next to her on the sofa. "Uh oh. You got sick? I didn't realize you drank so much. Did you have more after I left?"

She glared with her one good eye. "You left? I thought you said you were stalking me."

"I waited outside in my car and followed you two back to your place. Call it stalking if you want, but if he was a serial killer, you would be glad I'm bad with boundaries."

The chill from the ice pack seeping into her bones, she tugged the fuzzy blanket off the back of the sofa and snuggled beneath it. Well, almost. Her left arm had to stay out to keep the cold to her face. "So, you saw nothing, then?"

"I wouldn't say *nothing*." Carol shot her a sly smile. "I saw him walk you to the door and kiss your hand." She swayed from side to side in a swoon and batted her eyelashes. "So sweet. Tell me everything."

She shrugged the shoulder beneath the blanket. "He still thinks his life is too dangerous for me to be around. Just like Will. Of course, no one bothers to care what I think."

"What *do* you think?" There was the question again. Her friend kept asking it, and the answer should have been easy, but Liv's judgment sucked. Thankfully, Carol had been a steady beacon for months.

"I think...I want a chance to know him." Frustrated, she tossed the ice pack on the table and burrowed deeper beneath the blanket. "He's so gentle with me. And he looks at me like—I can't even explain it. He looks at me like I'm *everything*. When he does that, it doesn't even matter what he's doing when we're not together."

She flinched at her own words. "Maybe it should. I *know* it should, but it's like all the stuff I should worry about goes away. He acts like I'm a dream come true. Me. When have *I* ever been someone's dream come true?" She shook her head. "Never. I wasn't Ryan's for damn sure."

Carol slid under the blanket with her and grasped Liv's cold hand with her warm one. "What's his name?"

"Would you believe me if I told you I don't know? They call him Brick, but I don't know his real name." Acknowledging it aloud only highlighted how ridiculous it was. She steeled herself for Carol's inevitable laugh.

But it didn't come. Instead, her friend asked gently, "What *do* you know?"

"I know I want to keep feeling the way I do when he looks at me." She sighed. "I know he's a good guy underneath whatever shitty circumstances he's in. He wants to get away from it. He wants to keep *me* away from it. I know he's had a hard life."

She closed her eyes and leaned her head against the cushion, her hand slipping out of her friend's. "I think he lost his parents too, but he didn't have someone like Will or Izzy to make sure things would be okay."

"Are you going to see him again?"

She could hear no censure in Carol's voice. It was one of the things she loved best about her friend. Though Carol did sound tired and looked it, too.

She didn't even think before she answered. "Yes. I'm not sure how, but yeah, I'm going to see him again."

***

When she woke up the next morning, Liv found an eye patch on Carol's coffee table. Her friend must have planted it there during the night. Gamely, she tried it on, but she quickly ruled it out. First of all, the elastic rubbed against the bruise which had blossomed as she slept, making her more uncomfortable than ever. Secondly, the patch only covered about half of her swollen purple flesh.

Third, she looked like a fucking pirate.

A wannabe pirate with a black eye the size of Texas.

She dragged herself into Carol's bedroom, hoping to beg a ride home, but her friend had looked so exhausted last night, she couldn't bring herself to wake her. So, she Ubered. A quick shower and half a bottle of concealer later, she figured she could pass as someone who hadn't run into a fist the night before.

She was right. No one even glanced at her twice as she powered through the day. By lunchtime, she managed to even forget about it herself. It wasn't until Devon returned to her classroom at the end of the day, he gave her reason to remember.

He spoke softly, but his voice was ice cold. "Who hurt you?"

Her hand flew to her eye, and she flinched when her fingers ran over the tender skin.

"Make up doesn't last all day. It's starting to show."

Crap. She should have anticipated this on her own.

"You shouldn't be with somebody who puts his hands on you." His nostrils flared. "Tell me who did it, and I will make sure he never does it again."

"Oh honey, a man didn't do this to me."

He shook his head like she disappointed him. "You gonna tell me you walked into a door? You got hit with a ball?"

She sat down in one of the chairs and gestured for him to join her. "I got hit with my sister's fist when we sparred at the gym."

Devon's eyebrows shot up. "You fight?"

"Not very well, obviously. I weaved when I should have ducked, and she hit me even though she was trying to miss. Believe it or not, she actually teaches classes on this stuff." She pulled out her phone and pulled up her sister's profile page on the website for the gym before handing it to him.

It wasn't until he scrutinized at Izzy's picture, he finally relaxed his tensed features. "She looks so much like you."

She grinned. "Except for the black eye and all, sure."

He handed her phone back. "I'm glad it wasn't something else."

"Thanks. I appreciate you trying to look out for me, but it's *my* job to look out for *you*. Humor your teacher for a second while I've got you here. Have you given any thought to the ACT prep classes we talked about? You still have a few days to sign up for the summer session."

Devon's pursed lips gave her all the answer she needed.

"What can it hurt, Devon? I'll bet you can get a scholarship to a place close-by. You could stay home with your family if you're worried about leaving them."

He drew figure-eights on the top of the desk with his finger, staring intently at the wood littered with names and graffiti carved into the surface. "You don't understand. I'm gonna have to start working soon. I'm not going to have a choice."

"But you—"

"The answer is no." He looked up to face her. "It means a lot to me you want to help, but you can't. It only hurts more when you make me think about things I can't have. If you really want to do something for me, you'll stop bringing this up."

Tears prickled her eyes as Devon got up and walked toward the door.

"Thanks for believing in me, though." He didn't turn around. "I won't forget it."

CHAPTER TEN

Liv

Liv put her car in park outside Brick's work site an hour after school. She wasn't sure at first if he'd still be on the same build where she met him, but she recognized his truck the minute she pulled up. Her internal debate about whether to seek him out ended quickly once she realized the old Liv would've been too nervous to put herself out there.

Bonus points: she saw no sign of Will.

She'd barely made it two steps out of the car before Brick's long stride approached her. He'd stormed from the house, which now resembled a popsicle-stick version of itself. All the wood bones were in place, but not much else.

Her gaze soaked in the sight of him. Jeans hugged his thick legs, and an open blue flannel shirt covered a tight white T. His yellow hardhat did nothing to detract from the intensity written all over his face. Intensity that looked a whole lot more like fury the closer he got.

Had she made a mistake in coming here?

She took an involuntary step back. "I'm sorry. I shouldn't have showed up at your work without warning."

He lifted his hand to her face but stopped short of touching her. "Someone hit you," he growled. His eyes glowed with wrath.

She wrapped her hand around his and pulled it close to her chest. "My sister did it," she explained quickly. "It was an accident." She stepped in close to his rigid body. The tension poured off him in waves.

"Stay right there." He stomped back to the house and spoke tersely with the long-haired, tattooed guy she'd seen here before. Brick handed him his hardhat and returned in less than a minute. "I'll follow you home."

A dozen scenarios ran through her head on the short ride to her place. Each one ended with the two of them naked. She imagined Brick inside her space with his arm around her on the sofa. His big body covering her bed. The image still floated around her brain when she pulled into her parking spot.

She approached the door, but Brick didn't follow her. He still sat behind the wheel of his truck. Doubling back, she opened his creaking passenger door. "Aren't you coming?"

"No," he said tersely. "Get in."

She didn't hesitate. He broke at least a dozen traffic laws in the short distance to her sister's gym.

"Should I ask how you know about this place?"

He shrugged. "You told me she teaches Krav Maga. I looked her up. It's a nice place."

"So why are we here?"

Brick climbed out and passed around the front of the truck to open her door. "Because you need to train with someone who's not going to fuck up your face."

An explanation about how she brought on the black eye herself sat on the tip of her tongue. But she didn't want to waste her opportunity to spend time with him, so she kept her mouth shut, and they walked together into the gym. Cassie, the girl who worked reception, waved them both past the front desk.

"Not very worried about security," Brick muttered.

She tugged him into one of the empty training rooms. "She knows who I am. Cassie's worked with my sister for years."

Grunting, Brick surveyed the room. Not much to see. Only the standard mat on the floor. He stopped his inspection and faced her head-on. "Hit me."

"What? No."

"I need to know what I'm working with. Take a swing."

"Not. Going. To. Happen." To accentuate her point, she plopped down onto the floor, crossing her legs and her arms.

Putting his hands around her biceps, Brick lifted her to her feet like she was a ragdoll. He didn't let go and he drew his face only inches from hers when he spoke. "Do you have any idea what it's doing to me to see the shiner on your face?" His voice sounded calm, but his brown eyes flashed wild. "I need you to do this. If you won't do it for yourself, do it for me. Please."

It was the *please* that did it. She gritted her teeth and shook off his hands. "Fine." She squared her shoulders and threw a quick jab. He caught her fist in his hand, then let it go.

"Not good enough. Try again."

"What the hell did you expect?" This was pissing her off. "I'm half your size. I've only been taking classes for a few weeks. And I don't want to do this!" She pushed at his hard chest, but he didn't move an inch. It only made her irritation burn brighter.

Brick obviously wasn't happy, either. "You need to be able to protect yourself, Olivia. You're not even close."

She bit back her anger when she recognized his crazed expression for what it was: fear. Her hands crept up either side of his face.

He breathed in sharply, and his eyes drifted closed for a moment before he leveled his soulful gaze on her. His regard pressed against her like a physical touch. Though a real touch—one from those big hands—would be better.

"I know you live in a different world than I do. A scarier world. A violent one. But nothing is going to happen to me." She'd already faced the reaper and won. "I joined this class to get stronger and to make my sister happy. I suck at it, which is okay. I'm not trying to become a ninja."

Her fingertips traced his heavy jaw. "I'm a teacher. I grade papers. I go to the library. When I'm really living it up, I visit my brother or my sister at work." She left out the part about jumping out of planes and off cliffs. "I'm safe."

"Safe." His lips moved, but he barely made a sound.

Her eyes locked on those lips, and her breath quickened as his tongue swept over the bottom one. Moving slowly, she inched closer until her body hovered less than an inch from his. As he exhaled, the heat of his breath washed over her, and butterflies took off in her stomach.

She swallowed against the rising thump of her heartbeat. The tips of her fingers now rested on his shoulders and her thumbs feathered across his collarbone. Want shaped an iron vise squeezing her chest.

Forcing her stare away from his pink, full lips, she took in his entire face. Her need reflected in his stark expression. Unable to wait one second more, she lifted onto her toes and sought his mouth with her own.

He froze at first, his muscles rigid. But he didn't pull away.

She marveled at the softness of his lips, as she brushed her own across them, teasing, coaxing.

His pulse pounded beneath her hands. Was he breathing?

Was she?

Breaking contact with his mouth, she slid her cheek across his face, the stubble scraping gently against her skin. Her lips against his ear, she murmured, "Kiss me." It came out more breath than sound, but the words electrified him like live wire.

Those big hands he'd kept at his sides now framed her face. Banked coals glowed in his eyes.

He stared at her for a second—two—then pulled her forward to claim her mouth.

Her fantasies of him had nothing on the real thing. Brick kissed with more than just his lips; his whole body swept her up in passion.

The bulk of him overwhelmed her...exhilarated her. The heat and pressure at her mouth intensified with every breath, consuming her, burning her alive. He couldn't get close enough.

Neither could she.

Her hands clutched his hips, gripping his jeans, crushing him to her. She moaned at the intensity of the contact.

When his tongue finally slipped between her lips, her knees went weak. One of his arms snaked around her back.

No way he'd let her fall.

All her senses trained on this man, on this moment, as she tried to stamp the memory into her mind forever. The trace of cinnamon on his tongue. The scent of soap and sandalwood.

Want.

Need.

Fire.

It was all perfect.

He was fucking perfect.

Her nipples grew tight against the pressure of his chest. And God, why had no one kissed her this way before? Her head swam, and she swayed on her feet, unable to breathe or think or function. She could only drown in his touch.

As he pulled away, she sucked in a deep breath and stumbled right back into his arms. Holding tight to his waist, she buried her head into his chest until the world began to right itself again.

The way his ragged breaths slowly turned heavy and even helped her find her center. His gentle strokes over her hair soothed her.

It could have been seconds, minutes, or hours.

Or forever.

She could stay in his arms forever.

"You make it impossible to walk away from you," he murmured.

She smiled against his t-shirt. Beneath his regular scent, she caught a trace of sawdust he must have picked up at work. "You should stop trying." Reluctantly, she pulled back, searching for the control she'd lost when his tongue tangled with hers. "I'm hungry." The best idea occurred to her. "You ever been to the Majestic?"

Fifteen minutes later, they sat in a small booth. She had a Deluxe Burger with American cheese, and Brick got the Majestic Special.

She breathed in the comforting scents of the food and ran her hand reverently over the familiar vinyl seats. "I've loved this place since I was a kid."

He took a bite of his burger and looked around the place, not quite skeptically, but clearly not seeing beneath the surface of its old-school diner charm.

But he would.

"My dad took me to lunch here for my eighth birthday." She could still picture him as he looked then, so tall and healthy and strong. "We never told my mom he checked me out of school. He called it a father-daughter adventure."

She gestured to the shiny red counter and the padded stools. "We sat right there, and he told me I could have anything I wanted. *On the grown-up menu.* I had a giant cheeseburger and a chocolate milkshake." She'd felt so big.

Dad had shared memories about all the times *his* father had taken him here as a kid. The restaurant was a legacy of Turner memories. "He told the entire place it was my birthday and they all sang 'Happy Birthday' to me."

He nodded, setting down his half-eaten sandwich.

"After Dad died—and later, my mom too—coming here helped heal me." She hugged herself tightly, reliving the bear hugs her dad gave freely every day of her childhood.

"The Majestic is a hundred years old. It's an institution." It wasn't going anywhere. It wasn't changing. "I can still walk in twenty years from now and see the hanging lights or the vinyl booths. I can sit on the same stool where I sat with my dad, the table where I ate with Izzy after graduation." She released her arms. "Or this booth, where I ate with you for the first time. It will all stay the same. Accessible forever."

He dipped his head when she added the memory they were making now to her list of unforgettable moments. The way he'd watched her, transfixed during the story, made it clear he understood the significance.

The waitress stopped by and offered them refills.

He shifted uncomfortably in his seat and rearranged the ice cubes in his Coke with a straw. "I don't understand what you're doing here with me."

"I enjoy being with you," she said simply.

He said nothing, turning his attention back to his food.

She couldn't take her eyes off Brick as he demolished his double-decker burger in a handful of efficient bites. She chewed hers slowly, savoring the juicy ground beef and the cool sweet tang of ketchup before she swallowed.

"Hey, Mister." A little boy with curly carrot-colored hair and a striped shirt tugged on Brick's sleeve. "Are you in WWE? You look like a Superstar."

Brick smiled but didn't show any teeth. "Nah, buddy. I'm not a Superstar."

"But you're so big." The little boy's eyes were wide. "I want to be big like you someday. Then nobody can ever be mean to me no more. I could beat 'em up first."

"You'll be big one day," Brick assured him. "I'll tell you how to do it if you make me a promise."

The child nodded.

"The secret: you gotta practice lifting milk jugs filled with water above your head over and over again. You think you can try it? Lift 'em over and over until you can't anymore. Then do it again the next day and the next, until one day it's not even hard anymore."

"Milk jugs are the secret?" The little boy bounced.

"Mmm hmm. But now, here's your part of our deal. You've got to promise me when you get big, you use those muscles to protect people instead of pushing them around. A deal's a deal."

"Hey, Dad," the kid yelled, already running off. "We got any milk at home?"

Brick's cheeks darkened when he caught her beaming at him. He'd probably hate the idea he came off like a big teddy bear after his exchange with the boy. She needed a distraction…to get him talking. Besides, turnabout was fair play.

"I've told you my story. You know about my family, my favorite burger joint, my eighth birthday. And I don't even know your name. Doesn't seem very fair." She deliberately took another bite and waited for an answer.

His brow furrowed. "You know my name."

"Your name is not Brick. No one names their baby Brick."

"Oh." He started tearing his napkin into thin strips. It wasn't until he completely shredded it that he finally spoke. "Jonathan." He cleared his throat. "My mother named me Jonathan, but nobody uses it."

She tamped down on the satisfied smile threatening to take over her face. The last thing she wanted was to scare him off. It was a miracle she'd kept him here this long. "Speaking of calling you…" She pulled her phone out of her purse and slid it toward him. "Put your number in there."

He looked at it like it might bite him. "You want my phone number?" he echoed.

"Yes. Unless I need to stalk you on your worksite again, the next time I want to hear your voice."

He added his contact and slid the phone back to

her. She picked it up and called him on the spot. She let it ring once, then disconnected. "Now you have mine too." She waved the waitress over. "We're ready for the check, please."

Brick pulled his phone out of his back pocket and stared at the missed call, then back at her. "You want me...to call you."

"I want you to call me."

The waitress set the check on the table, and Liv reached for it, but Brick's hand shot out like a viper, grabbing it first. "You never pay with me." He stood and pulled some cash out of his wallet. "Not now. Not ever."

He reached out his hand and helped her to her feet. She warmed at the possibility there might be a next time, but she said nothing. For once with this guy, she wasn't going to push her luck.

Neither of them spoke on the short drive back to her place, but like before, Brick got out to walk her to her door. She didn't give him the chance to bolt. Instead, she stepped into him and wrapped her arms around his waist. Slowly, gently, he returned her embrace.

It was heaven.

"Thank you for tonight. I needed this."

He kissed the top of her head. "Thank *you*."

Resisting the urge to go for his lips again, she pulled back. It was one thing to make the first move; it was another to make them all. Skittish or not, the ball was in his court.

She unlocked the front door, flirting gently over her shoulder. "You thanking me for making your dreams come true again?"

He tipped his head and turned back to the truck. "Dreams I didn't even know I had."

***

Brick

Brick fought the urge to glance back at Olivia as he walked away. He didn't even let himself think about her during the drive home. He had to stay vigilant. Aware.

Thank God he didn't have any jobs lined up from Sucre. He didn't want anything to taint this perfect, precious night.

The security check at his apartment came up clean. No one had disturbed his home or his money. He took the napkin he'd swiped from the Majestic out of his pocket and placed it on his nightstand, smoothing out the wrinkles. Carefully, he removed the drawer with the false bottom and added the memento next to the toy car and his only photo of him with his grandma. It was the first thing he'd added to his small collection of treasures in years.

After setting everything back to rights, he grabbed a beer out of the fridge and sat on his old, comfortable recliner.

Now.

Now he could think about her.

When he'd seen the angry bruise bleeding through her make-up, his first thought was someone in Sucre's crew had found her. Someone was trying to get to him through her.

And in a fraction of a second, he determined that

person was going to die.

Thank God he'd been wrong. Her explanation about her sister made perfect sense, but he'd needed the ride to her house to get his shit together. Adrenaline pumping so hard doesn't just disappear.

He needed to do something. Something to keep anyone from hurting her ever again. Hardly a day went by where he didn't use his fists to pound the fuck out of something. He should be able to use his one fucking skill to help her, to teach her how to protect herself.

But Olivia had other ideas, didn't she?

His breath caught at the memory of her kiss, and his dick hardened all over again. The fucking thing stood at attention from the moment she put her hands on him. It was a goddamn miracle she didn't seem to notice.

So many times, he'd told himself to stay away from her. She wasn't for him. The promise of her kiss was all it took to blow his resolve to shit. He could still smell the hint of her vanilla scent lingering on his clothes, on his hands, his skin. For the life of him, he couldn't regret how anything played out tonight, even if he'd made a fool of himself trying to be a decent role model to some strange kid.

She was so soft, and the way she looked at him…no one had ever looked at him the way she did before—like he was worth something. Not the protection he could provide or the street cred he could give. Not even the connection he had to Sucre and his money and his drugs.

Just him.

Just Brick.

Jonathan.

He hadn't thought of himself as Jonathan since he was a kid. The name, it almost hurt to own it. No one had used it in fifteen years. Not even his grandma. Only his mother, and she died a long time ago.

Olivia was an orphan too. Even if she'd lost a very different kind of family than he had, she had suffered.

He was grateful she'd had Will. It didn't matter if the guy wanted to keep him away from her. More than anything, it proved the man cared about his sister. To make sure she had a home, to help her grow up and be successful, when he was barely more than a kid himself…plenty of adults couldn't pull off such a thing, his own parents included.

His gaze drifted to his phone. He could call her. Hear her voice whenever he wanted to. The idea was heady.

He pictured her bright blue eyes. How they focused on his mouth. How they broadcast her desire.

His heart sped up and his cock twitched in his pants, demanding satisfaction. Why fight it? He had nowhere to be.

He stripped off his clothes and dropped them on the floor in his wake as he moved toward the bathroom. Even if he didn't have hot water, a lukewarm shower would still do the trick. Stepping naked into the spray, his cock grew painful, as his body anticipated the relief it knew would come soon.

He lathered the soap in his hand, until he covered his palm in a thick foam. Only then did he wrap his fingers around his shaft and squeeze from base to tip.

He closed his eyes and focused on the faint remnants of vanilla he could still tease out on his skin. In his fantasy, he had her with him, her body bared, wet, and willing. Faster and faster, his hand moved. Harder and harder, he pulled, agony and ecstasy blending together as he approached his release.

Her name was on his lips, and the memory of her taste, in his mouth, as he finally came with a shuddering curse.

After tonight, he realized he would never be satisfied until he knew how it felt to be inside her. To touch every part of her, body and soul, until she belonged to him.

Forever.

CHAPTER ELEVEN

Brick

Brick couldn't keep the smile off his face as he pulled up to the Decatur site. The plumbers were working on the Burgundy Street house today, which meant he'd only be in the way there, but he could still do a lot to help the team here.

Kane raised his eyebrow as he settled in next to him in the space they would eventually turn into a garage. "Have a good night last night?"

He ignored the tease and rifled through the toolbox.

"I saw you leave with Will's sister. I thought you said nothing was happening there, brother."

Shit. He hadn't considered whether Kane or Matt might have seen Olivia at the site yesterday. The last thing he wanted was to hurt her reputation or for word of their meeting to get back to her brother. "I meant it," he sighed, "but she knows what she wants, and it's really fucking hard to tell her no."

Today Kane had his dark hair in a low ponytail

with a black bandana tied across the top of his head. Tugging at the fabric, he considered Brick's words. "It's only hard to tell her no because you don't want to. So, if she wants it and you want it, why are you fighting it? Will? Cause if you can make his sister happy, I think he could learn to live with it."

"It's not only about how Will feels. I wish he was just an overprotective brother who thinks I'm not good enough for his sister. The problem is, he's right. You know the kind of shit I'm involved with. Olivia's probably never even heard of Sucre de la Cruz, and I'm glad. I want her as far away from his cesspool of an existence as humanly possible. As long as she's around me, she's linked to it."

He rubbed at his eyes. The pressure building behind them sent sharp spikes into his brain. Saying this shit aloud made it real all over again. "All it takes is one fucking junkie to find out about her, and he'll use her to get to me or—even worse— Sucre could find out. He'd break her to remind me who's king. She hasn't lived like us. She'd never recover."

Kane dropped a hand on his shoulder. "You're talking some harsh shit, brother. Can't you get out? I mean, don't you *want* to get out?"

A dull laugh escaped his mouth. "You know, no one's ever asked me what I want before."

Kane shrugged. "People see what makes sense to them. They see a big guy like you, a killer, they don't understand how someone could trap you. You're the monster because you look like one." Gesturing to himself, Kane swept his hands down his body. "I get it. I also get what it's like to feel trapped by a certain kind of life. It's why we both come here and do this, am I right?"

He nodded sharply.

"Do you think you can stay away from her?"

"Truth?" He exhaled slowly. "No. I can't."

Kane spoke over the noise as he started hammering his two-by-four again. "Then you need to figure out how to keep your two worlds apart. Because you're right. She'll be your weak spot. The first person who finds it will destroy her. And you."

***

Kane's words still rattled around in Brick's head as he hit the street with Tre hours later.

He stole a peek at his trainee. Tre wore a bright red leather jacket, and it looked even shinier next to his dark skin. Most guys in this line of work dressed in black. They'd blend into the night, so their prey would never see them coming.

Tre was a different breed of predator. He *wanted* them to see him coming. He fed on the fear.

He held back a shudder as he imagined what someone like Tre would do with the knowledge of Olivia. He'd rape her, no doubt. Even worse, he'd hurt her as much as possible. He wouldn't kill her, though, at least not right away. Tre would find a quick death too merciful. He'd squeeze out as much pain as possible...to show Brick he could, but also because he'd fucking enjoy it.

Tre could never, ever know Olivia existed.

Unaware of his scrutiny, the kid scoped out Bennie's duplex. Their mark lived on the right side of the shotgun house.

As far as he knew, the other side sat empty. A weak light cast shadows against the thin curtains on Bennie's half of the house. The vague shapes of several men moved behind it, including the stocky frame of their Mexican target.

"How many of 'em do you think we can take?"

"Think smart, Tre. There's no need to walk into a free-for-all. We wait. We watch. It might mean we end up coming back tomorrow. It could be an ambush. When you work for Sucre, you're always going to have some dumb assholes plotting to get the better of you. Being stronger than them's not good enough. You've got to be smarter too."

Tre kicked a rock on the crumbling concrete at the curb. "So, he gets away with not paying because he invited his friends over? What kind of pussy are you?"

He growled and slapped the smaller man across the face. "You are reaching the end of my fucking patience."

The kid backed down, but the hate in his glare was unmistakable. "All I mean is, what kind of message are we sending by giving him a pass?"

"We're not giving him a pass. Sometimes you have to be a spider instead of a grizzly bear. One kills with cunning and the other, brute force. The outcome is the same. You have to think about which approach will serve you better."

Tre nodded, but it was obvious he only wanted to be the grizzly.

They didn't have to wait long. About thirty minutes later, half a dozen men filed out the door and down the steps on the porch. They piled into an old blue Delta 88. Bennie was among them.

Brick and Tre followed at a discreet distance as they drove to a dive bar down the street.

Bennie made a mistake in choosing his destination. Brick knew the guy who owned the place, and after a quick phone call, he and Tre slipped in the back door.

"So why is it okay to go after Bennie now when it wasn't before? He still has his crew with him." Tre's voice was like nails on a chalkboard.

How many times had he learned lessons the hard way? Tre had no idea how lucky he was to have someone show him the ropes. "The difference is now we can see what we're dealing with. In the apartment, there were too many unknowns. Now we know how many men he's got with him. We can see where they are, and the only place they'll be watching for us is the front door."

Proving his point, one of Bennie's guys headed their way, wandering alone to the bathroom. Even in such a small space, the guy had to weave through two dozen people to make his way back.

Brick grabbed him from behind and covered his mouth before he could make a sound. "You looking for trouble from me?" He used his stone-cold-killer voice.

The thin man shook his head emphatically.

"Hand my associate your phone and I'll let you wait this out in the storage room. Do something stupid, and I'll break something you're attached to."

The man's hands shook as he handed his phone to Tre.

"Pat him down for a weapon."

Tre did as Brick commanded and came up with a switchblade the size of his hand. Grinning, Tre shoved the knife into the pocket of his jacket. "You carrying anything else?" he sneered.

Again, the man shook his head, more frantically than ever.

He let the guy go. "In the closet. This shit goes south, I'll kill you first."

"Won't his friends come looking for him?" Tre lived to challenge him.

Rolling his eyes, he shrugged. "Maybe. Or they might think he bailed. If anyone gets curious, they'll come alone, and they'll end up in the closet too."

Sure enough, it happened twice more, which left Bennie with only two buddies next to him at the bar. Good enough odds for Brick to make his move. Judging by the expression on Bennie's face, he'd already reached the same conclusion on his own.

One of the guys with him flat out ran away as he stepped into the open. Bennie's other friend stood his ground, trying to seem tough. He failed.

Brick stared down the man with a diamond earring and fat dreds standing next to his quarry. "Is this the ditch you wanna die in?"

Blinking rapidly, the guy didn't even glance at Bennie before hightailing it out the front door.

Bennie dropped to his knees. Sweat dotted the skin above his quivering lip. "I was about to come see you, Brick, I swear."

"Don't talk to me, Bennie. Talk to Tre."

As Bennie turned to plead his case, Tre didn't wait for any words. He lifted his knee and kicked him square in the face. Then, when Bennie tried to roll up into a ball, Tre kicked him over and over and over again. "You think you can run from me, motherfucker?" Kick. "You think you can hide behind your friends?" Kick. "You spread the message Tre Lowry don't play."

Bennie whimpered at the brutal kick Tre delivered next but then fell silent and still. So did everyone else in the bar. They waited and watched to see what Tre would do next. So did Brick.

Tre was a loose cannon, as likely to kill Bennie as ask about the money he owed. At some point, though, the guy had to show what he was made of. Brick couldn't keep reminding him what was important.

With his shiny red leather coat, Tre was the loudest thing in the dark, dank room—the star of the show—and he wasn't finished with his performance. With the showmanship of a circus ringmaster, he unbuckled his pants and whipped out his dick.

Then pissed all over poor Bennie.

The guy lay there, soaked in blood and urine. Brick couldn't tell if the poor bastard was dead or alive.

Tre didn't seem to care. He swung around to face the crowd, cock still in hand. "Anybody else want a piece of this?"

Nobody said a word.

Stuffing his junk back into his pants, Tre puffed up like a proud peacock. "I didn't think so." He pulled out the switchblade he'd pocketed earlier and sliced off Bennie's index finger. He shoved it in his jacket pocket before strutting out the front door.

The last thing Brick wanted to do was stick his hands in Tre's piss.

No. The *last* thing he wanted to do was to face Sucre not knowing whether Bennie was dead or alive.

He reached down and checked for a pulse. There wasn't one. Then he dug out Bennie's wallet from his damp jacket, removed the forty dollars nestled inside, and dropped the fake leather on the dead man's chest.

Shit. His thoughts about Olivia had consumed him so much tonight, he'd forgotten his backpack. "I'm going to need a tarp."

The bartender cleared his throat. "I've, uh, got one in the bed of my truck."

"Get it. When I'm gone, you can let the guys locked in your storage room out. I've got no beef with them, but I don't think they'll take this very well."

It took him ten minutes to roll Bennie in the heavy plastic and toss his body in the back of his pickup. He drove straight to El Cabron, where Tre strutted around the bar like king of the fucking world.

"Took you long enough, man. Didn't think you wanted me to go see Sucre without you, but you know how the man hates to be kept waiting." Tre chuckled low and rubbed his tongue across his bottom lip.

Dumb fuck had no idea what he was in for.

He followed the kid silently to Sucre's throne, took his traditional seat, and waited for Tre to dig himself in deeper.

Tonight, Sucre wore a deep amber suit. He brushed at his lapel as Tre stood in front of him, practically bouncing on his feet. "I take it you had a successful evening, Tre?"

"Fucking A. Bennie thought he could get the drop on me. Set up a fucking ambush at his place, but I didn't fall for it. Nope. Tracked him and his hombres to some dive bar. Picked his guys off one by one, and *shazam*." He clapped his hands together. "Easy pickings."

Sucre shot him a bored look. "And my money?"

Tre swallowed, probably now beginning to realize the depth of his mistake.

"You *did* ask about my money. Right?"

"Obviously he didn't have it, boss, so he tried to get the jump on me."

Sucre narrowed his eyes. "So, he'll have it tomorrow? What did he say? Exactly."

Tre blinked quickly, his brain likely making all those connections he should have considered an hour ago. "He didn't say anything, boss."

Sucre stood, and the girls at his feet scattered. "Why not?"

Throwing his shoulders back, Tre went all in. "Because he was too busy getting his ass kicked. Fucker needed to learn you don't mess with me."

The deep, low laugh from Sucre's throat made the hair stand up on the back of his neck.

"He learned he doesn't mess with *you*?"

Sucre never looked away from Tre, but Brick knew what would come next. "Brick. Who exactly should people in this town know not to mess with?"

He rose to his feet and nodded with deference. "You, Sucre."

Tre spoke up. "I meant—"

Sucre wrapped his hand around the column of Tre's neck before he could finish making his excuse. The men stood about the same height, so they stared at each other eye-to-eye. "Tell me, Tre, what condition did you leave Bennie in after this lesson of yours?"

Tre didn't answer.

"Was he dead or alive?"

"I'm not sure." Finally, the bluster disappeared.

"Brick?" Sucre asked quietly.

"Dead."

Sucre moved his face so close to Tre's, he could have kissed him. "Let me make sure I understand this. You killed somebody who owed me money. You didn't get my cash. You didn't even try. And what? You left his fucking body in the middle of a public place?"

Silence.

"Answer me, *niño*," he breathed.

"Yes, sir."

For the first time, Sucre turned his head to face Brick, but his hand stayed planted firmly at the base of Tre's neck. "I assume you took care of this, Brick?"

"Of course."

"Where is the body now?"

"In the bed of my truck, parked out back." He dug out the two twenties he'd lifted off Bennie. "This was all the money he had on him."

"Bring it to my office. Bring Tre too. Someone

will take care of Bennie while we all…talk this through."

He knew Tre would be getting a lesson from Sucre tonight, but he'd hoped he wouldn't have to watch. He nodded at Sucre's words and guided Tre to the back room. The kid eyed the bed but didn't ask any questions.

Sucre joined them a minute later, loosening his tie as he came in the door. "You want to help me deliver this lesson, Brick?"

"No, sir. I don't." The very thought of it turned his stomach.

The boss lifted his eyebrow as he hung his jacket on the back of a chair. Brick almost never told him no, but the man had asked him what he wanted. He took a chance with the truth.

"All right, but if this lesson doesn't take, I might need your considerable, ah, assets to help drive home the message next time. Now get out of here."

Tre looked like a rabbit caught in a snare.

Brick dropped Bennie's money on one of the chairs, then backed out the door.

"Drop your pants, boy," Sucre purred. "This is going to hurt."

***

Brick spent twenty minutes in the shower, trying to wash off the horrors of the day. It never worked, but he couldn't stop trying. His skin turned red and raw from how hard he scrubbed, but nothing could erase the mental picture of what would happen to Tre tonight or the memories of what the kid did to

Bennie.

He'd seen a lot of fucked-up shit in his life, and he'd learned to lock it all up in a box inside his head. The box didn't usually leak until he was alone. Right now, it threatened to explode.

Wearing nothing but a pair of loose-fitting sweatpants, he ambled to the fridge and grabbed a beer. The cold, crisp taste normally helped soothe him, but tonight, he didn't think anything could distract him from the vile images crowding his mind.

Nothing, except Olivia.

He glanced at the clock on the microwave and shook his head at the display. Only nine o'clock. He would have guessed closer to midnight.

Early enough she was probably awake. She'd given him her number. He *could* call her.

But what could he say? *Hey baby, I watched a guy get beat to death tonight. How was* your *day?*

He shook his head and carried the cold glass bottle to his bed, where he propped himself up against the pillows on the headboard. His phone sat right there on the wobbly nightstand, a tempting distraction from the nasties assaulting his brain.

It wouldn't take much. He wanted to hear her voice. To feel like a normal man for a little while.

He didn't keep any contacts in his phone, so he went to his list of recent calls. Hers was the only number he hadn't erased. He resolved to memorize it, to minimize the possibility of exposing her.

His finger hovered over the touchscreen for several seconds, as his need for her warred with his conscience. His conscience lost. Before he could argue with himself any longer, he touched the screen, initiating the call.

She answered on the first ring, and her soft voice soothed like a gentle balm on his ragged soul. "Hello?"

"Olivia?" he rasped.

"You called. I—I didn't think you would, but I'm glad you did."

He took a long pull of his beer. "I just...wanted to hear your voice."

She made a small humming sound. "Bad night?" She didn't wait for an answer, which was a blessing. "I have a feeling your threshold is pretty high."

He made a noise somewhere between a grunt and a laugh. She had no idea.

Or maybe she did. The girl was pretty fucking perceptive. Beautiful and smart. The whole package.

He needed to lose himself in her for a while. "What are you doing right now?" he asked.

"Mmm. Grading papers. I'm glad you're giving me an excuse to take a break. How are things going at the construction site?"

"Not bad. I worked with your brother today." Though the man hadn't even spared him a glance. These days, Will treated him as though he didn't even exist. At least the guy didn't try to take a swing at him.

"How is it with him? He's not being an asshole, is he?"

He loved the bite in her voice. Like she would take her brother to task for him. He'd never ask her to, but the idea warmed him. "Nah. But things would probably change if he knew we were talking right now." Will could never know. Nobody could.

"I am going to tell him about us."

He sat up, tendrils of alarm wrapping around his chest. "Tell him what? There's nothing to tell."

She laughed softly. "Yes, there is. I'm going to tell him we're talking. He should know...I like you. I want his support."

"Olivia, you can't." Even one person knowing she mattered to him was one person too many. Even if Will would never intentionally hurt her, one wrong word said to one wrong person could be the difference between life and death.

"I can, and I will. Look, my family is important to me. You're not some dirty little secret I have to keep."

Another flash of warmth shot through him, but he shook it off. "I know, baby, but...there are bad people in my life." Understatement of the year. "We have to be careful or they'll hurt you to hurt me."

She said nothing for a moment, then she answered. "Someday, you're going to fill me in on those details, but I'll accept what you're saying for now. Still, you're not getting off the hook with my family. They won't spread our business to the underworld. I promise."

Will would lose his shit—and rightfully so—but Brick couldn't help the welling pride because this smart, beautiful woman wanted to claim him as her own. No one had wanted to claim him in, well, ever. "Your brother is not going to take this well."

Her laugh tinkled like bells. God, he loved the

sound of it. "You let me worry about my brother. We're having lunch together next Sunday. I'll break it to him in person."

At least he had a little more than a week before the inevitable fallout. "You'll call me if you need me before then?" he asked gruffly.

"I promise. Sweet dreams," she said before hanging up.

"They'll all be of you," he whispered into the silence.

CHAPTER TWELVE

Brick

Brick mopped the sweat off his face with the bandana he always kept in his back pocket. The plumbers finished up their part yesterday, and he was knocking out the punch list at the Burgundy house with the quiet guy, Matt. Kane worked at the other site, since this part didn't really require three men. Brick could've done it alone, but Robby never scheduled anyone to do stuff by themselves.

The kid had dropped by to check things out and deliver a cooler filled with red sports drinks. "Can you believe this heat? It's usually June before it gets this bad. How are you holding up, Brick?"

He took one of the offered bottles and unscrewed the cap. "The drinks help. Thanks, kid." Guzzling down some icy-cold Gatorade took some of the edge off the sweltering heat.

"The forecast says it will be better tomorrow." Robby shot him a winning grin. "You look like you're in a good mood this morning, which is awesome. I worried about you a little after the other day. I guess I'm not used to seeing you bummed out. You were kind of like a sad Incredible Hulk."

Wait. What?

Robby's thoughts had obviously moved on, his eyes shifting from side to side. "Um. Where's Matt? I, uh, I thought he might be thirsty too."

Ah. One mystery solved. "Matt, huh?"

Robby's expression looked like a kid with his hand caught in the cookie jar.

"Well, I'll be damned."

"What? No. I mean. Crap," Robby stammered. "I wanted to give the man a drink. No big deal."

Chuckling, he gestured toward the stairs. "He's on the second floor."

Robby pasted a bored expression on his face, but his eyes were still like a deer caught in headlights. Taking a deep breath in, then letting it out, he started toward the stairs.

"Hey, kid?"

Robby looked over his shoulder.

"You might want to bring the drinks."

Squeezing his eyes together tightly, Robby grabbed a bottle from the cooler and headed toward his target. Too bad the kid was barking up the wrong tree. Robby deserved a nice guy to make him happy.

He hadn't seen Matt so much as acknowledge Robby's existence. The man wasn't rude or anything, simply self-contained. And if the car seat in his sensible sedan gave any indication, he had a baby at home.

Still, Robby couldn't help how he felt about Matt

128

any more than Brick could about Olivia. Knowing something's impossible in your head doesn't really change what's in your heart. If it did, life would be a hell of a lot easier.

Robby came back down, carrying only a fraction of the high spirits he had before. He also still carried the Gatorade. "He already had a drink," he murmured as he dropped it back in the cooler.

"Sorry, kid."

Robby flinched a little with his words, and he resolved never to call him a kid again. "Robby," he said deliberately. "You can't take it personally. You're a great guy. Matt…just doesn't seem to be looking for a guy right now."

Robby didn't quite smile, but something in his face did change. "Thanks, Brick. I know I'm stupid sometimes, but you never make me feel ridiculous. I'm glad you're my friend."

For once, he didn't argue. He let the compliment wash over him as Robby patted him on the back and walked out to his truck a little bit lighter than when the day began.

Maybe he *could* be a good guy. If he could ever get away from his old life.

***

Liv

It had been way too long since Liv had shared a meal with Carol and her girlfriend. So, when they invited her to Alma Cocina for Mexican to celebrate the end of the school year, declining didn't even occur to her. Besides, Rosita said their carnitas were to die for.

She rushed home and washed off the stink from her visit to the gym. She made it to the restaurant at exactly seven-fifty-nine. One minute to spare before their agreed-upon time.

Rosita walked up right behind her. "Great timing." Carol's girlfriend folded her into a generous embrace. Rosita's short and round body presented the perfect complement to Carol's slender frame.

Dozens of other diners crowded the place, but Carol had been smart enough to grab them a reservation online, so they went straight to the table. They ordered margaritas as the server brought out their chips and salsa.

"We picked a busy night." Rosita crunched on a chip. "Thank God these tables are spread out, or I'd be claustrophobic right now."

She nodded and took in the atmosphere. The place had a modern feel with dark wood floors and a giant metal spherical light fixture hanging in the middle of the ceiling, which looked like an art piece to illuminate the room. Dozens of ongoing conversations generated a low-level buzz accompanied by an occasional clink from the busboy clearing plates.

She took a sip of her drink, and the tart taste of lime made her taste buds tingle. The aftertaste of the tequila made her shudder. "Holy cow, this is strong."

Rosita sipped hers and shook her shoulders in agreement. "Woo! The tequila packs a punch for sure. Only one for me tonight."

"Me too. Don't even get me started on the last time I had too much to drink. I could barely make it through the next day. One of my students had to lead the class." She eyed Carol with a trace of embarrassment, waiting for the inevitable teasing, then crammed a salsa-covered chip into her mouth.

Carol didn't take the bait but rubbed at her eyes instead. Maybe she was working too hard. God made a special place in heaven for social workers.

Before Liv could ask how things were going, though, her friend excused herself for a trip to the bathroom.

"I'm worried about her." Rosita massaged her temples. "She needs to go get a check-up."

She stilled, fear climbing into her throat.

No. Carol got a clean bill of health at the same time she did. They had their last round of chemo on the same day, months ago. "I think she must be overdoing it at work. Have you talked with her about it?"

Rosita shook her head. "You think it's work? She won't discuss it." She took a gulp of her margarita. "Sometimes, she seems fine. Great, even. Like when she's talking about the stupid list you two have. Or when she's telling a joke or when we dance. But then sometimes, it's like she's made of old paper liable to disintegrate if I touch her." She looked up, her eyes glassy with unshed tears. "I'm scared."

Carol approached the table now, her gait slow. But as other diners drifted in and out of her path, Liv couldn't tell if she would have moved differently without the crowd. "I'll talk to her. When we go shopping next weekend. I promise."

The waitress brought out their food, and it smelled so amazing they quit talking for a few minutes to dig in. She had taken Rosita's advice and ordered the carnita tacos. They were as delectable as promised. Some kind of pineapple salsa happening on top set off the pork to perfection.

They polished off their meal, and she watched Carol smile lovingly at Rosita. Her friend looked happy—tired, but happy. Everything would be fine.

She went home with a full belly and a light heart. Good friends. A sexy guy. A great job. Everything was falling into place, especially now, with her brother out of jail and part of the family again. The flat two-dimensional world she'd been living gained texture every day.

Smiling, she texted Brick.

Liv: Can u talk?

About five minutes later, he sent his reply.

Brick: Give me an hour.

After another minute, he sent a follow-up.

Brick: OK?

How cute.

Liv: I'll be here.

She changed into a pink cami and white capri pajama pants with little red hearts, then settled in on the couch with her Kindle. The hour flew by as she sank into the story filled with magic and swords, but when the phone rang, she had it to her ear in a second.

"Hello?" Did she sound breathless? Hopefully, he didn't notice.

"Sorry I couldn't talk before. Is everything okay?" He always worried about her.

"Everything is great. I had a fantastic night and I wanted to cap it off by talking to you."

"What made it so fantastic?" His words came out guarded.

"The company. I went out to dinner with Carol and her girlfriend. We ate and had margaritas. I've got a new book, and I'm curled up on the sofa, which by the way, is my favorite way to spend a Friday night. Now I'm talking to you. So yeah, fantastic." She ignored the temptation to ask him what he'd been doing tonight. She had a feeling he wouldn't want to share.

"I was…working."

"I figured," she said softly. "I know you don't want to talk about it."

"No. I want to keep the shit part of my life far away from this. From you."

She picked up one of the throw-pillows she'd tossed on the floor and hugged it to her. "I feel like you know everything about me, but I don't know anything about you. Tell me…about your childhood. What were you like as a kid?"

"I was poor." His response came quick and razor

sharp.

She refused to fill the silence afterward. It stretched for nearly a minute.

Eventually, he sighed. His words resumed haltingly. "My mom worked two jobs. Waitressing and cleaning houses. She was a first-generation *Machwaya* immigrant. Even though she grew up in Chicago, mostly in foster care, she was a Rom born in Serbia. I thought she was beautiful, but she looked different, sounded different from anyone around here. Even with a green card, good work was hard to come by." He paused. "My dad…was a junkie. Maybe he was less of a piece of shit when she married him, but who knows?"

He continued briskly. "I never saw much of either one of them. Mom did the best she could, but we had my grandma to take care of too. She slept on the sofa. I took the floor. Things were hard, but it was all I ever knew, you know?"

She wished she could see his face for this. Hold his hand. Then again, maybe this came easier for him when he didn't have to look at her.

"When my mom died, there was no money at all. My grandma has diabetes, and while Medicaid helped with her insulin, there had to be decent food in the house. There was no money for rent. There was nothing."

He cleared his throat. "Sucre was my dad's dealer. I went to him. I begged him to cut my father off. He said no, but he did offer me a job—doing little shit for him at first. Pushing pot on the corner. Selling it at school. It was enough to keep us off the street, but it wouldn't feed my grandma. Her legs were bad, so she couldn't stand up for very long. She had vision problems too, so she couldn't work. Eventually, I dropped out of school and got a job hauling lumber during the day and working for Sucre at night. It was okay, until Sucre noticed how big I was getting. Decided I'd be more valuable to him as muscle."

This was far more than she had expected to hear. It wasn't merely a story about a birthday lunch like she'd shared at the Majestic. This was how he came to be the kind of man her brother had warned her away from. She felt a pang she'd never told him about the cancer; happy memories were a whole lot easier to share.

His words came faster now. "I told him no the first time he asked me. The next day, my dad's tab ran out. Apparently, Sucre had only been keeping him alive as a 'favor' to me. It's what he told me anyway, and *did I think my grandma had the money to pay off my father's drug debt?* If she didn't, he was sure we could work something out if I started working for him full-time. It wasn't so much a question this time as an ultimatum."

Tears filled her eyes, but she kept her voice steady. "You sacrificed yourself for her."

"Don't make me into some saint," he growled. "I've done some really bad shit since then. I've worked for Sucre half my life now. You don't want to know what I do."

He drew a good enough picture she got the idea, but she pushed it down. "And your grandma?"

"She's in a nursing home now. I pay for it. The problem is, Sucre knows exactly where she is. He likes to remind me he can get to her at any time. Today, he sent me a picture of a bruise on her arm." He lowered his voice. "But I'm saving. Saving every cent to get her out of there. Some place where he can't find her, and he can't touch her."

"Until then, though," she whispered.

"Until then, he owns me, and if he ever finds out about you…"

"I'll be the person he holds over your head." No wonder he tried to stay away from her.

"I do fights on the side for extra cash. They're all fixed. Sucre thinks it's why I do construction too. The truth is, when I'm building houses, it's the only time I don't hate myself. Then and when I'm with you."

Her heart ached for all he'd been through. "I wish I could take it all away."

"Don't you understand?" He breathed deeply and gentled his voice. "You do."

Wow.

"When can I see you?" she choked out.

"Soon…but not tonight. I've got to get back out there. No rest for the wicked."

Her stomach wrenched at the idea he had to go back out into the night. To do God knows what for a man he hated.

"Be safe," she whispered. But he was already gone.

CHAPTER THIRTEEN

Brick

Brick didn't see Tre on the job Friday night, and he didn't ask where he was. Sucre would've told him if the kid was dead, which meant right now, Tre only *wished* he was dead. Brick wanted no part of it.

The first half of the night, he did simple collections. No one was too far in the hole, so it wasn't rough work. No doubt Sucre had planned it to work out that way because Brick had a fight at midnight.

Talking to Olivia had been a welcome diversion from slapping Fat Kenny around for the hundred bucks he owed. He considered their call as he stripped down for the match. For the life of him, he had no idea what possessed him to spill his guts over his pathetic history. But no one had ever actually wanted to know him before. He didn't count the people who thought they could leverage a friendship for drugs or protection.

Olivia was genuinely interested.

And he wanted her to know he wasn't a bad man by choice. Maybe he could have been someone better if his life had gone a different way.

He breathed in the miasma of sweat, cigar smoke, and beer as he approached the ring.

It was a moot point, anyway. This was his life.

Blood.

Brutality.

Climbing between the ropes, he pushed down thoughts of Olivia, locking them away. He reached for the cold stillness inside himself and faced the poor bastard he was about to destroy. His challenger, Paolo, appeared to be of Puerto Rican descent. A big motherfucker, maybe an inch or two taller than him and at least seventy-five pounds heavier. The man had a lazy eye and a mouth full of crooked, grey teeth.

Sucre wanted Paolo to go down in three and a half minutes. A challenge, but not an impossible one. The man swung wide as the bell rang, and as he expected, Paolo's size slowed him down. On fast feet, Brick danced out of the way.

The next time the man's meaty hand flew out, he ducked low and jabbed him in the side. It happened twice. Three times.

Sucre gave him the nod.

He had to speed things up. He faked another jab with his left, luring his opponent to step away, directly into the path of a viscous right hook. Before the guy could shake it off, he cracked into his temple again and again, driving him down to his knees, then slamming his head flat onto the floor.

Paolo didn't get up.

Sucre would make big bank tonight.

Brick walked out without so much as a scratch on him and a few hundred more dollars to add to his Grandma Fund.

***

Magnolia Green wasn't the swankiest nursing home around, but the staff kept it clean, and they had become a surrogate family to Brick's grandma during the years she'd lived there. The nurses waved in greeting as he walked the familiar pale blue halls on Saturday afternoon. He'd brought with him a bouquet of gardenias and his grandma's favorite sugar-free chocolate muffins from the bakery around the corner, the same place he got the tiramisu he liked so much.

This time, every week, Grandma usually hung out in the music room. She'd never learned to play any instruments, but she loved listening when volunteers came from a local church group to sing and play the piano.

He waited quietly, leaning against the wall at the back of the room as the ladies went through their set-list. He wouldn't interrupt, not when Grandma had looked forward to the music all week long. The piano player had more skill than the singer, who warbled through "Go Tell It on the Mountain" and a couple other songs he didn't know, but Grandma never stopped smiling the entire time.

This was why he endured working for Sucre.

He had never been especially close to his grandmother. She didn't coddle him as a child or protect him when her son got high. She was never cruel, though, and for most of his life, she was the only person who cared if he lived or died.

He waited until the church ladies let themselves out before approaching Grandma's wheelchair.

"Brick?" She spoke before he even reached her side. "Do I smell gardenias?"

Placing the bouquet in her lap, he tucked the box of muffins under his arm and took the handles of the chair. "Yes, ma'am. Picked them up fresh this morning."

Her hands shook as she lifted the flowers to her face. "Mighty fine. Smells mighty fine."

He looked for the bruise on her arm he'd seen in the photograph. He found it, though it had faded to a pale purple now. It wrapped around her slender arm like someone had squeezed her too hard. He thought about asking her how she had gotten it, but he didn't want to upset her.

Instead, he asked, "Would you like to go outside for a while? It's a beautiful day." He didn't know how often she felt the sun on her face. Not too much, he imagined, because she eagerly accepted whenever he offered to take her out.

"Yes, but I'd like to put my flowers in my room first. I want to enjoy them after you're gone."

He obliged her, and they took a trip down the hall so he could carefully place them in the clear, plastic vase on her nightstand. As always, he'd slip an orderly a few bucks to add water every day to help keep them fresh. Even if she couldn't see them, she wanted to enjoy the smell as long as she could.

"I brought some of those muffins you like too.

Do you want me to leave them here, or do you want to take one outside?"

She sighed softly. "Here's fine. I haven't had too much of an appetite lately."

He studied the old woman as he wheeled her out to the gazebo. She had lost weight, and she had the bruise, but she hadn't changed much otherwise since he'd visited last month. "Are you feeling okay?"

She waved her hand in the air impatiently. "I'm old. I feel...old. I don't feel much like talking today."

Didn't feel like talking? Usually, he spent his hours here listening to his grandma detail every single thing happening in the facility, from the contents of the dinner menu to which old devils had their sons smuggle them Viagra during their visits.

"You want me to go?"

Her unseeing eyes stared straight ahead as she lifted her chin toward the gentle breeze. "No. Stay a spell. I like it out here."

They sat together in silence.

It wasn't until about an hour later, as he wheeled her into her room, she finally spoke. "I don't know exactly what you have to do to keep me in this place. I imagine it's nothing pretty. Your daddy's dealer was already using you when you were a kid. I let it happen. I let you sacrifice to take care of me. That's my failing, my weakness. And I know you still answer to him. I hear their talk. They make their threats. I know they use me to get to you. They have, all these years." She shook her head sadly. "But it's almost over."

How did she know? The hidden money, the plan to get her to the nice place in Savannah, he had never told anyone, except for the little bit he'd shared with Olivia.

"I'm dying," she said softly.

What? "No. You're doing great." He sat at the foot of her twin bed. He picked up the soft, red, flannel blanket he'd bought her last Christmas and settled it on her lap.

She ran her gnarled fingers over the fabric. "You've got your mother's soft heart." Her face hardened. "It's how they'll break you."

The air conditioning kicked on with a loud rumble, and the icy breeze skittered down his neck. The chilled air made him shudder, not his grandmother's words. "No one's going to break me."

Grandma pulled the blanket up to her neck, and a shiver wracked her thin frame. "Only time will tell. Just don't forget the kind of people you're dealing with."

He nodded sharply and left her to her cupcakes and gardenias.

The old woman could have saved her breath with her warning. No chance in hell he'd ever forget he was swimming with the sharks. The second he stopped moving, they wouldn't hesitate to eat him alive.

Only one person in his life offered him a safe haven. Only one who he didn't have to pretend with, lie to, or posture for.

And in her arms was the only place he wanted to be.

***

Liv

Liv stared out the window of her apartment as lightning lit the dark sky. Rain beat a steady cadence on the rooftop, tempting her to close her eyes and set the papers on her table aside. She wasn't in the mood to grade final exams, and the last two essays she'd read were downright terrible.

For every standout student, she had two who could barely string words together into a sentence. For them to get this close to graduating, it was even more depressing. The system had failed them and soon they'd be out in the world trying to survive with only a fraction of the skills they should've been taught.

She rubbed her forehead, trying to dislodge the melancholy threatening to creep in. What she needed was a distraction.

She flipped on the TV and cycled through the channels. Cooking shows. Home makeovers. Nothing caught her interest, so she turned it off.

Truthfully, there was only one distraction she really wanted. But after all of Brick's revelations the night before, would he want her to call again so soon? Would he want space, or would he think she was rejecting him over the secrets he'd finally told her?

She picked up the phone, then put it down. Then picked it up again and held it to her chest. She was about to break down and call when a giant clap of thunder shook the walls, and the room went black.

Maybe someone was trying to tell her something. She smiled ruefully and used the light on her phone to dig out two fat candles from the top shelf of the cabinet where she kept her glasses. A matchbook hid under some Post-Its inside the junk drawer.

As she lit the wicks and inhaled the vanilla scent, she let her mind drift away to her fantasies. The candles set the stage for a night of slow seduction. Soft music. Maybe they would dance together.

There would definitely be kissing.

And she'd feel the weight of his body against hers.

Lightning flashed, bathing the room in bright white, and like a specter brought to life, Brick was suddenly visible outside the window. The rain had plastered his short, dark hair to his head. His black t-shirt clung to his body and streams of water poured over his skin.

The electricity flickered back on.

Dropping the matchbook to the table, she lunged for the door and threw it open. The rain came in sideways, soaking her pink pajama shirt and shorts in seconds.

Then Brick stepped inside, closing the door, locking out the elements behind him.

"You're soaked." She barely recognized her own voice, deep and breathy, as it came out. She ran to the bathroom, returning with two fluffy white towels in her arms and a pair of sweatpants hanging over her shoulder. Brick hadn't moved. She couldn't read his expression.

She stepped forward, her hand hovering over his midsection. "May I?"

He nodded and squeezed his eyes shut as she tugged his wet t-shirt out of his jeans, lifting it up to reveal his ridged abdomen and thick, muscled chest. Dark hair covered his pecs, and she bit back the impulse to run her fingers over them. Brick hunched forward, allowing her to pull the material over his head and away from his body.

It hit the ground with a wet slap.

She dropped to her knees, unlacing his heavy black work boots, then pulling them off one at a time. He grabbed her arm, pulling her gently back to her feet. His touch made her pounding heart beat even faster. Licking her lips, she reached for the button fly of his jeans.

Inch by agonizing inch, she removed his wet pants. His impressive cock strained toward her beneath his boxer briefs. It would be easy to take him in her hand, but he was cold and wet, and he clearly had something on his mind. So, her demanding libido would have to wait.

With care, she towel-dried his hair, then ran the soft terrycloth over his left shoulder and down his arm. She gave the same attention to the right side before dragging the material across his back and leaving it hooked around the back of his neck.

Putting the second towel in his hand, she walked to the window and closed the blinds. She didn't turn around. "Take the rest of your wet clothes off and get dry."

Though he didn't answer, she could hear him moving and more wet clothes hitting the floor. She counted to ten, then chanced a glance back. He had the second towel tied around his waist.

She handed him her brother's sweats. "Here. You can wear these while your stuff dries." Gathering his wet clothes off the floor, she checked all the pockets and placed his wallet, phone, keys, and a wicked-looking knife on top of the washing machine before tossing his clothes in the dryer.

She'd barely taken two steps back into the room when he spoke. "Why do you have a man's clothes in your apartment?" His eyebrows drew down sharply at her smile.

The idea he might be jealous felt like champagne bubbles in her chest, but she didn't tease him. He'd looked too worn down when she'd let him in the door. "My brother left them here a few weeks ago. I never got around to giving them back."

His face relaxed, and she allowed herself the luxury of taking a long look at his chiseled body. His torso reminded her of Henry Cavill's in the first *Superman* movie. Tan skin seemed to go on forever over his hard, cut stomach muscles.

And those sweatpants? They hung deliciously low on his hips, showing off a sculpted vee that disappeared beneath the drawstring waist.

She swallowed as her mouth began to water. Venturing forward, she finally allowed her fingers to drift over his broad chest. She wanted to look at him everywhere…touch him everywhere.

He growled deep in his throat, making her wonder if he knew the direction of her thoughts. Did he know how desperately she wanted to kiss him? To have him in her bed?

She tried to meet his gaze, but Brick had eyes for only one thing. Her mouth.

He stared unerringly at her lips for so long, she wondered if he'd ever close the distance between them. Then he was there, his mouth questing, his tongue darting against hers. Heat pooled in her belly as his hands splayed across her back and slid down to rest on her hips.

Finally.

Her nipples hardened as they rubbed against the cold, wet cotton of her shirt. What she really wanted—what she needed—was the connection of skin on skin. She wrenched herself away, long enough to peel her top over her head, then dove back into his arms. For a moment, she registered the heat of him, the abrasion of his chest hair against her tender breasts, but then he put his mouth on her again.

Dear God, the man knew how to kiss.

His tongue plunged in and out of her like he was making love to her mouth. He tasted faintly of chocolate and coffee, decadent and delicious. His calloused hands scratched gently along her arms, before descending to her ass and lifting her up and onto his body.

She struggled to catch her breath. Her heart jackhammered in her chest. Every nerve ending came alive with his touch.

If kissing him did this to her body, how would she survive when they made love? She desperately wanted to find out.

With her legs wrapped around his waist, she pressed closer, seeking friction against her aching core. There was little to be found. His hands, kneading her ass, and his mouth, now laving her neck with open-mouth kisses, had her panties thoroughly soaked.

Distantly, she heard a phone ringing, but whoever it was would have to wait. She only cared about the man setting her on fire from the inside out.

"Please," she moaned. "I need you."

He nipped gently at her ear, then slowly lowered her to the floor, her body sliding over his bulging arousal. She had never wanted any man as much as she wanted this one, this very second.

Brick reached forward and tenderly tucked a lock of her hair behind her ear. "You have no idea how much you tempt me, Livie-mine. I'm barely holding on to my self-control."

Gripping his hand, she pulled it to the top of her breast, close to her heart. "Stop fighting it. If you want me, take me. I'm right here."

The phone, which had quieted momentarily, started ringing again. He tugged away from her hold and raked his hand down his face. "I'll ruin you." His voice was gravelly. "I lie to myself sometimes. I let myself believe I can have you and I can keep you apart from all the putrid shit in my life, but I'm being selfish."

"No—"

"Yes. You make me feel like maybe I could be clean again, but it's a fantasy."

Her heart sank as he pulled further and further away. "Stay with me."

"There is nothing I want more, but it doesn't matter what I want. The phone you hear ringing? My boss is calling. There's no making him wait.

You don't understand what kind of man he is. I hope you never do." His smile held no joy. "I'm an idiot and an asshole for coming here. I'd say I'm sorry, but I won't lie to you."

He swiped his stuff off the washing machine and shoved it all in the pockets of Will's sweatpants, then turned toward the door.

"Will you be back?" As many times as he'd pushed her away, was this the final straw?

He paused, turned, then closed the distance between them. His touch was soft as he ran the back of his hand down her cheek. "Not tonight. Afterward...it depends on how well I can keep the promises I make to myself to stay away. God knows I've tried, but seeing you—touching you—it's like a drug. I go out there at night and do terrible things. Most of the time, I can barely look at my face in the mirror. But with you, it all goes away. It's the only time I don't feel like a monster."

No monster would have protected Robby's feelings at the bar or given advice to a strange little boy who only dreamed of one day being big.

She grabbed his arm. "Take this," she whispered, pulling the simple braided gold band off her thumb. It fit perfectly on his pinkie. "Next time you feel like a monster, remember there's somebody out there who knows you're a man." Forcing her shoulders back, she lifted her chin and let his hand go.

He blinked once slowly and turned away, grabbing his boots on the way out of her home and into the night.

CHAPTER FOURTEEN

Liv

When her phone rang in the middle of the night, Liv's first thought was Brick had changed his mind. It wasn't a fully formed idea, just a wish on the edge of a dream. A reason for her smile to carry in her voice when she answered.

"Hello?"

"Liv." The anguish rolled off Rosita in waves and her stomach sank like a stone. "She's gone." A sucked-in stuttered breath of air. "She's *gone.*

"Carol is dead."

***

Liv didn't cry at the funeral. She felt too empty inside to grieve.

Thank God for summer vacation. The last thing she could do right now was face a classroom of kids. She had nothing to offer them.

The service was small. Only Rosita, Carol's

twenty-year-old daughter Elise, and a few friends from work attended. Carol's parents had died long ago, and she had no other family. The preacher said some stuff about walking with the Almighty in the kingdom of Heaven. Not exactly Carol's jam, but it seemed to comfort Elise.

She watched it all in stunned silence. Shock and grief turned her into an observer watching from outside her body.

It wasn't until three weeks later, at Carol's attorney's office, her shock gave way to anger. Henry Beauchamp, Esquire, sat behind his large mahogany desk, facing Elise, Rosita, and Liv. The wrinkles at the sides of his eyes gave him a kindly, concerned appearance as he dropped the bomb no one saw coming.

"Thank you all for being here. I know this is a bit unorthodox, but I knew Miss Carol for a long time. She helped place my son with our family many years ago and we kept in touch." His cadence was Old World Georgia to the core. A genteel Foghorn Leghorn. "I hate to be the bearer of this news, but this is a favor she asked of me."

Elise laughed bitterly. "I'm pretty sure the worst news has already come and gone. What could be worse than my mama dying?"

"Of course, ma'am." He ran a pale, wrinkled hand over his thin white hair. "What I meant was, I'm afraid I knew Miss Carol was dying. Or more directly, so did she."

"Bullshit." Elise rose to her feet.

"Her last bout of cancer never went into remission." He gestured for Elise to return to her

151

shiny leather chair, and she sat in shocked silence, a pallor over her normally rich mahogany skin.

He couldn't be right. Her head spun. "We finished our chemo at the same time. I would *know* if she were still getting treatment."

"True, Miss Turner. She did stop treatment." He swiped at his iPad and peered at the screen. "In December of last year."

Rosita gripped the gold cross she always wore around her neck. "She wouldn't give up. Carol wanted to live."

The lawyer sighed, as if this conversation was harder on him than the women who loved Carol most. "Her cancer spread to her liver. The doctors could do nothing else except make her comfortable. She said she wanted to use the time she had left to live her life to the fullest."

"The fucking list," Elise muttered.

The Dare to Dream list.

The gut punch threatened to make her double over.

Carol's fucking bucket list, her last hurrah at living. And the worst part? They only managed to complete two goddamn things on it before she died.

"She knew you'd be angry," Mr. Beauchamp murmured. "But she made her choice, for good or for ill." He cleared his throat. "Miss Carol didn't have much in the way of material possessions. Her car, a 2015 Honda Accord, goes to her daughter Elise, along with some photo albums and home videos I have set aside in the back room. To Miss Suarez, she left the contents of her apartment: all furniture, clothing, electronics, et cetera. Miss

Turner, she left you this."

The lawyer opened his desk drawer and pulled out a black eight-by-ten frame and held it out to her. It was plastic and flimsy, feather-light in her hand. And inside, a handwritten copy of the list they'd come up with together so many months ago.

Dare to Dream
~~Cliff dive~~
~~Skydive~~
Drive a race car
Bungee jump
Scuba dive
Change Someone's Life
Fall in Love (trust your heart)

Two of those were new, and the last…unwelcome. She'd *tried* opening herself up and look how it turned out. He had never come back. Never called. Besides, romance had been the last thing on her mind the past few weeks.

And she'd made enough moves where Brick Barlow was concerned. Dammit.

She couldn't think straight; nothing made sense.

Her heart cracked open. As she stared at Carol's uneven print, the tears finally came. Her chest tightened against the soul-deep pain. Silent at first, her anguish gave way to a mournful cry, and she sobbed. For the lies. The crushing loneliness. For the plans they made and never saw through.

For a lifetime without her best friend. Her guiding star. Her mentor.

She cried until she had nothing left. It could have

been five minutes or fifty, but she finally caught her breath.

Clutching the frame in a death grip, she moved woodenly toward the exit.

"Are you going to finish the list?"

She paused at Rosita's question, the doorknob in her hand. "I don't know." Thinking about it hurt too much.

CHAPTER FIFTEEN

Brick

Six weeks later

"I told the new guy I'd have the money at the beginning of the week. Ask him; he'll tell you." Pam lifted her hands to stop Brick's approach.

"If you told Tre you couldn't pay, he would've told you the money's not due next week. It's due right now." He massaged the palm of his right hand with his left thumb.

Fucking Tre. Sucre let him do some work on his own now, but it was up to Brick to clean up any messes he made.

Pam dropped to her knees, and his stomach lurched. She whimpered as she reached for his belt buckle.

He took a step back. "Don't do this," he warned.

Her green eyes filled with tears as she lifted her head. She would've been a pretty girl if she didn't have sores all over her face. Meth fucked people up.

155

"I'm begging you. Please. Keep the new guy away from me. I can't—" Her voice broke. "I can't go through that again."

He had no doubt the terror in her eyes was real.

His mind started spinning. When exactly had Tre been here and why? Pam wasn't due a visit until today. He squatted down to her eye level. "Tell me exactly what happened."

"He *did things* to me." She trembled. "Last night. It was late, after midnight. He was so angry when he showed up. Said Sucre takes his money seriously." Her tears streamed down her face. "I told him I didn't have it all yet. I said I was going to go work the street tonight to get the rest, but he didn't want to hear it. Said he was going to…take it out of my ass."

A knot formed in his stomach. "Did he rape you?"

Her answer was to wrap her arms across her torso and start rocking.

He reached out to comfort her, but she scuttled back, her chest heaving with frantic breaths. Pam thought he was the same kind of beast as the man who broke her the night before. He twisted the shiny gold ring on his left pinkie. "I'm not going to hurt you."

Her eyes darted back and forth, like she couldn't make sense of his words. "Afterward, he said if I kept my mouth shut, he'd let me pay next week." Finally, her gaze landed on him. "He was lying, wasn't he?"

He nodded. "Just give me what you have, and we'll call it square." He'd use his own money to pay the difference.

Scrambling to her feet, Pam disappeared into her bedroom and returned with a handful of rumpled bills. "I can't face him again."

"You can't tell anyone about this." With a churning stomach, he took the cash and left.

The rain had finally stopped, but there were huge puddles he had to avoid on the way to his truck. The air hung heavy with the smell of wet garbage. His heart was even heavier.

Sucre's lesson may have worked in the short term, but the monster under Tre's skin was peeking out again. And his boss had been clear: next time Tre forgot the rules, Brick would be the one delivering the message.

He'd done terrible things, but he'd never raped anyone, and he refused to start now.

No. He'd keep his mouth shut and hope somehow, some way, he could get it through Tre's thick head to follow the rules, before they both lived to regret it.

***

Liv

Devon didn't show up for the first day of school. Or the second. When she saw still no sign of him after the first two weeks, Liv went to see the guidance counselor at lunch. She'd planned to do it back in May, and now she regretted the delay. Unfortunately, Mr. Barnes was out of the office. The administrative assistant said he had a bad case of the flu.

It didn't matter. She wasn't going to drag her heels again.

"You don't roll over and die when things get tough," Carol had told her once when Liv was so sick and weak, she could barely lift her cheek from the rim of the toilet bowl. *"You can't win the prize if you stop running the race."*

Helping this kid—changing his life—it mattered.

Not because Carol put it on her list. She still couldn't think about the damn list. But Devon had so much potential. She couldn't let him throw it away.

Even without Mr. Barnes, she could call Devon's parents. A quick search for his emergency contact sheet came up empty. A deeper dive into his electronic records failed to provide a single phone number, only an address in what she knew was a rough part of town.

She toyed with the idea of knocking on his door, but she didn't know how well it would go over with his parents. He'd given her the impression his family life left something to be desired, and unlike Carol, she was no social worker, but she did care about him.

Maybe she could find another way in.

Justin.

Every time she saw Devon last year, he and Justin Brown were thick as thieves. They ate lunch together. They left campus together at the end of every day. If anyone would know what was going on with Devon, Justin would.

She found him sitting alone, playing with his

phone on a bench in the quad. Surprisingly, there were no girls around. A cute kid with light hazel eyes and rich, dark skin, it was rare to see Justin without at least one girl hanging on his arm.

"Do you have a second?"

He glanced up, then gestured to the empty space on the bench next to him. His brows drew together. "Everything okay, Miss T?"

She took the offered seat. "I'm hoping you can tell me. I haven't seen Devon since school started back up. He was supposed to be in my Senior Advanced Lit class this year. Have you heard from him?"

Justin shifted uncomfortably. "He, uh, he's got some stuff going on at home."

"Yeah. I got the impression. Should I be worried?"

He closed his eyes and lifted his face to the breeze. She waited. She knew it was no small thing she was asking. It had to be bad for Justin to be even considering any answer besides *no.*

After a minute or two, he firmed his jaw and opened his eyes. "Yeah. I think we all need to be worried."

Shit. Part of her had hoped Justin would say everything was fine, or she had read too much into things and Devon only had a cold or something. "What's going on, Justin?"

He rubbed his forefinger across the seam of his mouth. "Can't tell you, Teach. Not my story to tell. Maybe you could talk to him. Convince him to come back. He liked you. He says you looked out for him and shit."

She let the curse word slide. "Can you help me find him?"

"Yeah. I can, but are you sure?" He tilted his head toward her. "You don't exactly look like you belong in our neighborhood, you know what I'm saying? And I'm not sure folks will appreciate some well-meaning white lady swooping in, trying to save the day."

He had a point. Her life was hardly a Michelle Pfeiffer movie with a Coolio soundtrack. She did care about Devon, though, and she didn't want him to fall through the cracks.

Change someone's life.

"You think you could get him to meet you somewhere? Grab a burger or something? I could run into you guys, try to talk to him."

Justin rubbed at his chin. "I think I could. Give me your number and I'll text you."

She rattled off the numbers, and he put them into his phone.

"He'll know it's not a coincidence," he warned, "but I'm hoping no one else will."

***

True to his word, Justin texted her around seven o'clock with the address of a Burger King ten minutes away. The teens were already halfway through their burgers when she walked in the door.

Liv walked straight to their table. "Fancy meeting you here."

The glower Devon gave Justin could strip paint from the wall. "Are you shitting me right now? You

160

narc'd me out to my *teacher*?" He tossed the rest of his hamburger onto the tray. "I should've known you didn't really want to buy Taylor a ring at the pawn shop tonight, even if her baby is yours."

"No telling who her kid belongs to, but no, I didn't tell anybody your business. Miss T wanted to talk to you is all. Nobody's here to see it. What's it gonna hurt?"

There weren't many people there, but she felt as though every one of them stared at her. "May I sit?"

"Whatever," Devon grumbled.

"I'll grab you a Whopper." Justin couldn't get out of his chair fast enough.

She sighed as she sat down. "Please don't blame him. I really did come asking about you."

Devon rubbed the back of his neck. "Well, you shouldn't. I don't need you to come in and save me."

"What *do* you need? Something's going on. You're not coming to school. I bet you didn't take your ACTs. You refuse to talk about college." It was such a waste.

She slapped the table. "You're too smart for this. You can do *anything* with your life, but only if you take the opportunities right in front of you."

The fire in his eyes dimmed a little. "I have responsibilities to my family, Miss T. I have to work. I'm not choosing to ignore my opportunities. What I'm telling you is I have no choice."

"What do you mean?"

He shrugged. "There's a guy in the neighborhood. He kinda runs things. When he says you have to work for him, you *have to work for*

161

him."

She held back a shudder. Those words sounded ominous. "What about your parents? Do they know you aren't coming to school?"

"No parents," he sighed. "Not for a long time now. It's only me and my brother."

"Can't you do both? If you have to work, can't you still come to school? At least graduate, Devon. You'll have your diploma, and no one can ever take it away from you." She lowered her voice. "If you want out of the situation you're in, I can help you. I can call—"

"No. I won't leave my brother. He's all I have."

She understood all too well. She would never leave Will or Izzy as long as she had a choice. "Will you at least think about coming back?"

"I'll think about it."

Justin returned to the table and held out a paper bag. "You, uh, might want to take your burger to go, ma'am."

Acutely aware of everyone looking at her, she accepted his offering and drew to her feet. "Thanks, Justin."

Suddenly, she felt very exposed. Was the man in the green car staring at her?

She returned quickly to her Corolla and sped away without even taking the time to put on her seat belt. Her unease followed her all the way home.

Still, if there was even a chance Devon would take her advice, the trip had been worth it.

CHAPTER SIXTEEN

Brick

The house on Burgundy was coming together. The team had completed the framing, along with the plumbing, electrical, and insulation. They would start to drywall today, which meant soon, they'd have real walls, and it would finally feel like a real house.

The guys had hit a problem on the other build. Something about the buyer wanting to make some changes. So, the project sat on hold until the higher-ups could get it all sorted out. Brick had heard Xander on the phone with his bosses off-and-on almost every day this week.

Poor bastard.

He studiously ignored Will when he pulled up outside. He hadn't seen him in months, but Liv's brother would be working upstairs, so there was no reason for them to cross paths. He took his time lingering at the ice chest while Will passed behind him and climbed up.

Kane slapped him on the back. "He's gone, brother, you can stop hiding."

He shot his friend a look that would make most guys wither. Kane just laughed. "Hey, I wouldn't want to face the guy, either, if I was the one who fucked his sister."

Before he knew what came over him, he had Kane up against the two-by-fours which would soon become a wall. "I didn't fuck her," he hissed.

Kane appeared totally unfazed. "Oh, I can tell there's absolutely *nothing* going on there."

He sucked in a deep breath and let go of Kane's shirt. "Sorry," he muttered. He'd been on edge for weeks.

A dozen times, he'd picked up the phone, tempted to call Olivia. Even more often, he caught himself staring at the ring she gave him, questioning whether he'd be a bigger fool to break things off or to keep putting his selfish desires ahead of her safety.

"I don't know what to do, man. You ever been involved with a woman who was too good for you? Someone who doesn't belong surrounded by the shit we live in?"

Kane's jaw tightened. "Once."

"I want her. More than fucking air sometimes. But having her feels selfish. She could be with some guy who's got class, some guy who doesn't have blood on his hands and dirt under his nails. A guy who—"

"She doesn't want some guy, though, dumbass. She wants *you*. Or at least she did." Kane tapped him lightly on the forehead. "If she wanted another kind of guy, she'd be with one. So, man up."

He almost let the conversation end there, but more words spilled out before he could stop them. "I don't even know how to be with her. What the fuck do I talk about? How do I act? I feel like I'm playing a part in a goddamn movie. Like I'm pretending to be a regular guy. One who calls her on the phone...or takes her to get ten-dollar hamburgers...or wears her fucking jewelry. That's not me."

Kane shrugged. "Isn't it? You did all those things, right? Her shiny gold band is right there on your finger, am I right?"

Cocky fucker.

"You feel like it's a part? Play it. Maybe it's not who you can be most of the time, but it's who you want to be when you're with her. There's no shame in it."

"Xander." A woman's voice rang out from the front of the house. It was strong, loud, and more than a little pissed off.

Kane's eyes widened, and Brick spun around to get a glimpse. The woman stood in the doorway as though she owned the place. She had thick, straight, dark red hair, which fell to the center of her back. Her skin glowed porcelain. A black pencil skirt ended right above her knees, and a cream-colored silky blouse tucked into the top.

Everything about her screamed power and class.

Her gaze flew right past him and landed on Kane. "Where is he?"

"What are you doing here?"

His head swiveled around and did a double-take

at the venom in Kane's eyes.

"It's still my company, Kane. Tracking problems is my responsibility." Her eyes were green with little flecks of gold, and her gaze fired with every bit of intensity as Kane's.

"I thought your brother was guaranteed to manage our crew."

Finally, a little chink appeared in her armor. Her throat bobbed as she swallowed. "Mike was in a car accident."

Kane stepped forward, the malice on his face replaced with concern.

The woman waved it off. "He'll be fine. For now, I'm responsible for everything, including this clusterfuck in Decatur. Can you please...tell me where to find Xander?"

"He's upstairs." Kane gestured toward the staircase, and she walked toward it. "Amanda?"

She stopped but didn't turn around.

"I'm sorry about Mike."

She nodded, then started to climb.

He waited until her shiny black pumps disappeared from view before approaching Kane. "What just happened?"

The man stomped out the front door, and Brick followed him into the street. "Wait up. Kane!"

Tattooed arms flexed as Kane pulled off his hard hat, and several strands of his dark hair came loose from the ponytail at the back of his neck. "Amanda and her brother Mike own the construction company. Seems like she's here to rip Xander a new one over the Decatur house, which is stupid because the delays aren't his fault."

Folding his arms, he stood still and watched Kane pace the pavement next to the curb. "So, what's the deal with the two of you?"

Kane's jaw flexed. "There's no *deal*."

"If you say so, man." He pulled a ten-dollar bill out of his wallet. "Why don't you take a run to the donut place and get us some coffee? My treat."

Kane scowled.

"She'll probably be gone before you get back."

Snatching the cash out of his hand, Kane stomped to his motorcycle. "Fine. I'll be back in twenty."

As the bike rumbled away, he wondered briefly how Kane would carry the coffee, but shrugged it off. The coffee had only been a smokescreen anyway.

He stepped back into the house, and raised voices echoed from upstairs. The entire crew had migrated to the backyard for an unscheduled break. Only Xander and Amanda remained unaccounted for. Robby paced nervously in and out of the French doors, which led to the rear patio.

"Robby."

The kid froze at the sound of his name.

"What's going on?"

Abandoning his post at the back door, Robby approached him. "Ms. Griffin is getting a lot of flak from the guy who commissioned the other house. He said we're not giving him what he wants."

"The guy signed off on the plans. How is it Xander's fault if he changed his mind? It's bullshit."

Robby snuck a glance at the staircase before

167

continuing. "Yeah, it is. Now, the man's threatening to pull out if we don't make the changes for free. The company takes a hit either way, and you know bad stuff rolls downhill."

The unmistakable sound of heels clicked down the stairs. "Get it done, Xander. I don't have time for excuses, and we can't afford any delays."

The older man followed her down. The sun-darkened olive skin on his face blanched. "We'll do our best, Amanda."

She shot a look at the men now crowded around the back door. "See that you do." She blew out the front door like a tornado and slammed it behind her.

Heat flooded his face. He liked Xander. The guy worked hard and gave things to you straight. Boss or no, the redhead had no right to talk to him the way she did. Judging from the expressions on the other guys' faces, they felt the same way.

"Stand down," Xander said tiredly. "We're all under a lot of pressure. Amanda too."

"But, Boss," Will began.

"No. No buts. Sometimes you've got to shove it down and keep moving. I'm going to need every one of you to get these projects done on time. Can I count on you?"

One by one, every man nodded.

"Great. If you guys could all work down here for a bit, I have a few calls to make upstairs."

Kane still hadn't returned, so he headed over to Matt to team up on the drywall. Together, they loaded the first piece of sheetrock onto the lift to install on the ceiling. Cyrus helped them tack it to the joists, and they made quick work of the dining room.

Robby brought pizza for lunch around one o'clock, and the guys fell onto the boxes like they'd been starving for days. The calories chipped away at the effects of their hard work and stress.

He tossed his trash into the big waste barrel. Before he could get back to work, Will grabbed his left arm.

"Where did you get that?"

He resisted his first instinct, the one to wrench free. The thought it would upset Olivia kept his temper in check. "I don't know what you're talking about, man."

Gripping his arm tighter, Will lifted it into the air and shook it. "The ring. You're wearing my sister's ring."

He had no idea how to respond, so he said nothing.

"Give it back to me, you dirty fuck."

Cyrus pulled Will back as he tried to rip it off Brick's finger.

Cradling his hand to his chest, Brick spoke softly. "She gave it to me."

Will's face darkened with fury. "Liar. Izzy bought that ring because it looked like one our mom used to wear. It was her good luck charm when she had fucking cancer because it made her feel like Mom was watching over her. She would never give it away. Never."

It didn't make any sense. Olivia hadn't told him the ring was special. "I don't know what to tell you." Cancer? "She wanted me to have it. If you don't believe me, call and ask her yourself."

Will tried to shake loose, but Cy kept him from lunging again. "Stay away from her. You're not fit to breathe the same air as my sister, you shit thug. You think I'm scared of you because you chop up people for Sucre de la Cruz?"

The words took the air out of the room.

"Yeah. I said it. I know what you are. Which is exactly why I will do whatever it takes to keep you away from her."

He couldn't even get mad. Will only spoke the truth. Still, hearing the words come from someone else hollowed him out. "We're not together." No one could know the truth.

"Let. Me. Go, Cy." Will's eyes glinted wildly. Cyrus didn't budge.

He wanted to tell Will he was crazy about his sister. He wanted to keep her safe. If the information got into the wrong hands, though, it could destroy the very thing he was fighting for. He liked the guys he worked with, but he didn't trust them with Olivia's life. So instead, he repeated, "We're not together, Will, and you don't want to do this here."

"Don't tell me what I want to do, motherfucker. What I want to do is bash your ugly face in. You are not good enough for my sister."

"You're right."

Finally, Will stopped struggling.

He shot Liv's brother a cold look and hardened his voice. "I'm everything you say I am, and your sister is a sweet little school teacher with a crush. But I don't even remember the last time I saw her." Lie. "We're not playing house. I didn't even fuck her. So, cool your jets." He stepped forward, crowding Will, but no one got in his way. His stone-cold killer voice fit like a glove. "Don't come at me again. There will be consequences."

Xander cleared his throat from the staircase. "Do we have a problem here?"

"No problem." He raised his eyebrows at Will, daring him to argue.

Silence.

"Let's keep it that way. We don't have time for petty squabbles. Let's get back to work."

Kane stomped back onto the property right as their boss made his pronouncement. Judging by the look on his face, the three-hour coffee run had done little to cool the heat of his anger.

There was no sign of any coffee, but Brick wasn't dumb enough to say a word.

CHAPTER SEVENTEEN

Liv

The banging outside Liv's front door had so much force behind it, the windows rattled in their frames. She hesitated to answer until Will's voice boomed from the front porch.

"Open up the goddamn door, Liv."

No matter how angry he sounded, she could never consider her brother a threat. An annoyance, yes, but the man was all bark and no bite.

The second she turned the knob, he barreled in, still dusty from his worksite. "You don't fucking listen! Dammit, Liv. I told you to stay away from Brick Barlow." His cheeks flushed red, and he paced with unspent anger.

She closed the door gently. "Calm down, Will." He didn't acknowledge her words, so she settled in on the sofa. "I can't talk to you when you're like this."

He slammed the heel of his hand against the wall, leaving a black smudge on the cream-colored paint. "You keep fooling around with Brick, you won't be talking to anybody." He wasn't getting calmer. "You'll be too busy getting ass-raped by one of Sucre's other goons, or if you're lucky, you'll only be dead."

"Will—"

"You don't understand the kind of people you're dealing with." He strode to the sofa then knelt in front of her. "When I went to prison, I learned fast, you don't mess with Sucre's crew. I saw one of his guys pop out somebody's eye with a fucking spoon, Liv."

His voice shook. Will never talked about the time he was in prison. "Those guys had no fear. They had no limits. They even scared the guards."

She reached out to cup his jaw. "He isn't like them."

He clenched her hand. "You don't understand. Brick was the one *those guys* whispered about. The one *they* were afraid of. You are letting a monster into your life." His eyes glistened with tears. "I can't protect you from these people, Liv. Please listen to me."

Her stomach churned with his warning.

She'd never seen her brother scared before, and he was clearly terrified right now. As she pulled him into a hug, the wetness from his cheek soaked through her shirt. "Whatever was between us is over. I haven't heard from him in months. Not since before Carol…"

He pulled back to search her face. "I don't get it.

I know he wants you. I'm not blind."

"He said he wanted to keep me safe. I guess you two have something in common."

Will climbed up from the floor and clasped his hands behind his neck. He stared up at the ceiling. "I pray to God what you say is true." His gaze cut back to her. "You and Izzy are everything to me. I'd die before I let something happen to either one of you. I couldn't do anything when you were sick; I was stuck in fucking jail. Please don't make me feel so fucking useless again."

He didn't wait for a reply. Gritting his teeth, he spun around and walked straight out the door.

She took a shuddering breath. She believed him when he said he would die to protect her. It was a promise she prayed he would never have to see through.

***

Thank God for Google Maps. Without the app, Liv would have never found her way to the address in Devon's student file. He hadn't come back to class, even after their chat at Burger King, and she couldn't help but wonder if his brother knew he'd been skipping out.

Will's meltdown reminded her big brothers tended to put their siblings first. No way would he have been okay with her ditching school. Will would've found a way to keep her in class, even if he had to work three jobs to do it. Maybe Devon's brother would feel the same way.

The apartment complex sprawled over a block,

but it desperately needed repairs. Boards covered several of the windows. The siding sagged, and a sheen of green mildew obscured the original color. One of the buildings had obviously been damaged in a fire and left in ruin. She stepped carefully over the broken concrete as she tried to figure out which section housed Building E. If there were ever markings on any of the structures, she saw no sign of it now.

She didn't spot anyone outside, strange for a Saturday afternoon, but the back of her neck prickled, the same way it had when she'd left the burger place. Even if she couldn't see who, someone watched her. Nerves crept up her spine.

She shook them off. Old Liv would have never set foot in this place.

Go big or go home. The expression had been one of Carol's favorites.

"You in the right place, lady?" The high-pitched voice almost made her jump out of her skin. Liv swiveled her head to the source, a gangly kid who looked about twelve.

She forced her voice to remain neutral, despite her unease. "Maybe you can tell me. Am I close to Building E?"

The boy narrowed his eyes. "Why you wanna know?"

"I'm looking for the Lowrys. I—"

The kid shook his head quickly and stepped back. "Sorry, lady. I can't help you." He moved away like his feet were on fire.

The feeling of someone watching her intensified. Still, she soldiered on, searching for any sign she was closing in on her destination. She spent ten minutes wandering around the ghost town of apartment buildings before finally giving in to the niggling voice she needed to leave.

Dark clouds gathered in the sky, and a clap of thunder in the distance made her surroundings feel even more menacing. She'd just turned into the stiff breeze and headed back toward her car when a man's voice cut through the silence. "I hear you're looking for me?"

The guy couldn't have been more than a few years older than Devon, but she had no doubt she'd found his big brother. He had the same arresting good looks, dark skin, and lean build, though there was something different in the eyes.

"Trevaughn? Trevaughn Lowry?" She approached him slowly.

He shot her a lazy smile. "Depends on who's asking."

"My name is Olivia Turner. I'm one of your brother Devon's teachers. I was hoping I could talk to you about him, if you have a minute. He's—he's one of my most gifted students."

Trevaughn lifted his eyebrows. "You want to talk about my little brother?"

She nodded.

"All right. Follow me."

He led her past the burned-out unit, toward the building behind a rusted basketball hoop without a net. It was nearly a block away from where she'd parked. They went in the second door on the left.

She wasn't exactly sure what she expected the inside to look like, but definitely not like this. Two lamps bathed the room in red light. A black leather sofa dominated the center of the room, and a giant plasma TV hung on the wall. A glass and chrome coffee table matched the end tables, one sporting a Bose sound system. The other had an Amazon Echo.

Devon's brother gestured to the sofa, and she sat down. "What seems to be the problem, Miss—"

"Turner." She cleared her throat. "As I told you, your brother is one of the brightest young men I've ever taught. He scores off the charts on the state benchmarks. I've told him many times, I think he's scholarship material."

"Scholarship, hmm?" Trevaughn joined her on the sofa, nodding for her to continue.

"Yes. He told me he couldn't leave home, and you needed him here."

He nodded. "All true."

"There are some wonderful schools right here in Atlanta, though. He could stay home and still go to college. All he would need to do is take his ACTs and apply." Her voice rose in earnest. "I would be happy to write him a recommendation. I know some of the other teachers would as well."

"You came all the way out here to talk about D going to college?" His voice sounded dubious.

"Yes and no. I mean, I would love it if you could help me convince him to go, but the more immediate reason I'm here is because Devon hasn't been in school for a while."

"What do you consider *a while*, Miss Turner?"

"Not at all this school year." She clasped her hands together in her lap. "I have an older brother, too. I kept thinking if something were going on with me, he'd want to know. He'd want to help fix it."

Trevaughn leaned back and propped his feet up on the glass table, crossing one ankle over the other. "I see. You make house calls for all of your students or only the special ones?"

She tried to ignore the heat creeping up her neck. "I've never gone to a student's home before. I guess I shouldn't have this time, either, but Devon *is* special. I'd hate to see him fall through the cracks."

"I had a teacher like you once." His eyes looked far away. "Mrs. Muniz. She tried to help me, get me on the right track when Moms died." He shook off the memory. "I remember her…fondly."

Muniz? The name sounded familiar, but she couldn't place it. "I'm sorry for your loss. My older brother took care of me, too, after our parents passed away."

Trevaughn didn't seem to be listening anymore.

"Mr. Lowry?"

His gaze focused on her again. This time his gaze looked sharper, more assessing. "Sorry. I got a little lost in the memory." He climbed to his feet, and Liv followed suit. "I appreciate your interest in my little brother. I promise, he and I are going to have a talk about this."

She smiled as he walked her to the door. "I'm so glad to hear it. I knew any young man as smart and special as Devon had to have someone at home who would want to know what's going on. It was a pleasure to meet you, Mr. Lowry."

This time, when he smiled, it wasn't relaxed or easy, the way it was before. Now, he looked more like a shark, his gold tooth glinting. The red lights and his red leather jacket only made him seem more like a predator.

"The pleasure was all mine. And please, call me Tre."

***

Tre

Tre laughed softly to himself as the pretty little blonde teacher scurried out the door.

Like a lamb to the slaughter.

Maybe he should've kept her here. Shown her some of the skills that made *him* so special. He didn't want to spoil the chase, though.

No. He'd give her a minute or two to try and make it to her car. Let her feel the hunt on her heels.

Then, he'd drag her back screaming.

His dick hardened in his jeans.

It was so much more fun when they ran.

CHAPTER EIGHTEEN

Brick

Brick couldn't believe his eyes when his Olivia walked out of Tre's apartment. He didn't know what she was doing there, and he didn't care. It was bad enough he had to spend so much time here collecting cash and busting ass—like he had already tonight—but this was exactly the kind of place he'd fought so hard to keep her away from. Nothing good could come of this.

He sped into the shadow of the neighboring building. As soon as she got close enough, he grabbed her by the arm and pulled her into the darkness beside him. He cut off her yelp of surprise with his hand over her mouth.

"Quiet," he hissed in her ear. "I need you to trust me."

Her tense muscles relaxed slightly against him, and she nodded beneath his hold. Her hand slid up to cover his and gently pulled his fingers from her mouth. She didn't make a sound.

Keeping her hand in his, he led her into the burned-out shell of Building D. He knew this place like the back of his hand and could navigate it easily, despite the quickly setting sun. He had no doubt in his mind Tre would be looking for her soon, if he wasn't already.

Sure enough, he could hear someone whistling "Time Is on My Side" moments after they stepped into the darkness. Heart in his throat, he pulled her deep into the back bathroom where the ceiling had given way, then readjusted his backpack and boosted her up to the second floor. An old toilet seat gave him enough height to grab hold of the broken boards above to pull himself up beside her. The place stank of charred wood, and there were probably rats, but Olivia was a hell of a lot safer in here than she'd be outside.

"I would take you higher, but there are some places in the building where the floor could give out on us. Especially in the third-floor hallway. This will have to be good enough for now. We have to stay out of sight," he breathed into her hair. "He won't give up easy."

Though he couldn't see her, he felt her lift her head toward his. "You mean Tre?"

He swallowed the lump in his throat. "You know his name. Does he know yours?"

"He knows it," she whispered, and he felt a shiver go through her small frame. He pulled her into his arms. For warmth, of course. Not because he needed to reassure himself she was all right. And definitely not because he'd been little better than an empty shell since he'd touched her last.

"Why did you pull me in here? What's going on?" Her voice cracked on the last word.

He needed answers first. "What are you doing here, baby?" Her cheek pressed tightly against his chest. She could probably hear his racing heart.

"I was worried about one of my students. Devon Lowry." Lowry? Shit. "He hasn't been in class since the school year began. I thought—" Her hands reached up to curl around his bicep. "I don't know what I thought."

He petted her hair. "You thought you could help. I love that you want to, but Tre is about as messed up as they come. I've met a lot of bad men. Some do bad things because they have to. Some do them because they don't care. Tre does them because he likes it."

Liv drew a sharp breath, her fingers now digging into his arms. "You're scaring me. What are you talking about?"

"You should be scared. I'd lay odds he's marked you as a target. If he had his way, he'd probably be torturing you right now...or raping you. Or both." He wished for at least a sliver of light, so he could see her face, but the darkness was his best bet to keep her safe. He kept his ears trained for a hint of any movement below, though he doubted Tre would think to check here. He would've expected Liv to go straight to her car.

"Why? Why would he want to hurt me?" Her breaths came out in short pants. "I'm trying to help his brother."

He wracked his brain, trying to remember

anything about Tre's family. Of course, his parents were dead. Sucre would have made sure of it before he recruited the kid. The little brother had to be how he asserted his leverage—or at least he would be if Tre were any kind of normal human being. "The guy is a sociopath, in the truest sense of the word. He doesn't feel things the way you or I do. I doubt his brother means any more to him than his favorite pair of shoes. Maybe less."

"H-how do you know him?"

He hesitated a moment before he answered. "We have the same employer."

She cursed under her breath. "Devon told me there was a guy in the neighborhood who said he had to work for him. It's the same bastard who trapped you, isn't it? He targets entire families."

"Sucre has a knack for finding a person's weak spot and exploiting it. Maybe at first, he thought your boy was a way to manipulate his brother. I'll bet you next week's paycheck now it's the other way around." It only got clearer as he thought things through. "Tre's a loose cannon. He messed up real bad once already, but Sucre didn't kill him. Fuck. He's keeping him alive to recruit the kid brother. You said he's smart, right?"

"One of my best," she whispered. Horror laced her words. "He's supposed to have a future."

"You can force someone to work for you, but you can't change who they are. Tre's not built right. He's got something…broken inside."

"Devon's only a kid, though." If she was trying to convince him, she was wasting her breath.

He answered quietly. "So was I. Kids are easier

to break down and build back up the way you want them. I'm sorry, baby. If Sucre's got him, the kid is lost."

"No." Liv tried to step back. "I refuse to accept that. He is not lost, and neither are you."

He circled her arms with his hands and shook her lightly. "Fuck, woman. What will it take to make you understand? We're talking about *killers*, Livie. *I am a killer*. Every person I've killed was someone's mother or husband or son. Yeah, they were addicts and criminals, but they were still people."

She whimpered softly. Then, with a shuddering breath, she reached up and cupped his jaw. "Have you ever said no?"

His teeth ground together. "Not in a long time."

"What happened if you did?"

"Nothing I'd want to remember in the light of day, much less here in the dark." Even the threat of those memories made his stomach churn. He needed to get her out of the building before Tre circled back, not relive the horrors of his life.

Her thumb soothed over his skin. "I know you've done bad things, things you regret." She stepped closer, her vanilla scent chasing away the traces of burned wood. "You can't convince me you're a monster, though. Monsters don't feel regret. They don't push away women they want. They take what they want. They don't care who gets hurt. That doesn't sound like you."

His muscles tightened as her body drew flush with his. It was clear she was scared, but not afraid of him.

She kept talking. "I know you want me. Still, you try to stay away. You try to keep me safe. The thing is, if you hadn't been here tonight—if you weren't in my life—God knows where I would be. You saved me."

It would be so easy to let himself believe her words. He'd love to be someone's savior for once, especially Olivia's.

He dipped his head and allowed himself the luxury of tasting her mouth. Kissing had never consumed him this way before. He wanted to sip from her lips. Worship her tongue. Show her with his mouth she was precious. Beautiful. Everything.

Her lower lip was plump and full. He sucked on it gently before sliding his tongue over the pillowy softness. Liv's body relaxed in surrender as he entered her mouth. Her hands climbed toward his neck.

No girl like her had ever even looked at him before. Why would she? Olivia was so far above him, he'd never survive the fall. But it would be worth it.

She would be worth it.

He wouldn't have her in this kind of place, though. The walls crumbling around them. Needles and bugs on the floor. And who knows when a junkie might wander in, looking for an empty space to get his fix?

He pulled back. "You need to get out of here. I've got an idea, but I'm going to need you to trust me."

"I trust you."

Together, they crept back down to the first floor.

185

From his backpack, he pulled out a folded black tarp.

"What are you going to do with that?"

With a flick of his wrist, he unfurled it across the floor. "Time to play dead."

She gasped. "There's got to be another way."

He hardened his jaw. "It might be the only way you make it out of here alive."

He was glad he couldn't see the expression on her face as he guided her onto the plastic and she allowed him to roll her loosely inside.

She stayed quiet, except for a small grunt when he heaved her over his shoulder.

"Keep it together a little longer. This will all be over soon." Just as he had a dozen times before, he hoisted up a tarp-wrapped body and walked right through the parking lot like he owned it. He could see at least a dozen guys out there now, shooting hoops, drinking, smoking. Yet not one pair of eyes drifted his way. He didn't walk fast. He moved as he would any other day, any other time—like he would if he wasn't carrying a body over his shoulder or smuggling a woman away from the guy who probably wanted to fuck her corpse.

He placed her in the bed of his truck and drove away. His apartment could be dangerous, and he didn't want to risk taking her home, so he navigated to a secluded spot, surrounded by trees. Once he was sure no one had followed them, he helped her get free.

Liv's hair plastered to her face; her skin was damp and pale. She stumbled from the truck bed, straight into his arms, and burst into tears. He had never comforted anyone before. He was usually the reason they were crying.

"I c-couldn't move," she sobbed. "It was like being buried alive. I used to have those nightmares back at the hospital."

Oh, God.

He held his hands in the air, afraid to touch her.

He'd tried not to wrap her too tightly, but obviously the tarp wasn't loose enough. Stupid. He had no business trying to be someone's protector. Liv was lucky he hadn't killed her by accident.

She should be running away. Instead, she held onto him like a lifeline. Her tears soaked his black t-shirt.

"I'm so sorry," he murmured.

Liv walked backward a few steps, her shining eyes, wide. "Are you kidding? You *saved me.*" She tilted her head back, held her arms open, and breathed in deeply. Her eyes glittered as she brought her chin down. "I don't know if you're trying to convince me or yourself this thing between us is wrong. It doesn't matter. You need to stop. Because this—" She gestured to the space between them. "This thing between us? I'm not walking away, and neither are you."

He didn't *want to* walk away. Every time he had her in his arms, it got harder to let her go.

"You're doing it right now. Stop thinking."

The breeze blew her hair behind her shoulders. He reached out and rubbed a lock between his fingers. So soft. "I can't stop thinking, Livie. If I let down my guard, you could end up dead, or worse. Believe me, there are worse things."

She ran her fingertips over his outstretched arm. "I believe you. So instead of thinking about how you can keep me safe by staying away, think about how you can keep me safe by being in my life."

"Are you sure you want this? You want me?" His heart pounded. "This is my life. I deal with people like Tre and Sucre every day. They'll *use* *you* to get to me."

"So, don't let them."

She made it sound so simple.

He groaned and took an involuntary step closer. "Don't you think I want to say fuck it all and just have you? To finally have one perfect fucking thing that's mine?"

"I'm not perfect." She met him halfway. "But I *am* yours. All you have to do is say yes."

Her earnest declaration was the last straw. No more fighting his feelings, denying himself.

"Yes," he breathed.

Liv was on him before he finished forming the word. She vaulted into his arms, wrapping her legs around his waist, the same way she had the rainy night weeks ago in her apartment. Her smile shined radiant as they held each other a long moment.

In the peace surrounding them, his mind finally registered something she'd said. He set her down and pulled back to look at her face. "You said you had nightmares when you were in the hospital."

She squeezed her eyes shut and tensed her jaw.

"Will said you'd been sick."

"I was diagnosed with Hodgkin's Lymphoma almost two years ago," she said tightly.

"Cancer."

"Yes. But they caught it early. My dad had it, so when I noticed I had an enlarged lymph node, I went to the doctor right away." She raked her fingers through her hair. "I did chemo and I'm in remission now. The doctors say I'm okay. I didn't want to tell you, because I didn't want to change the way you look at me." Her lip quivered. "I love the way you look at me."

He swept her back into his arms. "Nothing is going to change the way I look at you. Hell, I've got nothing but respect for you fighting death and winning." He rubbed her back. "You've got another fight on your hands with Tre. But you won't have to fight it alone. We're going to take it on together."

She nodded against him.

"Do you have someone you can stay with tonight? Your sister, maybe?"

"Sure, but why can't I go home?" Her fingers slid from his shoulders, down his arms, to grasp his hands.

"We don't know if Tre ID'd your car. He could've found your address on your registration. Which brings me to my next question. Do you have someone who can pick up your car for you? It needs to be a man, and one who can handle himself if he needs to."

Liv nodded. "Yeah. Take me to my sister's gym. I know exactly who to ask."

***

Olivia's self-defense instructor said he would be more than happy to go pick up her car after she explained the risk to her safety. She didn't go into the details, but the guy didn't push. So, he was all-fucking-right in Brick's book. When someone was willing to help him with no questions asked—no— he didn't know *anyone* willing to do such a thing.

They found Liv's sister at the gym too. Even without formal introductions, he couldn't miss the family resemblance. He stayed quiet as Olivia asked if she could sleep over and then promised to come right back after she walked him to his truck.

"What comes next? How will I know when it's safe to go home?" She shivered against the unseasonably cool night.

He grabbed his black hoodie from inside the cab and held it out to her. Would she—?

Liv accepted his offer without hesitation. Five seconds later, a sea of black cotton swallowed her tiny frame. For some reason he couldn't explain, the sight of it made him want to beat at his chest.

"Your, um, instructor is going to bring the car back here. If there's no sign anyone broke in, it means he doesn't know where you live, and you can go home tomorrow."

She burrowed deeper into the fabric. "What if someone did break in?"

He grimaced. "Then they'll have your address from your registration. You won't be safe there anymore." He kept going when she opened her mouth to argue. "Tre knows where you work. He might still come searching for you. I need you to promise you won't be walking to your car alone in the afternoons. Do you have someone who could walk with you?"

She sighed. "We have a resource officer. Technically, he's a cop, but he's more like our security guard. He would walk me out if I asked."

"You have to be careful about being followed too. I'll be at the construction site in the afternoons. I won't be able to keep Tre occupied."

"I'll be careful." She nodded reluctantly. "I'm going to tell Will about what happened. See if he has any suggestions."

More than anything he wanted to stay with her, protect her with the strength of his body, but he could do more good by working on the other side of this. He needed to get to Tre.

"I've got to go." He ghosted his fingers down her cheek. "We're going to get through this." He climbed in his truck and rolled down the window. "I'm going to keep you safe. No matter what it takes."

CHAPTER NINETEEN

Brick

Brick's head buzzed as he turned the key in the ignition. His tattered conscience branded him a liar and screamed that the only way to really keep Liv safe was to shove her in the truck and drive to a different time zone. But even if he didn't have his grandma to consider, no way she'd leave her brother or sister behind. He needed to do some serious recon. As far as he knew, nothing linked Olivia to him, so it shouldn't be too hard to get Tre talking, if only to see how much damage had been done. He gunned the accelerator and made it to El Cabron in ten minutes flat.

"Brick." Sucre greeted him with a raised snifter of Hennessy. A topless Asian girl sat on his lap. She looked about sixteen. "What a treat to see you this early. It's barely nine o'clock."

"Thought I'd get a jump on my rounds for tonight. The kid coming with me or are we working separately?"

Sucre pinched the girl's nipple, then soothed over it with the side of his thumb. "Tell me. What do you think I should do with young Tre?"

Kill him.

"It's not my job to think. It's my job to do what you tell me."

Over the course of the past decade, he'd seen too many people tell Sucre what he should do. It was a trick question. His boss laughed darkly when he refused to step into the trap.

"There's a reason you're my best, Brick. You're smart enough not to try to be smart." This time, he pinched the girl so hard she cried out.

Poor thing. She gave Sucre exactly what he wanted. He kept twisting the tender flesh as he regarded Brick. "I'm not sure whether I bet on the right horse this time. Maybe the younger Lowry boy would be a little less…"

Crazy?

"Independently motivated."

There were so many things he wanted to say, but the same words that might influence Sucre to focus on Tre one day might make him more determined to target his brother on the next. Even worse, it might be a tip off he cared one way or the other. Ignoring the Tre situation entirely, he asked, "What do we have on tap for tonight?"

"Two stops. Carolinda asked to meet. I think she's looking for a short-term loan." Sucre's hand snaked up the teenager's skirt. "Spread your legs, baby. Let Daddy play." The girl did as he told her.

Brick kept his attention on Sucre, unwilling to play the game.

"Find out what she needs the money for. Fifty percent interest. Due in two weeks." The boss looked at him expectantly. "You know the other one."

Oh yeah. "Lorenzo is due today." It was not likely to go well.

Sucre's arm jerked as he moved his hand roughly under the girl's skirt. Tears rolled down her face, and he licked up the side of her cheek. Laughing, he pushed her to the floor and pulled his phone from the inside pocket of his suit. Wisely, she stayed where she landed. Sucre fired off a text, then tucked the device back where it came from. "Tre will be here in five minutes. He is to *observe* you only. Am I clear?"

"Yes, sir."

Tre made it in four. Sweat dotted his forehead as the kid practically ran to the bar where he waited. "Boss says I'm going out with you?"

How quickly a predator could turn into prey.

"You're observing." They walked out the door together and climbed in his truck. He'd left the windows open to make sure Tre could pick up no trace of Olivia's vanilla scent. Glancing at his sidekick for the night, he cranked the engine. "I know you enjoy this shit, but what you've got to understand is it doesn't matter if you love it or you hate it. You do the job the exact same way no matter what. You want to instill fear? Make people piss themselves? You do it by creating an expectation of the same outcome every time."

The punk bristled. "You saying those guys weren't afraid of me when we went out before?"

194

He kept his focus on the dark road. "You don't want to make them too scared to work with you. This is a business, Tre. The same way they know you're going to break a bone if they don't pay, they've gotta know you'll leave them alone if they do. Or maybe they can live with the idea they'll get roughed up if they're a little late, but not somebody raping their sister. And Tre, you can't change the rules of the game. You can't take the money someone owes out of their ass. *You feel me?*"

Tre said nothing as they turned into the trailer park Carolinda called home. Brick sighed as the truck came to a stop. He knew none of this was sinking in. Still, he had to try. "C'mon. This is an easy one."

He led the way toward the second single-wide on the left. "Carolinda Ortega is a single mom with one kid who has problems finding someone to watch her baby while she's at work."

"So?" Tre sulked.

"*So,* it's our job to know everything we can about the people who want to borrow money. This girl's not an addict. She's not a whore. She cleans toilets to pay for diapers. Her terms are a little different. Right now, we're a last resort, but if this goes well, she might not wait so long to turn to us for help."

He rapped twice on the trailer, and the door swung open to reveal the girl in question. Carolinda was eighteen or nineteen years old, with tired eyes and a toddler on her hip. She acknowledged him with a nod but stepped back in alarm when she spotted Tre.

"I don't want any trouble," she murmured as she edged further into her home.

Brick spoke softly. "We're not here for any trouble."

The girl kept staring at Tre, like a scared rabbit. This was exactly what he'd been trying to explain on the way here. Tre's reputation affected potential clients. If Pam told even one person what Tre had done to her, every woman in the neighborhood would soon be running the other way.

"Hey. Eyes on me. Your business is with me."

She swallowed and did as he commanded. "I need to borrow two thousand dollars. Only for a few days. My boss doesn't pay me until Tuesday, but if I don't give my landlord the rent by tomorrow, he says he's going to throw me out. I can't have Esperanza on the street and I don't feel safe at the shelter."

"We can loan you the money, but you need to understand the terms. Are you listening?"

She nodded.

"You have two weeks to pay it back, but it's not cheap. Interest is fifty percent. So, if you borrow two thousand, you pay back three."

She gasped, and the baby squirmed in her arms.

"If you don't have the money when it's due, I'm going to come searching for you. I will find you. I find everyone." He narrowed his eyes. "I'll have to remind you about the commitment you made. It will be…uncomfortable. If you don't have it two days after that, I'll have to break something. And if I have to come back a third time…I hope you've made arrangements for your little girl."

Tears poured down her face as she put her child in the playpen next to the worn loveseat. "Are there any other, um, ways to pay?" Her voice shook, and Tre laughed softly from behind him.

"Sometimes Sucre allows some alternate arrangements." He thought back to the girl at the bar. Someone had probably paid his debt using his daughter. "I wouldn't recommend it, but if you want me to take the offer to him, I will."

"I'm not sure I have any other choice." She wiped her tears with the back of her hand. "I won't have three thousand dollars in two weeks."

The poor girl had no idea what she was in for, but it was her choice to make. He texted Sucre, and the response came instantly. "He said yes. He gets you for twenty-four hours and it will cancel out the interest. You'll need to find a place for Esperanza, and there's no changing your mind. Do you understand?"

She lifted her chin. "I understand."

He counted out a hundred twenty-dollar bills and placed them in her hand. "Your service begins the day the money is due. Five p.m. at El Cabron. Please don't be late."

Tre waited until she closed the door behind him before he spoke. "Why did you try to talk her out of it?"

He climbed into the driver's seat. "I didn't. I wanted to make sure she understood what she was agreeing to. For the record, though, it's better business for them to take the high interest. Sucre can fuck anybody he wants."

Tre flinched.

"The high interest option gives him money in the bank. Cash is more valuable than pussy any day of the week."

True, but not the real reason he warned women against paying with their bodies. Some things you simply couldn't come back from the same way you went in. A night as Sucre's plaything neared the top of the list.

Tre ran his tongue over the back of his teeth and made a sucking sound. "I don't know. I ran into a prime piece of ass tonight, man. Might be worth losing some cash to rip into her pretty pussy."

His fingers dug hard into the steering wheel. Tre was talking about Olivia. He should just kill the worthless fuck right now and get it over with.

Unaware he was taking his life in his hands, Tre kept talking. "She was one of those pristine little blonde numbers. Thinks she's gonna save the world. I'm gonna tear into her until she can't walk. Afterward, I might tie her up and keep her under my bed for a while—pull her out whenever I want to stick it in another hole."

A red haze coated his vision. Tre had no idea how lucky he was they were already at Lorenzo's place.

Ignoring his preening protégé, he stomped toward the apartment door and kicked it open. Lorenzo would get something broken tonight.

The strung-out twenty-something white dude jumped to his feet and backed toward the wall. "Brick! I only need a little more time."

"You're out of time," he growled. "Give me the money, Lorenzo."

"I don't have it."

He advanced toward him. "Wrong answer."

Lorenzo reached into his waistband and pulled out a revolver his ratty t-shirt had hidden. His mouth opened, likely for some kind of pithy response, but Brick moved fast, knocking the gun out of his hand, onto the floor. He slammed his fist into Lorenzo's stomach, and the guy doubled over before dropping to the floor.

They always pretended to pass out.

Dumb fuck. A gut punch wouldn't knock anyone out.

"Get up."

Lorenzo didn't move.

"Get. Up." He spoke through clenched teeth. He would be well within his rights to kill the guy after he pulled a gun, but he didn't want to send Tre the wrong message.

When Lorenzo refused to budge, he lifted him off the floor by his neck. Lorenzo's eyes flew open, and they immediately bulged in their sockets.

"Oh. So, you're awake now?" Keeping his grip on Lorenzo's neck, he used his other hand to snap the man's wrist. "This is what happens when you don't pay."

A smarter man would've been grateful to escape with his life. Lorenzo wasn't smart. Digging a switchblade from his pocket, he swung the weapon at Brick's torso.

He let go of Lorenzo's neck and used both hands to hyperextend his elbow. The man made an inhuman noise when the loud pop signaled it had left its socket. "*This* is what happens when you try to fight back." Lorenzo slid to the floor, cradling his arm against his chest. "You have two more days to pay what you owe. You know what happens on the third."

Much as he tried, he couldn't ignore the tent in Tre's pants when he turned toward the door. God, he hated this life.

"That was the fucking shit, Brick." Tre adjusted himself as he took his place in the passenger seat. "*That* is what I want to do. I want to be like *you*, man."

"Then stop being such a creepy fuck. This job's not about keeping some girl under your bed to rape when you feel like it." He struggled to rein himself in. He couldn't let Tre see it was personal. "It's about collecting Sucre's money. You want a future as something other than his fuck-toy, you will get your head on straight." He fired up the engine and flicked his gaze toward Tre. The kid had murder in his eyes. "You got something to say to me, son? You dumb shit, I'm trying to help you survive this."

Whatever he was going to say, Tre thought better of it and deliberately turned his head to gaze out the window, which suited him fine. At least he'd kept the twisted fucker away from Olivia tonight. He'd figure out the rest later.

CHAPTER TWENTY

Liv

Liv stared out the window of Izzy's apartment, painfully aware she'd made a colossal mistake the night before. Eduardo said her car had been intact, so she planned to go back to her own place tonight.

Izzy handed her a cup of coffee and joined her on the sofa. "How long until he gets here?"

"He said he'd be here for lunch around twelve-thirty." She sipped at the dark roast, the flavor washing over her tongue. "I know he loves me, but the last thing I want to do is explain myself to Will right now."

"I support you, Liv, but I won't lie for you. If this Brick guy—"

"Jonathan." More and more often, in the moments when she allowed herself to think of him, he stopped being *Brick*. He was more than the scary hunk of muscle other people could see. Calling him Jonathan—knowing she was the only one—made it feel as though a secret part of him was hers.

"If this *Jonathan* is who you have your heart set on, you can't hide this from our brother. We're family. We've got to have each other's backs."

Iz was right, as usual.

"You've got to tell him about what happened last night, Nugget. While you're at it, you need to fill in some blanks for me, too. You barely told me anything, only something about your car getting stuck in a bad part of town and you needing to crash here. I didn't push then, but I'm pushing now."

She sighed. "I fucked up, but it had nothing to do with Jonathan. He actually saved me from my own stupidity." She sipped her coffee, then set the mug on the table. "Remember I told you about my student, Devon, last year?"

Iz nodded.

"I went to his apartment last night."

"Didn't you tell me he lives in the Bluff—*That's* why your car was there?"

"Yeah. Turns out his brother is a total psycho, and now I'm on his radar. How fucking naïve, right? If Jonathan hadn't seen me walking out—if he didn't know the kind of guy I was dealing with—I probably wouldn't have made it home."

"Motherfucker," Iz muttered.

"The guy still knows where I work, and I'm not sure what I can do about it. I *will* tell Will…all of it." She set her coffee on the table. "Let's just start cooking." Going through the motions would soothe her.

They washed their hands in silence. Iz had already told her she planned to stuff bell peppers for lunch, so she unwrapped the ground beef and gave it to her sister to brown it in the pan. She'd been cooking with her sister for years. The rhythm of it took her mind off her troubles.

"What was your guy even doing there?" Iz stopped stirring the meat. "You sure he's not stalking you?"

She wanted to throw the onion she was peeling at her sister. Instead, she set it on the chopping board. "He's not stalking me. I haven't seen him in months. He works in Devon's neighborhood sometimes."

Her sister's expression dripped with skepticism. Iz grabbed a knife from the big wooden block on the counter and started chopping. "Have you heard from him since last night?"

She shook her head.

Iz stopped chopping the onion and paused with the knife in the air. "Do you even know what he did when he left here? Exactly what kind of work is he doing?"

"No. He doesn't like to talk about the stuff he does for his boss." She didn't look at her sister as she dipped stale bread into a bowl of beaten egg and milk.

Stern-faced, Izzy scraped her onions into the pan. "Let me guess. You don't want to know." Iz elbowed her in the arm. "You can't keep the blinders on with this guy. I know you're into him, but it sounds like he's involved with some serious shit. If he's what you want, I've got your back, but don't lie to yourself. Accepting him in your life means accepting all the fucked-up shit he does when he's not with you."

Her mouth ran dry as she considered Izzy's words. A million doubts crowded her mind while she questioned her perceptions of the man. Hell, she questioned her perceptions of every man. Every*one*. She hadn't even known her best friend had been lying to her for months. Some judge of character she was.

She stepped away from the stove to grab a bottled water from the fridge and watched her sister tear the bread pieces apart and add them in with the meat.

In her head, she knew Jonathan hurt people— killed people. He'd said so himself. It was one thing to know it. It was another to let herself feel it.

He had taken people's lives.

Her throat closed on the water as she tried to swallow, but she forced it down. "He's so gentle with me. It doesn't make sense." She tried to picture him hurting her, and she couldn't do it. "It's not who he is. There's kindness in him. I've seen it. I know it's what he does, but it's not who he is. He's protecting his grandmother, Iz."

Izzy shot her a glance before spooning the meat into the hollowed green peppers. "For how long? Are you going to live like this forever? Until she dies?"

"I don't know, but what happened last night wasn't even about him. It was all me." Suddenly, the stress-filled night caught up with her. Exhaustion hit her like a freight train, and she struggled to hold her head up against the protesting muscles of her neck. "I'm going to go lie down for a bit, m'kay?"

"Okay," Iz said gently. "Rest. I have a feeling you're going to need all the strength you can muster to face our big brother."

It only felt as though she'd closed her eyes for a moment, but the clock said it was twelve-fifteen when Izzy shook her awake. She'd slept forty-five minutes.

"Look sharp. He's on his way."

She stumbled to the bathroom and splashed water on her face. Her eyes were still a little bleary from sleep, but other than a few wrinkles in the clothes she'd borrowed from her sister this morning, she didn't think Will would notice anything out of the ordinary. Right as she finished running a comb through her hair, his voice drifted in from the living room.

No time like the present.

Will's gaze zeroed in on her the moment she walked into the living room. He gave her the same assessing look he'd given her in high school when she'd hit the neighbor's mailbox with her car. Like he had a sixth sense for bad news.

He folded his arms. "What's going on?"

She climbed on the sofa and hugged her knees. "I did something stupid. You're going to be mad. I need your help, though. Can you please listen?"

He nodded, but the suspicion didn't leave his eyes.

She braced for impact. "How can I protect myself if a really scary guy knows where I work?"

A vein pulsed in Will's temple. "Are you talking about Barlow? Why does it keep coming back to that thug?" His hand curled into a fist. "Is he

205

threatening you?"

"Jonathan would never hurt me," she murmured, then forced her voice to steady. "I paid a house call to check on one of my students. His brother is a total psycho. I'm lucky I got out of there in one piece."

Will shook his head, like he was trying to make his brain catch up to her words. "How do you know this guy's crazy? Did he put his hands on you?"

She shivered. "No. Thank God, Jonathan was there. He helped me escape. He told me the guy— Tre—works for Sucre de la Cruz, and he's really bad news, Will."

"Jona—are you talking about *Brick*?"

She nodded. "Eduardo says no one broke into my car, so Tre probably doesn't know where I live, but he knows I'm Devon's teacher, which means he can find me at work. It doesn't seem real it would happen, but…"

"Who the fuck is Eduardo?" Will raked his hand across his scalp. "Liv, I'm about to lose my shit here."

She gripped her legs tighter. "He's my self-defense instructor. Jonathan snuck me out of the neighborhood in his truck and brought me to Izzy's gym. We sent Eduardo to get my car so Tre wouldn't see me again. I'm hoping maybe I'll be out of sight, out of mind, but Jonathan says he's still a threat."

The confusion lifted from his eyes, leaving steely resolve in its place. "He's right. This Tre guy can still get to you. All he has to do is stake out the parking lot at the high school." He paused. "They think someone snatched a teacher there a couple years ago, right? I read about it in the paper. What was her name?"

"Mrs. Muniz." Her eyes widened in horror, the memory flooding back. She sat up straight. "Oh my God, Tre said something about her while I was there. I didn't make the connection."

Izzy gasped. "They found her a month after she disappeared. The news said she'd been kept alive. Raped. Tortured. She was missing one of her fingers."

"I'm scared, Will," she whimpered. "Part of me thought things weren't so bad if he didn't know where I lived. I mean, Jonathan *told* me Tre was a monster, but I *remember* when they found Mrs. Muniz. The police chief cried on the news."

Will spoke through clenched teeth. "The name Tre doesn't ring any bells, but if he was the guy responsible for what happened to that teacher, I know enough." His jaw ticked. "Are you and Brick together, Liv?"

"Yes. I wasn't lying to you before. We just—"

He waved away her nervous chatter. "It doesn't matter. He cares about you? Are you sure?"

"I'm sure."

Will nodded resolutely. "He is not the kind of guy I want for you, but if anyone can help keep you safe, it's a big motherfucker like him. What did he say you should do about all this?"

"He said I needed to have the security guard walk me to my car every day, and he said I needed to tell you everything."

"You have a security guard? Let me guess, they

hired him after the teacher went missing."

She nodded miserably. "Jonathan can't come to the school to watch out for me. He's got the build for the construction company, but the bigger issue is things will get even worse if Tre realizes we're together. I'll end up leverage for Sucre. He'll use me to make Jonathan do whatever he wants. *If* Tre doesn't try to keep me for himself." She covered her hand with her mouth as her stomach churned.

"It's *not* going to happen. You're going to come straight to me after work every day." He knelt in front of her. "I'll make sure you get home safely. I'll build a fucking fortress around you if I have to."

"You can't protect me forever."

"The fuck I can't." He gripped her hand. "I'll do it as long as it takes."

***

Liv curled into a tight ball on the bed in her sister's guest room. Even though she'd probably be safe at home, she couldn't bear the thought of being alone. Every time she closed her eyes, she saw the face of Jennifer Muniz.

She hadn't been friends with the woman, but they'd spoken a few times in the faculty lounge. What she remembered most about her was the passionate speech the woman had given at a PTA meeting the year she disappeared.

"These kids need us," she'd said. "We could turn them toward a real future instead of a life slinging burgers or selling weed."

How could she have missed the connection when Tre brought her up?

She shivered and pulled the nest of blankets tighter around herself. She had stood barely a few feet away from the man who extinguished the light in Jennifer's eyes. The man who violated her and threw her away like garbage.

"I'm so stupid," she whimpered.

She'd resolved to live bigger, make better choices. What a joke. Last year, she was planning her future by checking off boxes, and now she was doing the exact same thing. Except instead of picking Mr. Perfect or the right vacation spot, she marked boxes off a bucket list she didn't even make...and still didn't think about whether her choices would really make her life better. She only asked herself what Old Liv would do, then did the opposite.

But there was no *Old Liv*—or new one for that matter. Only one Liv existed, and she was long overdue on facing reality.

Surviving cancer didn't make her invincible, but maybe a small part of her felt entitled to give danger the middle finger. She lived through her treatment when so many didn't. But what did it prove? Carol had kicked cancer before, but beating death once didn't guarantee you could beat it a second time.

No more jumping out of planes.

No more home visits in a terrible neighborhood.

No more being reckless.

She had to be smart. From now on, she would think things through, consider the end result, and commit to the path to get herself there.

She wouldn't keep taking Krav Maga to satisfy Izzy or prove she was tough; she would use it to learn to really protect herself. Starting tonight.

And she wasn't staying with Jonathan simply because he was so different than Ryan or because Carol put falling in love on the list. Not even because he made her heart race and her pulse pound. She wanted to be with him because he was a good man and she cared about him. He could make her happy.

If she had been unsure at all about what a monster looked like before, thanks to Tre Lowry, she knew now.

Jonathan's hands may not be clean, but he wanted to change. He *would* change, and she'd be there with him to celebrate when he did.

If her mistake with Tre hadn't already sealed her fate.

***

Two hours later, Liv faced her sister at the gym, warming up her muscles.

She peeked over at Izzy as she dropped into a lunge. "I'm sorry you got stuck in the middle of all my drama."

Her sister sat on the floor with her legs spread, leaning over to hold her right foot. She sat up fully with Liv's apology. "Are you kidding me? I'm your big sister. I want to help you with your problems. You've hardly talked to me at all since we lost Carol."

We. The word grated.

Carol wasn't your friend. She was mine.

She almost said it aloud before she realized how awful it would sound. Her grief had consumed her so much, it never even occurred to her Iz considered Carol a friend too. Maybe not the same way, but her death affected every life she touched. "I'm sorry. It was too hard. It's still too hard, really. I need you, though. I need you to help me be strong. Help me feel safe."

Iz resumed her stretching, her face carefully blank. "This Jonathan makes you feel safe?"

"Someone would have to go through him to get to me. He's always been worried about keeping me safe. So yeah. But I want to do the same for him. I get the idea no one has ever fought for him before. Hell, *he* doesn't even think he's worth fighting for, but he is." She clucked her tongue on the roof of her mouth. "Maybe it sounds dumb, but Mom said love doesn't always make sense."

Iz switched her stretch to the other side with a wistful smile. "Yes, she did."

Giving up any pretense of stretching, she squatted down to get eye level with her sister. "Even though I feel safe with him, Iz, I need to feel safe alone too. Will you help me?"

Izzy completed her stretch, then gracefully came to her feet. "How about I start with showing you how to escape a chokehold from behind?" Her sister stepped behind her and locked a forearm against her throat.

Instinctively, her hands reached up to pry it off. No matter how hard she struggled, Iz didn't budge. When her sister finally let go, she did it because she chose to.

"You're never going to free yourself by thrashing around. In most cases, your attacker will be bigger than you. Stronger. You compensate by being smarter and faster." Iz stood in front of her. "This time, you come behind me."

She wrapped her arm around Izzy's neck the same way her sister had done to her, but in seconds, Iz had escaped her grasp. She had no idea how it happened.

"We'll do it again, but in slow motion."

She returned to her position behind Iz.

"Start by bringing your hands up, on your attacker's hand, the other on his forearm." Slowly, Iz showed her where to put her hands. "Tuck your chin to the left. Then push your left shoulder into the guy's chest. It's going to put a little space between you." Izzy's body moved in time with her explanation. "Now step back around him with your left foot and duck out under his arm."

Like fucking Houdini, Iz got out.

"Now you, Nugget." They went through the steps three more times, until finally she managed to shimmy loose, and Iz called it a night.

For the first time, she'd learned something at the gym that gave her hope she might be able to protect herself if she had to.

Iz joined her as they headed for the door. "You said *love* a minute ago. Love doesn't always make sense. Are you in love with Jonathan, Liv?"

"I think I might be." She hefted her bag onto her shoulder. "But one thing I know for sure—I'm not going to give up the chance to find out."

***

Brick

The crowd at El Cabron swelled a little thicker on a Sunday night during football season. Not because many of the guys in Brick's neighborhood were Falcons fans, but because most of them had a bet on the books over the point spread. Sucre took in as much cash making books as he did pushing drugs or loaning cash.

Before Brick even settled in his regular chair, Sucre got down to business. "I need a cleanup on Lorenzo."

Did he hear Sucre right? Lorenzo was supposed to have one more day to pay off his debt.

Sucre ran his hand over the lapel of his burgundy suit jacket. "He's been running his mouth. And he pulled a gun on you."

"Yes, sir. I fucked up his wrist and his elbow for the disrespect."

"I want him dead. You and I both know he doesn't have the money. He lost it all on the ponies. I want you to take Tre and make an example of Señor Carpenter."

His boss meant for him to leave a mess behind. This shit would never end. "Consider it done." He returned to his feet, ready to get his dirty job started.

Tre waited for him by the bar. "Dude is finally gonna get what's coming to him."

"Yeah, but what you've got to take away from this is, Sucre made the call to pull the plug on this guy. It's never our call. You kill somebody when

213

it's not ordered, and you set yourself up for a world of pain."

Tre nodded darkly. "Yeah. I got it."

It occurred to him Sucre hadn't specified Tre's role for the night. Maybe he could save himself a little more blackness on his soul and channel the kid's darker impulses at the same time. "Sucre said to make this one dirty. Seems to me, you might enjoy that sort of thing. You want to take the lead tonight?"

The kid's eyes darkened with excitement. "For real? Fuck yeah, man. I live for making things dirty."

***

Dirty didn't begin to describe what Tre did to Lorenzo Carpenter. Brick was grateful he didn't have to clean up the mess left behind. He let Tre run the whole operation. Watching it unfold was one of the most heinous things he'd ever witnessed.

When Tre completed his task, blood coated his skin and clothes. He smiled at the carnage he'd made of what was once a man and smirked. "Now that's what I call a lesson."

The kid pulled out his switchblade and sliced off Lorenzo's index finger. "You got your tarp, man? I'll roll him up."

True to his word, Tre did all the heavy lifting. They left Lorenzo's door wide open. No one could doubt he'd died screaming. Even without a body, no one could miss the blood, gore, and other bodily fluids covering the floor.

214

He drove to the backwoods property Sucre owned, where he kept drums of sulfuric acid. Tre heaved the wrapped body into one of the barrels, and laughed so loud, it echoed into the night. "I don't know how to thank you, man. I needed to blow off some steam like you wouldn't believe."

Holding onto the mask he'd perfected with Sucre all these years, he nodded. "Just keep it channeled on the job." *Stay away from my girl.* "You don't want to do anything to jeopardize Sucre's operation. Follow the rules and this kind of job will come around every now and then."

Tre rubbed his hands together, the dried blood flaking off onto the ground. "Guess it would be too much to walk through the bar like this."

"Now you're thinking." *Sick, sick fucker.* "I'll take you home to clean up before we report back in. You can take the lead, make sure you get the credit for the job."

Tre rode in the bed, as he had with the body. Brick sprayed it down and treated it with bleach, while Tre showered inside his apartment. It was almost eleven o'clock by the time they gave their report to Sucre, and he could finally head home.

His security sweep showed no one had been inside. He wanted to fall into bed, but traces of blood dotted his skin, and even though exhaustion dragged him down, the reminder of the night's brutality would keep him awake.

He thought of Liv in the shower. He needed to be with her, to take a break from all this shit, even for one fucking day. How he felt about her was the only thing tethering him to his humanity these days.

He needed a getaway—even a temporary one—and he needed it with her.

Rust-colored water circled the drain as he scrubbed off the reminders of what had happened at Lorenzo's apartment. He'd seen some brutal shit in his life, but what he'd witnessed tonight left him more convinced than ever Tre was a deeply disturbed motherfucker.

And he would die before he let the sick bastard put one finger on his girl.

CHAPTER TWENTY-ONE

Liv

The smell of freshly cut grass mingled with the thicker scents of motor oil and exhaust, and Liv held back a sneeze. The bright sun, the loud rumble of the engines filling her ears...everything about the race track assaulted her senses.

She surveyed the open space. Busy, huge, and raucous, Carol would have absolutely loved it.

Jonathan stepped up beside her, his deep voice drowning out the noise. "I've got our helmets. They also sell something called head socks. I grabbed those too." He held a bright blue racing helmet in each hand, the fabric from his additional purchase stuck inside.

She accepted the headgear he offered, then threaded the fingers of her free hand with his. "You know where we're going?"

His palm radiated warmth; his fingers, strong

against hers. Tugging her gently, he led her to the starting line. About a half-dozen other racers already waited to begin. She swallowed against the rising butterflies in her stomach and climbed into her go-kart. They'd chosen the single-seaters, though a few people sat in karts for two.

He settled into the kart in front of her, then slid the fabric covering over his head, followed by his helmet. Lifting his arm in the air, he shot her a thumbs-up.

The heat beat against her as she donned her own headgear. The backs of her legs stuck to the seat. But she had no time to give much thought to any discomfort, because suddenly, Jonathan's kart moved, and the guy who worked there beckoned her forward and through the aisle created by a plastic guardrail on one side and a wall of tires on the other.

Then she was *moving*. She couldn't tell how fast she sped along the course, but she put her foot down hard on the pedal. The kart responded like a dream, zooming forward, beside Jonathan.

His head turned slightly, taking her in, then he gunned ahead of her, and tried to hug the inside of the track as he took a curve. It didn't quite work. His kart skidded to the very edge, but somehow, he stayed on the pavement.

She eased off the accelerator long enough to take the turn, then darted back in front. Her heart raced, her grin so wide, her cheeks hurt. She wished she could feel the wind in her hair. The exhilaration pumped through her like a drug.

She finished a hair's breadth ahead of Jonathan,

the ten minutes on the track passing more like ten seconds. He lifted his visor, revealing the laughter in his eyes. "Rematch," he growled, as they got into position again.

He beat her the second race. She won again in the third.

Why had she never done this before?

His face was flushed when he pulled his helmet off, then reached out his hand to help her out. "Holy shit. That rocked."

The cool air against her damp skin when she removed the helmet was the only reminder of how hot she'd been. She could smile forever. Once clear of the track, she threw herself against him in a tackle hug. "I loved it."

She felt more than heard his laughter as he indulged the embrace for a few seconds. "C'mon." He pulled back and retook her hand. "I'm starving."

Me too. I could eat you alive. Adrenaline fueled her jacked-up libido. Now, she wanted to climb him like a tree.

Two teenage boys streaked past them, howling like a pair of monkeys.

Okay, obviously this wasn't the place. She followed his lead back to the truck, forcing herself to calm her breathing and take in their tree-lined surroundings.

A sub taught her fourth-period students at school right now. She couldn't remember the last time she'd played hooky from work. Sure, she'd missed some days last year when she'd been sick, but she never blew off her classes.

When Jonathan called her last night, though,

there was something in his voice she couldn't refuse. Besides, she didn't *want* to say no. He'd promised her a real date, a day with only the two of them—no distractions. A day out of time. And she knew exactly what she wanted to do.

He held open the door for her to climb in when they reached his truck, then he walked around the front before settling in behind the wheel.

"Not bad for a first date." The corners of his lips tugged up at the word *date*. "No girl's ever asked me to take her to Motorsports Park before."

"Not what you expected, huh? You don't mind, do you?" She searched for a sign he might be disappointed, but his expression gave no hint of displeasure.

If anything, his eyes twinkled. "Do I look like I mind, sweetheart?" He winked, and her worry melted away. "You like ribs?"

"Wha—? Uh, yeah. I like ribs."

He nodded toward the sign for a barbeque place, and within minutes, they had their orders wrapped up and back with them on the road. Though she did like ribs, she opted for the BLT. Easier to eat in the car.

Jonathan must've been on the same wavelength because he got a burger on Texas toast. He ate it in four man-sized bites while he drove one-handed. Though not as fast as him, she polished off her sandwich in minutes. It had the perfect amount of mayo, enough to moisten the bread without making a sloppy mess. They'd just finished their shared order of fries when they completed their fifteen-minute journey up Highway 183.

Amicalola Falls boasted majestic views, hiking trails, and the state's highest waterfall. It was too hot for a hike, but they got a parking spot near enough to the top they only had a short walk to view the falls.

It took her breath away. The water trickled over the rocks going down, down, down. Trees lined either side, their foliage thick and green. People loitered along the wooden walkways, taking videos and selfies, but as Jonathan wrapped his arms around her waist from behind, they all disappeared.

He kissed the side of her neck and goosebumps prickled her skin. She turned toward him, her lips seeking his. His mouth brushed hers, feather-light.

"Don't tease me." She grabbed his t-shirt and pulled him closer, only for a second kiss as chaste as the first. "Please, Jonathan."

He pulled her away from the falls onto an almost-deserted trail, and this time when he kissed her, she got everything she wanted. Heat. Passion. Ownership. His tongue swept into her mouth and tangled with hers. God, how she wanted this man. All too soon, he pulled away and tucked a strand of her loose hair behind her ear. She liked him growing more comfortable with touching her.

"You don't have to call me that, you know."

She traced her fingers over her lips, still feeling the tingles left by his kiss. "Hmm?"

"You can call me Brick. Everyone does."

"Do you *want* me to call you Brick?" she asked carefully.

He shook his head slowly.

"Good. I don't want to call you that either. It's

221

not how I think of you. You're Jonathan. In here." She tapped her head, then slid down her hand down to rub her chest. "And here."

Covering her hand with his own, he grasped her fingers and slowly pulled them toward his mouth. His breath fanned hot over her skin as he kissed her palm.

Something tightened low in her stomach. Her lips parted.

And a passel of kids came tearing down the path, one screaming he was about to make the other "it." The boy leading the charge ran so close to Liv, she had to sidestep quickly in order to avoid being run over.

Effective as a bucket of ice water in killing the moment. Kids must be united in some kind of cock-blocking mission today.

She growled at the intrusion, but it only made Jonathan chuckle. Raising her eyebrows, she cocked her head to the side.

He rubbed his big hand across his forehead. "If they would have come through five minutes later, we might have traumatized them for life."

"Fine by me," she muttered, but she didn't mean it. She had no desire to put on a show for a group of eight-year-olds.

Jonathan tugged her toward the truck. "Now you've gotten me all hot and bothered, let's cool off in the a/c."

The truck may have looked old, but thankfully, the air conditioner worked fine. She stuck her face right in front of the vent.

"Why go-kart racing?" He shifted in his seat.

"Don't get me wrong. I had a great time. Was it another one of the places you went with your dad?"

The cool air, which felt like a relief a moment earlier, now felt icy cold. She leaned back and looked out the window. "No." She exhaled. "It was kind of a promise to a friend."

He waited for her to continue.

Damn. I guess we're going to do this now.

"I told you about the cancer." He nodded. "I met my best friend in treatment. You met her once at Moe's. Her name is—was—her name was Carol. She died."

The air turned warm again. Or she was warm, but the air was cold. Fuck. This sucked. "Anyway, when we finished our chemo, we made a list of all the things we wanted to do."

"A bucket list," he acknowledged.

"Yeah. I thought she was better, like I was, but it was a lie. She knew she was dying." She could hear the bitterness in her voice. She shook her head, trying to find her center. "We called it the Dare to Dream list. The first thing on it was cliff diving."

His fingers latched around her knee. "Please tell me you're not jumping off a cliff."

The nerves in his voice pushed away her melancholy. "Too late. We did it before I met you."

"You jumped off a *cliff*?" It came out strangled.

"Out of a plane too. It felt like flying. Words can't describe it." She chuckled at his expression and patted his arm. "Don't get me wrong. I was terrified."

"Then why did you do it?"

She thought about his question. The answer was

one she was only now coming to understand, herself. "I thought that was what it meant to really live. Do crazy shit. Or maybe just do things because I never would have done them before I got sick."

"Like jump out of a plane."

"Jump out of a plane. Show up at a student's house." She shuddered. Hesitated. "Fall for a different kind of guy."

She stole a peek of Jonathan from the corner of her eye. He looked gobsmacked.

"And riding go-karts was on your list?" he asked slowly, ignoring the more obvious question.

"Not exactly." She turned to face him fully. "After what happened the other night, I realized *living* doesn't have to mean jumping blindly into crazy shit. It means figuring out what I want, then going after it, because it's right for me.

"The next thing on the list was driving a race car. But I don't need to go two hundred miles an hour, or whatever it is they go. I don't need to risk my life to feel alive."

Jonathan shook his head. "Please don't."

"The go-karts felt like a way to honor the spirit of the list. And even if you didn't know why, I guess I wanted to share the experience with you."

"Thank you." He blinked. "What else is on the list?"

"Bungee jumping."

He shook his head deliberately. "Uh-uh. What else?"

"Scuba diving?" He gave her the side eye. "Though I thought maybe I could change it to snorkeling. And don't worry, I'm not bungee

224

jumping. The sky-diving was close enough."

"Anything else?"

"One I really liked was 'change someone's life.' I thought I could do it with Devon. I really wanted to." She licked her lips. "The last one was to fall in love. Carol added it at the end. A little surprise for me after she died."

"The last one might be the most dangerous, you know."

"And probably the one most worth the risk."

The tips of his ears turned red, and for a moment, silence reigned. His gaze flicked to the steering wheel, down to his lap, and over to a bag from the BBQ place on the floor. The corner of his mouth quirked. "I don't suppose there's anything on the list about indulging in something sinful every now and again."

He lifted the bag and pulled out the container left inside. "I ordered it while you stepped into the ladies' room. Pecan pie for two."

The second he opened the carton, she could smell the irresistible blend of decadence and vanilla. "Oh my God, yes." Snatching the bag, she rifled for the forks inside and made quick work of the plastic covering on hers. The rich flavors exploded on her tongue.

Jonathan paused with his bite halfway up to his mouth.

"What?" she mumbled, covering her mouth with a napkin.

"No. Don't stop. Watching you eat your pie gave me an idea of what your face must look like when—" His cheeks colored, and he turned his attention to his own food.

She laughed. "You mean what I look like when I come." Her voice was husky.

His blush grew even darker. "You, um, seemed like you were really enjoying it."

The poor guy was obviously embarrassed, so she threw him a bone. "Best pecan pie I've ever eaten. Could have something to do with the fact we worked up such an appetite together." She shook her head at her own double entendre. "Sorry, guess we've both got sex on the brain."

"It's hard not to."

"Heh. Hard, huh? Well, maybe we should head to a bar and order a *stiff* drink."

He caught on. "I like it. I could go for something *wet* right about now."

"Maybe Sex on the Beach? Or we could do shots. I always did love sucking back a creamy Blow Job."

He held up his hands in surrender. "I give up. Unless you want me to embarrass us both by having you right here in the parking lot, I suggest you accept your victory and allow me to keep some dignity."

She speared another forkful, then held it up to her mouth. "Where's the fun there?"

He grabbed her hand and wrapped his lips around her fork. His tongue peeked out in the process, raising the hair on the back of her arms. "Someday soon I'm going to find out what *you* taste like, Livie-mine." His voice came out so deep and gravelly, he barely sounded like himself.

She thrilled at the possessive nickname he used

when she turned him on. "How long are we going to keep teasing each other?" she whispered. Dozens of people milled around the cars outside, but it was getting harder to remember they were in public.

A text chimed on his phone before he could answer. He grimaced as he checked the screen. "All good things must come to an end." Dropping his fork in the bag they used for trash, he signaled dessert was over.

It had to be his boss calling.

She drooped as she swallowed one more bite. There was still a little pie left, but she'd lost her appetite. Of course, she knew this day couldn't last forever, but it didn't make it any better when reality reared its ugly head. Neither of them spoke as she shoved the remainder of the food into the bag and buckled her seatbelt.

They drove for a while in silence. After about ten minutes, he turned on the radio, the volume barely loud enough to hear. Scott Weiland crooned about being half the man he used to be.

She leaned back on the seat and closed her eyes, soaking in the warmth of the sun through the window. Stone Temple Pilots gave way to Staind, and she hummed along.

And Jonathan's low baritone joined in with Aaron Lewis.

She blinked.

His voice was beautiful, though he kept it low, and his focus stayed planted firmly on the road in front of him the entire time he sang. She held her breath, staring, mesmerized by him. She'd grown up on car-karaoke, but she'd bet a week's pay it wasn't something Jonathan usually did in front of anyone.

Warmed, she unbuckled, slid to the center of the bench, and snuggled into his side. His arm came down around her shoulder. "We're going to figure this out. I'm not going to let you go."

Pressed against his body, she barely noticed as they drove into her apartment complex. Jonathan insisted on walking her inside.

She'd barely opened the door when she came face to face with Izzy. "What are you doing here?" It came out an octave or two too high. No one was supposed to be in her apartment, and seeing someone—even her sister—shook her more than she cared to admit.

"Just picking up the boots you stole from me to bring on my trip." Iz held up the footwear in question.

She wrinkled her nose, her heart rate returning to normal. "I didn't steal them. I borrowed them."

Iz shoved them into the duffel bag hanging from her shoulder.

"Hey, before you go, I want to officially introduce you to someone." She tilted her head from her sister to the quiet man beside her. "This is my sister, Isobel. Iz, this is Jonathan." His eyes widened at the use of his given name. It looked like it would take some getting used to.

Izzy didn't hesitate. Her sister reached out and grasped his hand in a firm handshake, then gave her a chastening look. "I did see him at the gym, you know."

"You did such a good job ignoring him, I wasn't sure."

Iz grunted and returned her attention to Jonathan. "My sister says you saved her ass the other night."

He gave a short nod. "I guess I did."

Iz tilted her head. "Of course, my brother says you're nothing but trouble."

"Also true."

Izzy tugged on his hand and pulled him closer. Pure flint reflected in her ice-blue eyes. "Are you going to take care of her—or am I going to have to take care of you?"

She grabbed her sister's shoulder and tugged. "Iz."

Jonathan lifted his free hand. "It's okay. I want to answer her." His gaze met her sister's. "I *am* trouble. It's why I tried so hard to stay away from her, but there's a reason we keep coming together. I'm tired of fighting it." He stood straighter. "I want this. I want *her*. So, yes, I will take care of her. I will do everything in my power to make sure she's not touched by who I am and what I do. Anyone who wants to do her harm will have to get through me first."

Izzy gave him a cool once-over. "Good enough. Liv sees something in you worth taking a chance on. You're welcome here as long as you do right by her."

"Uh, guys?" She wiggled her fingers in front of her face. "I'm standing right here." She shooed her sister out of the door. "See ya when you get back from your trip, Iz."

Izzy smirked and waved as she walked away.

She closed the door behind her.

"Your sister's going somewhere?"

"Only for a few days; some kind of martial arts expo. She wanted to cancel, but I'll tell you what I told her: Don't worry. We've already established Tre doesn't know where I live, and Will is going to be watching me like a hawk."

"She was right to question me, you know. She only wants to protect you." His deep voice was quiet.

"I know. She's been looking out for me for as long as I can remember."

"You're lucky to have her."

"I am. She didn't say anything I didn't expect."

He tucked another wayward lock of hair behind her ear. "I'm not going to give up on us."

"Promise me," she whispered.

He kissed the top of her head. "I promise, but I need you to promise something too. You're going to be on guard when you go back to work tomorrow."

"Oh, I promise. I already went through this with Will. He signed off on the security guard. He's not even banging the drum for me to stop seeing you anymore. I'm surprised he didn't want me to hire my own personal bodyguard."

"It wouldn't be the worst idea."

Spoken like another overprotective male. "You two have more in common than you think."

He hugged her closer against him. "Oh, we've got something in common. Both of us would take a bullet to keep you safe."

***

Brick

Brick reported directly to his boss after he dropped Olivia back home. It had been two hours since Sucre had texted him, and though he'd answered him right away, the man did not like waiting for anyone.

"Ah, Brick." Sucre rose from his throne and held his arms open. "Glad to see you could finally join us." The boss reached to the table beside him, where two chocolate muffins rested. One was half-eaten. Sucre lifted the other and offered it to him. "Muffin? They're sugar free."

And unmistakably from the bakery where he shopped for his grandmother. Were those *her* muffins? He refused to ask, but his blood pressure soared.

Bowing his head, he played the game. "No, thank you. Sorry to keep you waiting, Boss." When he got the call to come in, he'd texted Sucre he went out of town scouting for a hunting cabin. Olivia had done some quick research on her phone before he left her apartment, finding a few places for sale or for rent. He had a list in case Sucre pushed for more details. He'd wait until Sucre asked, though. Offering too much information without prompting would look squirrely.

Sucre sniffed. "I don't know why you want to be out in nature. We've got everything you need right here."

It wasn't a question. He stared at the floor, waiting submissively for instructions.

"I have some new product coming in tonight. Go

stand at the bar and look intimidating."

Motherfucker. There wasn't even a reason to call him in. Sucre had only done it to interrupt whatever he'd been doing.

Shaking his head, he turned toward his assigned destination.

"Oh, and Brick?"

He stopped.

"Maybe I do need to think about spending some time in the great outdoors. Send me some addresses." His voice hardened. "Or better yet, show me the GPS in your phone."

This is where it paid to be prepared. He had already cleared his history from the track and the falls and punched in four of the cabins Olivia had found on Zillow. He pulled up his GPS app and handed the phone over to his boss.

Sucre narrowed his eyes and gave the phone right back. "Just go. And next time, don't keep me waiting."

CHAPTER TWENTY-TWO

Brick

Brick didn't have to face Will for several days. He'd talked with Olivia every night since their date, and she'd told him her brother knew everything they were dealing with. As much as he dreaded facing the fallout it would bring, he was glad Will kept her safe in the afternoons. He was doing his part by keeping Tre occupied at night.

The electricians were installing the light trim at the house on Burgundy Street, which had the entire construction team focused on the Decatur house for the rest of the week. Will stood waiting for him by the front door when he pulled up Thursday morning.

"Let's go out back."

He followed Liv's brother around the property to the backyard that butted up against a wooded area.

Will lit a cigarette and took a deep drag. "You

know how I feel about the idea of you and my sister."

"I think the whole crew knows. I get it. I know she deserves a regular guy, one who doesn't do the shit I do. I swear, I tried to stay away from her, but I can't."

Will was sucking down his cigarette so fast, it was already halfway gone. "Tell me you are not a danger to her."

He wished he could, but it would be a lie. "I promise you I will never hurt her, and I will do everything in my power to keep her safe from anyone who would try."

Will tossed the filter in the dirt and ground it in with his heavy boot. "This Tre guy. He's bad?"

"The worst I've ever seen." Which said a lot.

"You have no idea what I've been through to keep my sisters away from this kind of shit." Will kicked over one of the barrels of construction debris. Chunks of sheetrock, nails, and two-by-fours spilled out on the ground. "I failed once with Izzy. I'll be damned if I come up short with Liv too."

He bent over to right the now-dented can. "You didn't fail her," he said gently. "She told me how you stepped up after your parents died. You mean the world to her."

"I wasn't there when she got sick." Will cursed under his breath, and they worked together to clean up the mess on the ground. "I heard a lot about you when I was inside. Can you at least tell me you're not as bad as your reputation makes you sound?"

"No. I've done some bad shit. I still do. The only thing I can tell you—something hardly anyone knows—is I hate every second of it. I always have, but I'll use it, you feel me? I'll use the reputation, the skills, whatever. I will fucking *break* anyone who touches her with a goddamn smile on my face. We do what we have to do to protect the people we love. You understand."

"Better than you even know." Will sighed. "I won't stand in your way. Not like it would have made a difference anyway."

He offered Will his hand, and they shook. "It will make a difference to her. Thank you."

Will stayed behind, already pulling another cigarette from the pack, while Brick made his way inside the house. He could see significant changes in the layout since the last time he'd been here. The man who'd commissioned the build had decided he wanted an additional bedroom downstairs with an attached bathroom. So, they'd had to extend the foundation and plumbing before they could even start adjusting the framing, which they worked on today. At least, he was working on it with Kane and Matt. Will and Cyrus focused on some task in the backyard.

Kane raised his hand in greeting. "Seems like you're still in one piece. Should I congratulate you on surviving your conversation with Will? It looked intense."

"We've reached an understanding." Kane didn't push for more, which was one of the qualities he liked best about him.

About an hour into the job, Matt's phone rang, and he stepped away to answer the call. The man spoke too quietly to give anything away, but his face said it all. The dude looked ready to set the room on fire. Gritting his teeth, he walked back over. "I've got to go. Family emergency. Will you guys let Xander know I'll call him?"

"Sure, man." Kane gripped his shoulder. "Anything I can do to help?"

Matt shook his head and strode out the door.

Robby bustled over to them seconds after he was gone. "What's going on? Is he okay?"

Kane raised his eyebrows, and Brick shook his head at him subtly.

"I'm not sure." He caught himself before he called Robby *kid*. "He only said he had a family emergency." He lowered his voice. "You ever try talking to him?"

Robby shot Kane a nervous look, but the biker was intently measuring the support beam he'd been working on. "I've said *hi* and stuff. I bring him Nestea; he doesn't really like soda."

"Not what I meant."

"I know." The kid sounded dejected. "I'd rather keep my distance than be disappointed, you know? If he doesn't have a chance to reject me, I can keep the dream alive."

A month ago, he would have never even imagined he could be with a woman like Olivia. "You never know what life can bring. I can tell you this, though, if you want something, you have to reach out and take it. You deserve to be happy, Robby."

A blush crept up Robby's neck. "Thanks, Brick. You're a better big brother than my real one ever was."

He had never had a little brother, but with Robby, he was getting an idea of what it might be like. "Any time."

Kane finally looked up when Robby walked away. "He's got a thing for *Matt*? Baby-mama-drama-every-other-week Matt York?"

"C'mon, you know as well as anyone we can't help who we want." The heat in Kane's WTF expression could melt the paint off the walls, if the house actually had walls, but Brick shrugged it off. "You think I didn't notice whatever was between you and the boss lady the other day?"

"You don't know what you're talking about, brother." Kane issued a warning with his voice.

"I'm not trying to bust your balls, man. Really. I didn't go out looking to fall for Will's sister either." Holy shit. He'd said it out loud, but it was too late to back out now. "That's my whole point. Maybe we give into it and maybe we don't, but we don't get to choose who we fall for. It just is."

"Doesn't mean it's good for us," Kane grunted. "The kid's probably in for a world of hurt."

He slapped his friend on the back. "Probably. Or maybe he and Matt will end up friends. I'm starting to learn they're kind of nice to have around."

Together, they lifted the wood into place and secured it.

By the end of the day, the additional framing was complete. They walked together toward the area where they had both parked.

Kane paused to fasten his helmet. "I'm thinking you might make a pretty decent drinking buddy, man. Come have a beer with me tomorrow night."

It surprised him how much he wanted to say yes. Kane had really grown on him in the past few weeks. It might be nice to hang out, like regular people did. "I wish I could, but I've got a fight tomorrow night."

"I heard you fight. I'd love to see a match. Would it be cool for me to come check it out?"

It had never even occurred to him anyone outside of Sucre's orbit would even be interested. "Sure." He rattled off the address of the gym. "The matches start at ten. I'm usually at the end, though."

"This is going to be awesome, brother. I'll see you then." He climbed on his bike.

"Hey—aren't you working tomorrow?"

"Nah. I've got club business. I've already cleared it with Xander." He grabbed the clutch and pushed the ignition button, bringing the engine to life. "Gotta make a run with my guys, but I'll be back in time for your fight." He grinned widely before taking off down the street.

***

The gym was packed Friday night even tighter than usual. Brick scanned the crowd for Kane's face, but too many bodies kept him from seeing clearly. It didn't really matter if the guy made it there or not. The fight would go the same, either way.

Sucre had paid him a visit while he warmed up in the little office which belonged to Freddy, the old guy who ran the place. Sucre didn't tell him to lose, but he *did* want him to take a beating. It was an instruction he didn't get often, but sometimes, Sucre liked to bet against the odds to make a little extra cash. What most people didn't realize—or at least they didn't talk about—was the fact that the boss controlled the outcome of every bout he fought in.

Tonight, he would let Antonio Reyes beat the crap out of him for at least twenty-two minutes before he took the guy down. His stomach turned even thinking about it. Reyes had a reputation as a solid fighter. This was going to hurt.

The big digital clock above the ring showed five after midnight when the ref called him up. By then the place reeked from the press of unwashed bodies and booze. Almost everyone watching was either buzzed or blitzed, and they roared when he entered the ring. The cheers didn't fool him. They wanted to see him bleed, and they were about to get their wish.

Reyes faced him with clear eyes and cool composure. When the bell rang, the guy led off with a powerful punch, leaving him gasping for breath. He had to fight back or he wouldn't make it two minutes, much less twenty-two. He planned to volley a blow for a blow but save his hardest hits for the end.

The strategy sucked balls.

In the first five minutes, Reyes clocked him in the eye, and blood trickled down with the sweat threatening his vision. A minute after that, the guy punched him in the ear, leaving a tinny ring in his wake. By the fifteen-minute mark, his body ached, and his head was swimming. If he didn't start hitting hard soon, he wouldn't be able to at all.

He threw all his weight into a blow to the ribs, sending Reyes hunched to his side. He followed it up with an elbow to the nose, gushing blood from his opponent's nostrils. A quick glance at the clock showed him he still needed to kill five more minutes. But how?

The crowd had grown rabid, roaring with each punch—even the weak ones both fighters threw now. He'd busted up his hands so completely, it hurt as much to hit Reyes as it did to take a hit. He could barely make a fist, so he started hitting with the heel of his hand.

Two more minutes.

He swayed on his feet. The noise got further and further away. Swinging wide, he missed his target completely. Before he could regroup, Reyes delivered a one-two punch, making him stagger back.

Would this fucking fight ever end?

Finally, Sucre gave him the signal. But he had nothing left. He struggled to stay on his feet. Thank God, Reyes was in the same boat. He was listing like a drunken sailor.

This had to end now.

Ignoring the pain, he curled his hand into the tightest fist he could make and punched Reyes square in the jaw. He followed the hit with a strike to the nose, and the man dropped like a bag of concrete.

He only waited long enough for the ref to call out his name before he lurched toward the door. Two steps out into the street and the world went black.

***

Liv

Liv curled herself around her pillow, the bed a warm cocoon, as she held the phone to her ear. Though they'd texted, it was the first time she'd spoken to her sister in days, and Izzy's voice relieved some of the anxiety that came with her absence. With Carol gone, she'd had no one to tell about her date with Jonathan, and she was busting at the seams.

"It was actually really amazing." She wanted to share every perfect detail, but a tiny part of her wanted to hoard it all in a little secret place inside her heart.

Iz didn't push, one of the reasons it was so easy to talk to her. "We drove go-karts, then we went to the falls. It was so beautiful with all the trees and the trails. We laughed, and he *sang*. He held my hand, and he kissed me."

"Sounds like a Disney movie, Nugget. Any birds flying around with ribbon or dwarves marching past?" Iz snickered.

"No, but there was pecan pie."

A beep announced she had a call on another line. She squinted at the clock on her nightstand.

Twelve-forty-five. Normally she'd already have been asleep two hours. Jonathan's picture she'd taken on their nature date filled the screen. He never called this late.

Saying goodnight to her sister, she clicked over. "H'lo?"

An unfamiliar voice answered. "Is this Olivia?"

She sat straight up in the bed. A thousand possibilities surrounded the identity of the person on the other end of the line. None of them were good. "Who is this?" she asked sharply.

"My name is Kane. I work with Brick and your brother. You probably saw me at the bar for Will's birthday. Long hair. Brick's in trouble and yours was the only number in his call log."

Her stomach fell, and her self-protective instincts warred with concern for her man. "What's wrong? Is he okay?" He said he had a fight tonight, but he'd sworn they were all fixed, and he always won.

Kane paused. "He's in pretty bad shape. He probably needs a trip to the hospital, but something tells me he wouldn't want to go."

"Bring him here." She rattled off her address. "But Kane? Make sure no one follows you."

"I promise. I'll be there in ten."

They made it in eight. Enough time for her to dig out her first aid kit. She opened the front door as soon as a car pulled up outside.

In the shadows, she spotted the big frame of the biker-looking guy she remembered seeing at Will's work site. He practically dragged an even larger man who had one arm crooked behind his neck for support.

Jonathan.

She ran out and met them three feet in front of the doorway. As they moved together into the apartment, the light gave her a first look at Jonathan's face. Her attempts to prepare herself failed, and her eyes filled with tears.

His entire face was swollen and misshapen, but his left cheekbone looked the worst. She guessed it was the cheekbone, but it could have been his eye; it was hard to tell because it was swollen shut. A cut above his eyebrow was bleeding and it appeared it had been for a while. Wet and dried blood trailed down his cheek and smeared on his neck and bare chest. He only wore a pair of knee-length shorts.

He was clearly out of it. The one eye she could see appeared tired and unfocused. She didn't think he even knew where he was because he didn't so much as glance at her when Kane settled him down on the sofa.

"How do I help him?" she murmured.

The grim expression on Kane's face only made it worse. "Keep him awake until you're sure he's coherent. No doubt he's got a concussion. Get some ice on the swelling. Clean him up. Not much else you can do." A horn honked outside. "My buddy Cue Ball is outside waiting." He moved toward the door. "If it gets too bad, call 911. He won't be happy about it, but you do what you've got to do, hear me?"

He didn't even wait for an answer before he let himself out. She stared at the closed door for a heartbeat, until a groan from the sofa snapped her attention back where it belonged. With Jonathan.

She moved quickly to the kitchen, where she filled a large bowl with warm water and grabbed a washcloth. She could only assess the damage underneath the blood if she cleaned him up first. As she knelt in front of him, she wondered whether he might do better in the bathtub, but even if she got him in, she wasn't sure she could get him out. No, it would have to be a sponge bath for now.

She ran the warm wet cloth over his forehead, and he made a noise in the back of his throat. "Jonathan?" Her voice came out small and thin. He didn't respond, so she cleared her throat and tried again. "Jonathan." She said it louder this time, and the lid on his right eye fluttered. She rinsed the cloth in the water, then returned it to his face. "It's Liv. I need you to wake up, sweetheart. Look at me."

His eye opened slowly. He licked his lips, then opened his mouth, but instead of speaking, he broke out in a fit of coughing.

As quickly as she could, she grabbed the water bottle she'd left on the coffee table before bed. She held it to his lips. "Here. Drink. Don't try to talk." She tilted the bottle up, and though a little dribbled down his chin, his throat moved as he swallowed.

The coughing died out.

"I need to clean this cut before I bandage it." She lifted an alcohol pad to his face. "This is going to hurt."

He squeezed his eye closed, but didn't flinch, as she gently ran the astringent over the gash. She pulled out two butterfly bandages and did her best to close the cut. The bleeding had almost stopped.

"Okay. The hard part's done. Keep your eyes on me."

His lid rose again. This time, his gaze appeared sharper. She finished cleaning his face, then moved down to his throat. He lifted his chin to give her better access, and she wondered if he allowed many others to get this close. His breathing changed subtly as she rubbed the cloth down and across his chest.

She froze. "Am I hurting you?"

"In the best way, baby," he rasped.

Her face heated, and she bit back a smile. If he could flirt, surely, he wasn't dying. "None of your swagger, Mister. Not when you look like you've been hit by a train."

The air in the room suddenly felt a little lighter. "You think you could stand long enough for a quick shower? I could help you."

He looked like he was trying to raise his eyebrow, but with his swollen face, he couldn't quite pull it off.

"Don't give me that look. I need to make sure you're alert, and the shower might help. Come on." She reached for his hand. Her fingers had barely touched his when he yelped and jerked away.

Holy shit. His hands were destroyed. She leaned closer so she could see better. His fingers were fat and distorted, the skin mottled. Dried blood crusted across his split knuckles. A few still oozed.

"It's okay," she soothed. Her stomach churned, but she fought to keep her nerves out of her voice. "You can shower in the morning. We'll take care of your hands now."

He groaned. "Good. I'm not sure I can get off the sofa."

***

Brick

Liv relaxed against him after doctoring his hands, and Brick kissed the top of her head. No one had ever fussed over him this way before. It humbled him. "Thank you for taking care of me. You're giving me exactly what I need right now."

She burrowed deeper into his side. "What happened tonight?"

He didn't want to think about the clusterfuck in the ring, but he wouldn't ignore her question. "A fight. I told you earlier."

"You told me the fights were fixed. You said you always won." With the strain in her voice, he couldn't tell if she was angry or upset.

"I did win."

She pulled back and shot him a critical look.

"Really. The other guy looks as bad as I do. Maybe worse."

"You made it sound like this wasn't a big deal. Like I didn't have to worry about you getting hurt. Why didn't you warn me it might be this bad? I care about what happens to you."

He decided she was angry *and* upset. He needed to make things better. Fast. "I didn't mean to trick you, Livie. I swear. The fights *are* fixed. Sucre decides how long they last, so he can cash in on his bets. I could have taken the guy down quickly, but I had to make it last." His jaw tightened. "I had to let him hit me. By the time I'd been in there long enough, I could barely pull out the win."

The horrified expression on her face warmed his heart. "He forced you to—How long? *How long* did he make you stay in there?"

"Twenty-two minutes."

Her face darkened as she considered his words. Minutes passed before she finally spoke. "You're a toy to him. A tool he uses to line his pockets and build his empire. It doesn't even matter what it does to you along the way." She didn't even know the worst of it. "You hurt people. You kill people."

Shit. This was it. The truth of who he was—what his life was like—it was finally sinking into her brain. The blood drained from his face. He was going to lose her, but he wasn't going to lie. "Yes." He locked his muscles, steeling himself for rejection.

"You do it for him. Why don't you do it for yourself? Kill *him* and be done with it all."

It took a moment for her words to make sense. "You mean, why haven't I killed *Sucre*?"

"Yes." Her eyes flashed as her fingers gripped his thigh. "If he were dead, you would be free." Her lips thinned. "I'd do it myself if I could. I won't lose another person I care about."

She looked like she meant every word and he had to swallow the lump in his throat. "Taking somebody's life puts a stain on your soul you can never get clean. I don't ever want you to know how it feels." He rested his worthless hand on top of hers. "You don't know what it means to me you want to protect me. No one else ever has. I need you to hear me, though. You've got to stay far away from Sucre. Promise me, Livie. If he got his hands on you, both our lives would be over."

"What kind of life do you have *now*? You act

like he owns you, but you're strong. You're powerful. Why don't you crush him or at least run?" Olivia pulled her hand away and stomped to the kitchen. She put some ice in a towel, then yanked a glass-bottled drink out of the fridge and popped it open. It wasn't until she returned, he could see the label. She'd brought out one of those fruity Hard Lemonade drinks. She handed him the ice, and he held it to his left eye.

"You didn't promise." Did she think he wouldn't notice?

She took a long pull of her drink. "Fine. I promise." She plopped back down on the sofa. "It's not as though I would be able to kill someone anyway. Even if he does deserve it."

"It's not as simple as killing him." He'd fantasized about it plenty, though. "If something happens to Sucre, someone will kill my grandmother. I'm not Sucre's only muscle, you know. I'm the best, but the boss has made it very clear he has people in place to execute his final wishes. He sends me pictures of her almost every day to remind me. Once, he sent me a piece of her fucking nightgown. If I run, she dies. If I kill him, she dies. Otherwise, I'd have taken the sick fucker out years ago."

The cold, hard pressure of the ice against his face sent sharp spikes of pain into his head, but he pushed down the discomfort. "I've done so much to keep her safe, I can't give up now. It has to mean something. She's comfortable now, but she's still exposed. I can't get her free until I save enough money to get her in a good facility, somewhere

Sucre can't get to her. My goal was fifty thousand. I always thought I'd go with her, start my life over somewhere. Now, with you—"

He sighed. "If I stay here, there needs to be enough money to take care of her the rest of her life. And I have to figure out which assholes at Magnolia Green are on Sucre's payroll. If the wrong person tips him off I'm pulling her out, we'll both be dead before we're out of the city."

The corners of her mouth drooped as she set her drink on the coffee table. "Do you have *any* happy memories? Has this man stolen your entire life from you?"

He set the ice in his lap, then used his palms to pick up the drink and take a sip. It tasted like almost pure corn syrup. Gross. He cringed as he put the ice back on his face. "I can't blame him for every bad thing in my life. My dad was an addict. He would've been an addict whether Sucre was his dealer or it was some other guy on the street. Kids with a drugged-out parent always have it rough. There's never enough money, never enough food." He shrugged. "But there were some good times. Before my mom died, sometimes she'd sing to me or take me to the park. She worked a lot, but I loved her."

He furrowed his brow, trying to grasp a memory. "One time, she bought me a little red toy racecar. I must have been about six or seven. I was so proud of that thing. I carried it everywhere."

"Do you still have it?"

He shrugged. "My father stepped on it barefoot in the middle of the night once. Threw it against the wall. I should've put it somewhere safe."

Olivia's eyes were wet, but her tears didn't fall. He was grateful for the small mercy. Her tears might break his heart in a way he'd successfully avoided for years.

She nestled back into his side, her hand resting over his heart. In minutes, her breathing shifted to the heavy rhythm of sleep. It was after two o'clock. The poor thing was exhausted.

Climbing to his feet, he scooped her into his arms and carried her to her room. The bed was a double; it would be a tight fit, but they could both squeeze in. He noticed the indention on the right side of the mattress, so he placed her there and climbed in beside her. He barely had to wait a second before she rolled up next to him, curled against his side.

He had never slept with anyone before. He'd had sex, sure, but he'd never spent the night in a woman's bed.

As Olivia tangled her smooth legs with his and threw her arm across his waist, he was glad she'd be the first. Somehow, he suspected it wouldn't be the same with anyone else.

CHAPTER TWENTY-THREE

Liv

Liv woke up Saturday morning in the pale light of dawn with a blazing heat against her back and an iron band around her waist. For a moment, she froze. Then Jonathan's breath fanned in her ear. She recognized the crisp hair of his leg rubbing against hers, and his stone-hard arousal nestled against her ass.

She wiggled her backside, and he groaned.

"You're teasing me on purpose."

Laughing, she rolled over to see him. His face looked worse than it had been the night before. Bruises had time to fully bloom on his skin, and none of the swelling had gone down. She should have made him hold the ice on it longer. Biting her lip, she held her fingers over his cheek, but didn't touch. "Does it hurt?"

"Nothing I can't handle."

She rolled her eyes. "You don't have to be a badass every single second."

Pulling himself to a sitting position, he revealed the pillowcase he'd slept on was now dotted with dried blood. "I'm sore, but I'm feeling better than I did last night."

She ran her fingertips over his swollen face, but he didn't flinch. "You ready to give the shower a try?" She slid out of the bed and walked around to his side. "Put your arm around my shoulder. We'll do it together."

Gritting his teeth, he did as she asked. Carefully, they moved into the small bathroom. Even a fraction of his weight on her shoulders felt like carrying a boulder.

He leaned against the door frame as she turned on the spray.

"Can I, um, help you with your shorts?" She gestured vaguely at the only clothes he had on his body.

He guarded his expression as he nodded, and averting her eyes, she gently eased them down. "You're killing me, Livie," he moaned.

Blushing hotly, she stood and forced her gaze to stay on his face. "Let me help you in."

He didn't move. "You're keeping your clothes on?" He scowled. "Every time I've ever thought about showering with you, both of us were naked."

She chuckled at the trace of whine in his voice. "Hush." She wrapped her arm behind his back and pulled him toward the bathtub where the shower ran. He allowed her to help him inside and groaned when he stepped under the spray.

Even though she was in the shower with him, Liv stayed mostly dry. Jonathan's big body blocked the water. She grabbed the soap and got to work, gently massaging the Dove bar into suds on his back, shoulders, and arms. His muscles slowly relaxed under her fingers.

"Turn around," she whispered. Hard as she tried to prepare herself for the full-frontal view, she couldn't help but suck in a breath when he faced her. She fought to keep her attention firmly above his waist. Remnants of the soap rinsing from his neck and back slid over his defined pecs and tangled in his chest hair.

She stepped closer, and his eyes flared as she began to lather his chest. Her hands slid over his nipples and up to his collarbone. The last time she'd seen him without a shirt stayed burned into her memory, and seeing him this way, without even the sweatpants he'd worn before, threatened to stop her heart. The man's body was perfectly made. His shoulders were broad. His chest and torso sculpted like a statue.

Despite her resolve, her gaze slid down, and her soapy hand followed.

He had a trim waist, and a narrow line of hair dipped down, leading the way to what was now a thick, proud erection.

He shuddered as she took him in her hand. The skin of his cock was hot and smooth. The soap on her hands made the glide effortless, and she began to pump him.

He swayed on his feet and closed his eyes. "Livie," he groaned, but he didn't protest. Instead, he leaned his shoulder against the wall and let her have her way with his body.

God, she wanted to fuck him. With every encounter, the need to feel him inside her grew. It reached a fever pitch now, feeling the weight of him in her hand, knowing how he'd fill the aching void between her legs.

He'd recovered some since the night before, but he was still hurt. He couldn't touch her; he could barely even move his hands.

His pleasure would be her pleasure.

She tightened her hand and pumped harder. Faster.

Her own arousal was getting harder to ignore. She squeezed her thighs together involuntarily. Much more of this and she'd have to use her other hand on herself.

"Let me take care of you," she whispered. Leaning forward, she ran her tongue along the pulse of his neck.

His body tensed against her, and he came with a shout.

Her hand relaxed, but she didn't let him go until he pulled away. She felt breathless, needful. But there would be no help for it. She'd brought this on herself.

Laughing softly, she pulled back the shower curtain and stepped out. "I guess you can rinse the front now."

***

Brick

As sluggish as he'd felt when he woke up, Brick was wide awake after his shower. His face still ached, and he still couldn't close his fat fingers into a fist, but who the fuck cared when he could still feel Olivia's fingers wrapped around his cock?

She changed her clothes while he shuffled to the sofa in a towel. He'd gotten jizz all over her pajamas, which he should probably feel guilty about, but he couldn't regret what they'd just shared.

Olivia was already in a pair of soft shorts and a t-shirt heading toward him before he could sit down. "Wait. I've got some clothes for you." He stopped his descent into the cushions and waited while she pulled a set of clothes from her small laundry room. "Do you need help getting dressed?"

She held a pair of his jeans, boxer briefs, and a t-shirt. They were all folded neatly.

How did she...oh, yeah. He'd left them in her dryer after the storm that night.

"I can do it." He held out his hand, but when she offered the clothes out to him, he couldn't get a grip. They tumbled to the floor.

Immediately, she knelt and scooped them up. "Let me help you, Jonathan."

His name on her lips melted his insides every time. He braced his hand on her shoulder and stepped into the underwear she held open at his feet. Once she got them to his knees, he pulled them the rest of the way into place with his thumbs. "I don't care about the clothes."

Her eyes flared as her gaze skittered across his bare chest. Thank God. She wanted him too.

He ran his thumb over her bottom lip. "I want to finish what we started, but I want to do it right." Trailing his hand down to her collarbone, he rubbed across it, and her nipples pebbled in response.

Grasping his hand as gently as she could, she pulled it toward her and kissed the pad of each finger. "We have all the time in the world. I can be patient."

"Or." He licked his lips. "You could let me take the edge off." Without waiting for a response, he leaned in for a kiss.

She shivered beneath him as he licked over her bottom lip, then bit it gently.

"Let's go back to your bed."

Liv led him to her private space, the need he saw in her eyes during the shower glowing brighter than ever.

"I want to see you. Show me your body. Let me worship you." She deserved so much more than a wreck like him, but this was something he could do. He could serve her like the goddess she was.

Her eyes closed as she tugged her T-shirt over her head. Her full breasts called out to be touched. If only his fucking hands would work.

"Shorts too," he growled. "Then get on the bed." His cock was already waking again despite the pleasure it had just spent.

Pushing them down slowly, Olivia revealed the heaven he'd only dreamt of. Fully nude, she was perfection. Freckles dotted her pale shoulders, but the rest of her skin was a sea of peaches and cream.

She stepped backward toward the bed, then lay down, waiting for him to give her what she so clearly craved.

His hungry gaze locked between her legs. The thin strip of blond hair covering her mound ended at the top of her slit. Beneath, she was totally bare. Her pussy was already wet and gleaming, the moisture seeping down to the sheets below.

He couldn't wait another second. He needed to taste her, to drive her crazy with the same pleasure she'd given him.

Climbing onto the bed, he positioned himself between her legs, his face, a fraction of an inch from the place he craved most. "So beautiful," he murmured, his breath hot on her private flesh.

Her pussy clenched.

"So pink." He ran his thumb up her slit. "So smooth."

She squirmed beneath his touch.

He chuckled. "And so impatient." Using both thumbs, he spread her lips apart and slipped his tongue between her folds. He wanted to make his movements slow and teasing, but her taste drove him wild. He speared his tongue inside her, the way he wanted to thrust inside her with his cock.

But this wasn't about him. It was about her. Forcing himself to slow, he lapped at her wetness, reveling at the tiny noises escaping the back of her throat.

He raised his head, his thumb rubbing slowly over her clit. "Tell me what you want."

She groaned. "I want you. I want everything."

Everything. He wanted it too. Her words made

his heart race, but he wasn't sure if it was from excitement, fear, or some combination of the two.

Ignoring the ache in his hands, he lifted her ass off the bed. His tongue swept over her asshole. Circled it. Then dove back into her wet heat. He fucked her with his mouth. But it wasn't enough. It would never be enough.

"Touch yourself, Livie. My hands don't work, but yours do. Make yourself come while I taste you."

Her hand shot straight to her center, separating her folds, finding the treasure within.

He didn't move for a few seconds. His eyes locked on the movement of her fingers. How they disappeared inside her to emerge covered in her own silky essence, then rose to the hidden pearl above.

His head dropped between her thighs again, and his lips brushed her skin as he spoke. "Ride my tongue, baby. You're not going to hurt me."

Her knees fell open as his tongue speared deep. She quickly found her rhythm, her middle and index fingers circling her clit, while her hips rose and fell with each stroke. She did as he instructed, meeting each thrust of his tongue with abandon.

No one had ever made him burn this way before. There was nothing else in the world but this woman and the orgasm building between her legs.

When the rising tide broke, she cried out his name, her muscles locking in place.

He stayed motionless until the last shudder went through her body, then he climbed back to the top of the bed and opened his arms for her to collapse inside.

Everything about the moment felt right. She was spent and satisfied…and *he* was responsible. Now he had her in his arms.

They were together in her bed.

If only they could stay this way forever.

CHAPTER TWENTY-FOUR

Brick

The last thing Brick wanted to do was leave Olivia's side, but he could only escape his real life for so long before it would seek him out. Better if he faced it head on—and he would in a few more minutes. It wouldn't be the end of the world if he let himself revel in this perfect moment.

Would it?

He'd thought falling asleep with her was extraordinary, but waking up with her was every bit as precious. Now she lay here next to him naked with perfect trust.

When had anyone ever trusted him?

The responsibility was staggering. It was foreign, a gift.

Eventually, he pulled on his jeans, fumbling awkwardly with the zipper, then tugged on his t-shirt. It occurred to him quickly he had no shoes, no truck, and no wallet to get himself home.

Fuck.

It would take at least an hour to walk to his place, and doing it barefoot would destroy his feet. Shame tainted the amazing morning he'd had as he returned to Olivia's bedroom to wake her up. "Livie?"

"Mmmm," she hummed and turned toward his voice. Her eyelids fluttered open, and she smiled at his ugly face. "Morning, baby." Her lower lip stuck out as she took in his fully dressed state. "You're leaving?"

He sat on the edge of the bed. "I have to. Or they'll start looking for me."

Her teasing pout turned into a real frown.

He cleared his throat. "I don't have a way to get home, though. I hate to ask, believe me, but do you think your brother would give me a ride?"

"Are you kidding? You want to explain to Will you spent the night, or should I?" Olivia rolled her eyes. "Grab my purse off the kitchen counter."

"No way. I'm not taking your money."

She climbed out of bed without a hint of modesty and swiped her purse from the kitchen. She fished out a twenty-dollar bill and folded it into his hand. "I don't care about the money, Jonathan. There's plenty of other stuff to worry about." She sighed. "I hate the idea of you going back there."

His heart warmed at her concern. "I'll be okay. But I'm going to pay you back." He kissed her forehead, then ordered his ride. "Thanks for taking care of me last night."

With gentle fingers, she lifted his fucked-up

hand to her lips and feathered it with kisses. "You never have to thank me. I'm glad Kane had the sense to call me when he found you. *He* is the one we should both be thanking."

"Trust me. I will. But Liv, this is important, we're lucky he was the person who tracked you down. If you ever get a call from a number you don't know, don't answer it."

"But he called me from your phone."

He shook his head. "From now on, when I call, wait for me to talk first, okay? If it had been anyone else on the other end of the line, I don't want to even think about what could have happened." The horn honked outside, and he drew to his feet.

Liv kissed his cheek as he headed for the car. He really did owe Kane for looking out for him. It seemed he didn't only have one person who cared about him, but two.

At least he didn't have to worry his screwed-up life would be a threat to Kane Hale. That motherfucker could take care of himself.

***

The driver dropped Brick at the gym, where Freddy had set aside his forgotten shoes and keys.

"Where you been, man? Rumor mill's been churning 'bout you wiping out in the middle of the street. You all right?" Freddy wasn't a bad guy, but you couldn't find a bigger gossip around. If you wanted a story to spread, he was the guy to tell.

He spread his arms wide. "It would take more than what Antonio Reyes could dish out to put me down. I was the one who won the fight last night."

The old man lifted his cap to rub over the top of his bald head. "You don't have to tell me. I watched them carry his sorry ass out of here last night on a stretcher. At least you walked out on your own two feet."

Yes, Freddy. Build me up.

"Damn right I did. Might've had a bit too much to drink. Made me a little sloppy, but hey, lesson learned, you know?"

"I figured it had to be something along those lines, Brick. Nothing else makes any sense," Freddy agreed, buying in deeper to the story with every word. "So where did you get to after the fight?"

"Buddy of mine showed up. Maybe you saw him. A biker dude." He paused while Freddy nodded eagerly. "He picked me up. Took me out." His voice dropped to a conspiratorial whisper. "Between you and me, I barely remember *what* I did last night. I only remember waking up wearing nothing but a smile…and finding a pink pair of panties on the floor."

Freddy whooped. "Nights like those were the best ones of my youth. Enjoy 'em while you can, Brick. Enjoy 'em while you can."

He chuckled. "Fucking right, my man. Now, I'd better get my ass home for a shower. I smell like day-old pussy. Did you save my shoes for me?" He gestured to his bare feet and Freddy scurried to his office.

Handing over the shoes, Freddy patted him on the back. "You're a lucky bastard."

He smiled and turned for the door.

"Hey, Brick?" He stopped. "Lay off the booze before the match next time. You don't want folks to get the wrong idea."

He lifted his hand in a wave as he made his way out into the street.

Mission accomplished.

He texted Liv.

Brick: Made it home. Will call you later.

Fishing his keys out of his left shoe, he looped the keyring on his pinkie until he strode up to his apartment. He held his head high and his shoulders, back. There was no room to show weakness. No letting his guard down until he could close the door behind him.

As he jammed his key in the lock, he could already hear the theme song from *The Golden Girls* coming from his neighbor's TV. The guy watched TV Land every weekend. The walls were thin, but he could ignore the noise. He just wanted to collapse in his well-worn recliner.

Only, someone else already sat there. "Sucre." Fear skittered up his spine. Forcing himself to appear unconcerned, he pulled his phone from his back pocket and glanced at the screen. "Were you trying to reach me?"

His boss wore his shiny green suit, one ankle resting on the opposite knee. He looked like a Mexican Wizard of Oz. "Word on the street said you disappeared last night. You didn't come home. But you didn't make a run for it." He lifted the black ornamental cane with the silver handle he had leaning against the chair and tapped the hollow leg of the table. "I knew because you left your precious stash of money here."

He choked back the wave of nausea churning with what Sucre's words revealed. Where had he gone wrong? He'd been so careful. Canned laughter from his neighbor's TV show filled the short silence.

"Didn't think I knew about the money, did you?" The bastard shot him an evil grin. "There's not much I don't know about you. I'm a businessman, and *you* are my business. So, satisfy my curiosity. Where were you last night?"

Fuck.

Bullshitting Freddy was one thing. He thought he'd have more time before he'd have to face Sucre. "A friend of mine from my day job picked me up after the fight."

His boss steepled his fingers beneath his chin. "The long-haired man with the beard."

He prayed it would be the end of the conversation, but he knew Sucre better.

"Are you fucking him?"

For a second, he couldn't even respond. The question stunned him. "Sir?"

"Are you. Fucking. That biker?"

"No, sir."

Sucre dropped his hands to his lap and began rubbing them together. "I ask because I don't see you taking advantage of any of our local merchandise. No girls." He raised his eyebrows. "No boys. I figure you've got a side-piece somewhere nobody knows about. A special someone."

It took everything he had to hold a neutral expression on his face. "No special someone."

"Excellent. Then, I have a little surprise for you." Sucre snapped his fingers and three nude women walked out of his bathroom. They must have been waiting for the signal. A blonde, a brunette, and a red-head. Of course. "You worked hard for me last night. Let me show you my appreciation." He gestured to the women. "Pick one."

It wasn't a question. A hundred denials ran through his mind. None of them would hold water with Sucre. The man was trying to prove something. If he turned down the offer, it meant he had something to hide. Once Sucre caught wind of a secret, he would be a dog with a bone until he uncovered it.

The laugh track from next door felt like fate crowing at his misery.

He pointed to one of the girls without even looking. "Her. Thanks, boss." The woman stepped forward, and he started leading her toward the bedroom. Hopefully, he could figure out a way to buy her silence.

"Ah. Ah. Ah. Now you wouldn't rob me of the chance to watch you unwrap your present. You can fuck her right here on the couch, no?"

He couldn't have sex with another woman.

He couldn't.

Turning down this *gift*, however, practically shined a spotlight on Olivia. Sucre might not find her today, or even tomorrow, but he wouldn't stop until he figured out who had stolen his heart. He'd be putting a loaded gun to her head for the rest of her life.

The girl he'd selected, who he could see now was a buxom brunette with bright red lipstick, rubbed against him. "Maybe just a little blow-job, Papi?"

His hands moved to his belt, but he froze as bile churned in his stomach. Sucre had broken him in a hundred different ways over the years. Some were big, like the times he'd fucked him to prove he could. Others were subtle—or at least as subtle as Sucre could be—like when the doctors "couldn't find" his grandma for a couple of hours last year after he'd disagreed with Sucre over how many fingers needed breaking on Paul Franco's left hand.

But this? This was, perhaps, the worst cruelty of all.

He finally had something good in his life. Someone who cared about him. Someone who someday might even love him.

And Sucre was forcing him to destroy it.

"No," he murmured.

"What did you say?" Sucre narrowed his eyes.

"I don't want a blow job. I don't want a girl. I want to go to sleep."

Sucre grabbed the brunette by her upper arm and jerked her back. "Get out," he hissed. All three women grabbed the clothes piled on the sofa and scrambled out the door. The moment it slammed shut, the boss turned all his venom on him. "Who the fuck do you think I am? *Un pinche idiota?*" Spittle flew from his lips with the force of his words.

"No, sir." He kept his voice calm and even.

Sucre slammed his walking stick into the old mug Brick had left on the coffee table the day before. It bounced onto the carpet, the handle snapping off in the process. In stages, he drew his rage inward until his face was once again a placid mask. "Give me your phone."

On instinct, he did as Sucre commanded. Only then, did he question what might be there for the man to find.

His boss clenched his teeth as he swiped through the screens.

No GPS. No contacts. He'd cleared the call history—

A satisfied smile lit Sucre's face. "Tell me, Brick, who exactly did you text when you got home?"

Fuck. Why hadn't he erased it the second after he sent it?

He couldn't think. His ears locked in on the commercial playing the familiar *Andy Griffith* whistle. None of this felt real. It was some kind of fucked-up nightmare.

Only it wasn't.

"Cat got your tongue?" Sucre tutted. "Why don't we call and find out?"

Before his words could sink in, Sucre had connected the call, and turned on the speaker.

Please don't answer. Please don't answer. Let it go to—shit—not voicemail.

The phone stopped ringing, but thank fuck, Liv stayed silent.

"Don't you want to say hello, Dove?" Sucre's

voice came out syrupy sweet, but his face contorted when Olivia refused to take the bait. He shoved the phone into his pocket. "*No me importa.* You think you're so smart. Let's see what your lover thinks of the real you." He spun on his heel, then smirked over his shoulder. "It always pays to have insurance, Brick."

Abruptly, the TV turned off next door as the slam of his front door echoed in the small living room.

When had he heard Sucre say those words before?

Oh fuck.

He had to get back to Liv's place before Sucre made his move.

***

Liv

Liv trembled as she disconnected the call. She had no doubt one of Jonathan's associates had just tried to figure out who she was.

Could he trace her through her phone? Should she get out of the apartment?

She forced her labored breathing to slow. Panic wouldn't help anything.

It hadn't been Tre. She would have known his voice anywhere. And even if Sucre himself had been on the other end of the line, and he was trying to figure out who she was, she hadn't taken the bait. He couldn't identify her, and more importantly, he couldn't find her.

Still, it wouldn't hurt to keep a knife from the kitchen next to her on the sofa.

She texted Will to be on the safe side. He agreed with her conclusions, but he promised to come over anyway. In the meantime, she needed a distraction. The pictures from Amicalola Falls always made her smile. She mirrored her phone onto the TV and scrolled through them. The warm memories soothed a little of the chill seeping into her bones.

Until a text flashed across the screen. A video?

She tapped the vidbox and brought it full-screen, then pressed play. The video quality was terrible. Someone obviously had shot it on a dark street, the low light making everything grainy. Still, Jonathan was unmistakable as he charged a smaller man in a torn white T-shirt, standing in front of a nondescript building.

The guy dropped to his knees, but Jonathan didn't slow. He held something black in his hand. A crowbar, maybe.

Her stomach turned as he cracked it over the man's head.

Jonathan towered over him, then kicked him hard in the midsection. "Get up." She could barely hear him, but she understood his growl.

The man stayed motionless. Even as Jonathan picked him up by the throat. Even as his face grew mangled by one hit after another…after another. His white T-shirt darkened with blood.

Jonathan slammed the back of the guy's head into the bricks behind him.

Then the screen cut to another scene. It was Jonathan again, only this time, he was inside someone's home. The camera watched from outside a window.

This time, the image looked clearer because there were lights on, which only made it worse. There was no sound, but the black guy in the hoodie was shaking his head. His eyes were pleading.

Jonathan backhanded him. Then hit him again and again and again before twisting the man's arm in an unnatural direction and leaving him in a heap on the floor.

The video cut to another scene, then another. They were all different, but still the same. More violence, more blood. More begging and crying. And more of Jonathan's relentless fists.

Everything inside her screamed to turn it off, but she didn't. She couldn't.

She lifted her thumb to swipe the horrors away when Jonathan's face filled her screen. Here, he looked different. Younger. His hair was a little longer; it had a bit of wave to it. Here, he wasn't some punishing machine. He looked relaxed. His eyes were closed, his jaw slack. He lay on a red silk pillow.

The camera panned down to reveal a woman riding him. A dirty blonde with fake boobs way too round and big to be real. They bounced unnaturally with each rise and fall of her body. Jonathan was silent, but the wet sounds coming from the blonde's movements were deafening.

Her breathing grew shallow as another woman crawled into the frame. The newcomer showed no sign of expression; her bare skin was light brown and her body, long and lean. She straddled

Jonathan's face, then rolled her hips. The blonde leaned toward her, and the women lapped at each other's tongues.

Was this better or worse than watching Jonathan beat a man to death?

A bald Hispanic man wearing only gold chains and diamond rings joined the three of them on the bed. A man who had to be the boss Jonathan so loathed and feared. Then, she knew the answer to her question.

This was worse. So much worse than she'd ever imagined.

***

Brick

Brick's heart sank as he watched the horror play over Olivia's face. He was such a fucking stalker, watching her through the window, hidden in the shadows of some tall bushes, but he couldn't bring himself to knock on the door.

The mirror on the far wall revealed the nightmare that played on her screen. One of the nights he'd spent in Sucre's "office."

He barely remembered the details. In a small mercy, he'd had a lot to drink both before and after. But he remembered the worst of it.

Olivia's hand covered her mouth, and her shoulders jerked forward. Her face twisted, and tears streamed from her eyes.

Hot shame washed over him. How could he ever face her after this?

It was one thing for her to *think* she knew the worst of him. It was another for her to see it with her own eyes.

Tires squealing in the parking lot had him crouching deeper into the foliage. Will strode to Liv's front door and into the apartment without bothering to knock. She turned off the TV, jumping to her feet and falling into his arms.

Even if she had a broken heart, at least she'd be safe.

He shuffled back to his truck, the filth and despair of that night and others like it, threatening to drown him. The ride home passed in a blur.

Once inside, he shed his clothes and shuffled into the bathroom. He turned on the shower and climbed inside. He knew from years of experience, he couldn't wash any of the memories away. Still, he tried.

As always, the water was lukewarm.

But the tears rolling down his face boiled blistering hot.

***

Liv

Jonathan didn't call her Saturday night or Sunday. Afraid of who might answer his phone, she didn't call him either. But she needed to talk to him about what she'd seen. It couldn't wait another day.

Her stomach still churned over what played out on the video file she received. Not because she'd seen him in bed with someone else or even because it was a man. It was the absence of horror in his face over what he had to endure. The absence of anything, really. It was the dead emptiness in his eyes as he'd followed every command his boss had issued. A blank stare and an obedience without hesitation.

After bearing witness to even a sliver of their dynamic, she had no doubt there was nothing Jonathan wouldn't do for his boss. The monster's control over his creation was excruciatingly complete.

But that wasn't entirely true now, was it?

He was risking everything to be with her, and not only did Sucre have some inkling about it, he was obviously displeased. What kind of punishment would he think of to fit the crime?

Heart in her throat, she drove to the house on Burgundy Street before her first class on Monday morning. She saw no sign of Jonathan's blue truck. Still, she got out and peeked in the open front door.

Kane stopped working on the kitchen cabinets and ambled her way, his eyes pinched with concern. "Everything okay, sweetheart? Did Brick take a turn for the worse? I got worried when I heard he wouldn't be in this week."

All week? Could Sucre have him? "He looked fine when he left me Saturday morning. I mean, he was still sore and swollen, but he was walking around...talking."

"Was it the last time you heard from him?"

She nodded miserably, debating how much to tell him. "I think his boss tried to call me. Sent me some really nasty videos. I'm really worried."

Kane grimaced. "If it was really his boss, you should be."

"I'm afraid to call him. I don't even know where he lives." What if he was hurt? What if Sucre was torturing him for information about her? She couldn't breathe as the possibilities rained down on her.

"The best thing you can do for him is to sit tight." He touched her shoulder. "I'll go down to his neighborhood. I'm not sure which apartment is his, but I've been to his gym. Let me sniff around. See what I can find out. I promise, I'll let you know, okay?"

She didn't like it, but she didn't have a choice. "Give me your phone, and I'll put in my number." Once he handed it over, and she'd saved her contact, she gave it back. "You'll call me? As soon as you can?"

"I'll call you. Whether I find him or not."

***

Brick

The longer Brick took refuge inside his apartment, the more the dingy walls threatened to close in on him. A hundred times, he relived his exchange with Sucre, looking for a way he could have handled it better, but there'd been no way to stomach any intimacy with the girl his boss offered. Anything short of letting her suck his dick—well, the particulars might have changed, but the outcome would have remained the same.

275

Sucre would have still seen through him, and Olivia would still know his deepest shame.

He shuffled to the refrigerator and looked inside. The very idea of food made his stomach lurch, but a Budweiser longneck wasn't out of the question. His hand was an inch away from the closest bottle when a knock sounded at the front door.

The temptation to ignore it overwhelmed him, but if Sucre stood outside, it would be a bad idea to make him wait. He had already met his lifetime quota on bad ideas.

He abandoned the promise of a little alcohol-induced oblivion as the banging grew faster and louder. An apology died on his lips when he caught sight of Kane at the threshold. "What the fuck are you doing here, man?"

"Fine way to greet a friend." Kane shouldered his way into the room.

He kept the door open behind him. "How did you even find me?" He shook himself. "Doesn't matter. You need to leave."

Kane brushed at some imaginary lint on the sleeve of his leather jacket. "Some old bald guy at the gym pointed out the way. Apparently, he thinks I'm doing something to help you get laid." He dropped the casual façade, his face turning to stone. "And I'm not leaving, so you can hang that shit up right now."

The guy meant well, but Kane didn't understand the kind of clusterfuck he was stepping into. Brick dropped his voice to a whisper. "I think my place is bugged, or there are cameras; I don't know. It's not safe."

"Fine. Then take a ride with me. We need to talk. I'm not going without you."

Growling, he followed Kane to his bike. "No way we're both going to fit on there."

Kane climbed on. "Just get behind me, asshole. I'm not trying to be your boyfriend. Let's go."

It was a tight squeeze, but he managed to balance on the seat. They drove several blocks to an empty playground with wooden benches. Playground wasn't the right word. There were two swings and a single basketball hoop. A bent-up old baseball bat lay discarded in the grass.

He strode away from the bike and kicked over one of the heavy benches. "My whole life is *fucked*." Bellowing into the open field, he channeled the hate, the shame, the hopelessness into a roar that sent the birds squawking into the cloudy sky.

Sitting on one of the benches still standing upright, Kane waited and watched.

He stomped the overturned bench again, then picked up the old bat and tore into the wood. All the while, he yelled at the top of his lungs. When he had no energy left, he slid to the ground. "He ruined the only good thing I've ever had." It came out ragged. "No. I ruined it...before I ever even met her."

Kane gave up the bench to sit next to him in the dirt. "I assume you're talking about your girl. She says you're not answering her calls."

"She knows what I am now." His stare drilled holes into the ground.

"She probably knows who you are better than

you do, brother." Kane sighed. "Tell me the whole story."

"It was a test." He laughed brokenly. "Sucre gave me a girl to make me prove I had no one special in my life. He was looking for a clue I had someone he could use against me."

"And?"

"And I fucking failed. I couldn't cheat on Olivia. *I couldn't.*" He flexed his hands then shook them out. "I told him no, so he played his trump card. He showed her what I am."

"I still don't understand."

"Sucre fucking owns me. He's owned me for years," he gritted. "He tells me to kill somebody, I kill them. He tells me to fuck somebody, I fuck 'em."

"Not this time."

"No. Not this time, but enough times he has an arsenal to use against me whenever he needs a weapon. I knew he had videos of me on the job. I figured he'd use them to threaten me with the cops if I ever stepped out of line. I figured the videos he took in bed were just another way to break me down."

Had he really just slipped his worst shame? Did it even matter anymore? No. He laughed darkly. "He says it always pays to have insurance. I guess it paid off for him this time."

Kane gripped his shoulder. "You have to talk to her."

"How could she possibly look me in the eye?" He buried his face in his hands. "You don't know what was on the video she saw."

Kane squeezed, then let go. "I have a pretty good idea. But as for your girl, I can't say how it will go once you see her. I do know she's looking for you, and she's scared. And for what it's worth, it sounds to me like you didn't have much of a choice. About any of it."

"I don't think she's going to see it the same way."

Kane climbed to his feet and held out his hand. "There's only one way to find out, brother. Let's get back on the bike."

CHAPTER TWENTY-FIVE

Liv

Liv gave up her attempts to marshal her thoughts into lesson plans as a knock came at her door. When she opened it up, Brick stood outside, his expression a blank mask.

"Can I come in?" His voice was stilted, formal.

She ushered him in and led him to the sofa. "I've been so worried. I was afraid to call you."

"I know. I'm sorry. I wasn't ready to face you. I'm still not, but here I am." He didn't so much as glance at her while he spoke. His gaze fixed somewhere over her shoulder.

His dead stare looked so much like the one she'd seen at the beginning—and later—the end of the video. It was like he'd sealed himself off to what was happening; he'd resigned himself to his fate.

"I guess you know I've seen the videos."

He nodded his head.

"You know what was on them?"

"Some of it. I've got a pretty good idea about the rest." His fingers dug into the coarse denim covering his thighs. "I'm sorry I'm not the man you thought I was." He never turned his gaze from the wall.

It only made the pressure on her lungs intensify. It hurt to breathe. "Look at me," she whispered. When he ignored her, she spoke in a louder voice. "*Look at me.*"

"I can't!" he roared, but his actions betrayed his words. His wide, frantic eyes swung to her face. "How can I look at you when you've seen—when you *know?*" There was so much anguish in his question. The blank expression replaced by something twisted and broken.

She fought the threatening tears. "I already knew what you did for him. The business parts." Though nothing could have prepared her for seeing it. "You've been up front with me about the violence from day one."

"But not the sex. I never told you I—" His big body shuddered.

She couldn't hold back the tears any longer.

With a deep sigh, Brick drew to his feet, then pushed his shoulders back. "I'll go."

No. Everything inside of her cried out in protest. If he walked out the door, he might never come back. "Wait." She leapt off the sofa and grabbed his arm. Pain gripped her chest. She couldn't shake the image of him in the bed with those women…and that man.

But he hadn't wanted it—any sign of pleasure on

his face in the video evaporated the moment Sucre touched him. Only the mask remained. He may not have let his misery show, but she had no doubt about what she'd seen. The idea of this breaking him, of it breaking *them*…

Not going to happen.

She shoved it all down. "Do you want to be with me?" Her voice sounded surprisingly level to her own ears.

He finally looked at her. His eyes were haunted. "More than anything. The worst part is I have no idea what kind of shit he'll put me through next. I can't ask you to live with that. I can barely live with it myself."

She swallowed the lump in her throat. "I don't want to give up on this." Her hand slid down his arm to grip his palm. "I don't want to give up on *us*."

"I'm not worth it," he whispered. His hopelessness strengthened her resolve.

"You're wrong. Would you blame *me* if someone forced me into sex?"

His voice hardened. "It's not the same."

She tugged on his hand. "The hell it's not. You don't need my forgiveness, or my acceptance. You need to forgive yourself. He raped you."

"Did you see a gun to my head?" he shouted. "I'm bigger. I'm stronger—"

"And he's controlled you since you were a kid. He. Raped. You." She stepped toward him, and he stepped back.

"Don't pity me," he gritted out.

Slowly, she raised her hand and cupped his jaw.

Her insides were flayed open, and her heart, bleeding. How much could one man take?

"It's not pity. I hurt for your hurt. I want to take it away. I want you to feel how much you mean to me." Her hand slid behind his neck. "Please don't give up on us."

He stared into her eyes for two heartbeats, then swept her into his arms. Crushing her against his chest, he murmured into her hair. "I don't deserve it. I don't deserve *you*. But if you want me, I'm yours. For as long as you want, however you want, I am yours."

She was starting to get light-headed when he finally eased his grip.

"I don't know how we're going to make this work," he breathed, "but I swear I'll do anything I can to find a way."

He leaned down and placed a chaste kiss on her lips.

Her mouth still tingled as he let himself out the front door.

***

Brick

Brick returned to work the next day, though he had some trouble holding on to his tools. His hands had come a long way since the fight Friday, but they still had some healing left to do. Kane quietly stepped in whenever he struggled.

He tried to call his grandma at lunch, but the nurse gave him the runaround with some bullshit about how the doctor would call him. It would have made him nervous if he hadn't received a picture of her in her dressing gown taking a bite of what appeared to be oatmeal for breakfast. If he couldn't get her on the phone, he'd go visit in a few days. As much as he hated those pictures, occasionally they were as much of a blessing as a curse.

Wednesday night, Sucre summoned him to El Cabron. He went with his heart in his throat, sure his bastard of a boss would have some other degrading hoop for him to jump through.

When he arrived, though, Sucre, missing his regular gaggle of girls, sat on his throne with Tre on one side and a younger guy on the other.

He only spared the kid a glance at first, but something pushed him to do a double-take. The boy looked eerily similar to Tre, but instead of projecting bravado, his face was very serious. No flashy clothes, he wore jeans and a dark hoodie and stared at the wall across the room.

Damn.

He would bet all the cash in his coffee table he was looking at Olivia's missing student. Gaze focused back on his boss, he advanced toward the throne. "Sir."

Sucre tossed him the phone he'd taken at the apartment. "Brick, I want to introduce you to the newest member of our little family." He gestured to the teenager in the hoodie. "This is Devon. He's going to be learning the ropes over the next few weeks."

The kid flashed a look at him briefly, and Brick nodded his head. In his peripheral vision, he could make out Tre's clenched fists and tight jaw.

"Young Devon is Tre's brother by blood. I'm sure they'll both be able to bring something special to the table." Sucre turned to Tre. "You'll welcome your little brother to the fold with open arms, won't you?"

For a moment, he thought the fool would be crazy enough to tell Sucre *no*. Tre's eyes drew to slits and his mouth, a thin line. Ultimately, though, he managed to grit out an unconvincing, "Yes, sir."

Sucre clapped his hands together. "Excellent. Devon's already been doing some small assignments for me. We'll start revving things up a little later in the week. Brick, I want you to go over the outstanding accounts with Tre. His brother and I have some quality time we need to spend together now."

Apparently, Sucre wasn't going to say anything about the scene he'd made Saturday or the video he'd texted from his phone. Fine. But Brick wasn't fool enough to think his boss had let it go.

As Sucre led Devon toward his office, Brick could only hope the man's harem waited back there as a surprise for the boy. The alternative was too disheartening to consider. Either way, there was nothing he could do to affect the outcome.

He motioned Tre to the bar where the bartender was already popping open two longnecks. They sat on the old leather stools.

"Where are you on your collections?" he asked before taking a swig of his Budweiser.

Tre didn't answer. His fingernails dug into the scuffed wood in front of them.

Brick cleared his throat. "I understand if you're worried about your brother."

"Worried?" Tre scoffed. "I'm not fucking worried. I'm pissed." He gripped his beer and guzzled it down. "This is *my* gig. Last thing I need is perfect little D coming along and trying to do it better than me. He needs to stick to his own shit."

"You think he *wants* to be here right now?"

"Why wouldn't he? This job means good money, respect, and all the free pussy you could ever ask for. And it's supposed to be *mine*."

"There's plenty of it all to go around," he said quietly. "We'd better focus on those accounts, though, unless you want a different scenario to play out."

Tre nodded reluctantly. "Fine. But brother or not, if Devon tries to take even a little of what's mine, he won't live to regret it."

***

Liv

Liv had been uneasy all day, like someone had been watching her at work. She could've gone to Will's construction site as she had been for more than a week, but instead she called Iz and met her for a sparring session. People packed the gym this time of day and all the other people gave her at least the illusion of safety.

Izzy linked arms with her as they walked into the gym. "I'm glad you called me. I like sparring with you, Nugget, even if you do still whine sometimes about the shiner I gave you once."

Though it was true the black eye was still an occasional sore spot, at least practicing self-defense gave her a proactive thing to do. Her resolution about making good choices wasn't bullshit. She would help herself by taking these lessons seriously, like she should have done from the start.

God knows she was flailing in every other part in her life. She couldn't remember the last time she saw Devon. She'd lost him.

Then there was Jonathan. She was falling hard for the guy, and she was pretty sure he felt the same. Still, she felt as though she could lose him any second. What if his drug lord boss kept him in a fight too long? Or what if some junkie came at him with a gun? And she refused to even think about the possibility of Sucre putting his hands on him again.

Jonathan was so big and strong and capable, but even he had been a victim. Without training, what chance did she have?

She rubbed at her sternum. "I kind of hoped we could work on grappling holds and escape techniques."

Izzy stopped a few feet into the building and cocked her head to the left. "Is there something you want to tell me about?"

Not even a little. "You wanted me to learn how to defend myself, right? I don't need offensive techniques. I don't even really need to deflect a punch, Iz. If anyone were to come at me, they'd grab me, right? What I need is to be able to get away. I liked the stuff where you showed me how to escape a hold from behind. I want to go over it again, and anything else you think would be good."

Iz rubbed her hands together briskly as they faced off on the mat. "I'm not going to go easy on you."

"You wouldn't be helping me if you did."

Over and over, they ran through the drills. The first half hour they did only attacks from behind. They must have done it twenty times. When the arm came around Liv's neck, she'd tuck her chin and push out her shoulder, step out and duck under it. Tuck. Push. Step. Duck.

Tuck. Push. Step. Duck.

Determined to get it right, she pushed herself.

Soon, her muscles responded without thought.

Tuck. Push. Step. Duck.

She pulled the elastic band from her hair to reform her ponytail. The hair framing her face and neck was damp with sweat. "What do I do once I get out of the hold?"

"Hurt him. Then run."

"Like, kick him in the junk?"

Izzy shook her head. "It's not always as easy as it sounds. I'd jab him in the throat if you can. Don't make a fist. Keep your fingers extended." Her sister gave a quick demonstration, then gave her a chance to try it herself. "If you have something sharp, go for an eye, but you can't be squeamish. What was it Carol liked to say? Go big or go home."

The idea of popping someone's eye turned her stomach. She frowned. "I don't know if I could pop somebody's eye."

"Then punch him in the ear or slam the heel of your hand up into his nose. Either one will hurt like a motherfucker. Strike hard, then run fast."

They never did get around to front-facing grappling attacks, but she felt a lot more confident walking out than she did walking in. "You have time for dinner with your now-badass little sister? My treat."

"As long as it's not Chipotle."

"Spoilsport."

***

The next day at work, Liv's nagging feeling came back, and it followed her all day long. She couldn't quite put her finger on what bothered her, but her sister had told her a hundred times never to ignore an instinct.

Getting backup would be the smart approach.

It only took a few minutes to find Dave, the school resource officer/security guard, to walk her out. Even with him right there, her stomach did a slow flip when she spotted her car. There were key-marks scratched in either side, footprints and a deep crater caved in on the hood, and all four tires were flat. Someone had attacked her little Corolla.

She whipped her head around the parking lot, searching for clues to the perpetrator, but deep in her heart, she knew who to blame. She'd let herself believe Devon's brother had forgotten about her. Obviously, it was too much to hope for.

"You have someone you can call, Ms. Turner? A husband? Your father?" Dave asked sympathetically. "I could help you file a report."

She blinked back tears. "Let me try my brother."

She dialed Will's number, but the call went straight to voicemail. Afterward, she called the gym, looking for Eduardo, but it was his day off. Briefly, she considered calling Izzy, but in truth, there was only one person who could make her feel safe right now.

Jonathan answered the phone on the first ring. "Livie?"

"I need you to come," she whispered. "He came to my school. Slashed my tires. Trashed my car. I can't drive it."

She imagined a rage building in the silence before he spoke. "Let me make sure he's not watching you. Do you have somewhere safe to wait for me?"

"I'll wait in the office. Jonathan?" She swallowed. "I'm scared."

"Hold tight. I'll be there soon."

Though she stayed busy filling out a police report with Dave, the hour she waited for Jonathan seemed to last forever. He texted her when he arrived outside.

Brick: Stay where you are. I'm changing your tires.

A fresh wave of terror washed over her. What if Tre was still out there? What if he was watching Jonathan right now?

No. Her man was too careful. Still, the wait stretched in front of her like melted wax.

Another fifteen minutes passed before she heard from him again.

Brick: Have someone walk you out. I'm going to follow you home.

She spotted his truck a few parking spaces away as she got behind the wheel. For the first time in an hour, the panic began to subside. With Jonathan in her rearview mirror, she knew, at least today, she'd make it home safely.

CHAPTER TWENTY-SIX

Brick

The minute Brick followed Olivia into her apartment, he had to touch her. To assure himself in the most basic way she was safe and unharmed. Snatching her into his arms, he molded her body against his.

When she'd called him, he'd known something was wrong. But he forced himself to take the time to track down Tre and make sure he was long gone before allowing himself to run to her rescue. It took even longer because he had to stop and buy four new tires for her car.

Now with her here in his arms, he couldn't let her go. "Tell me you're okay," he gritted.

She'd buried her face in his T-shirt, and the fabric muffled her reply. "Now that you're with me, I can finally breathe."

He pulled back enough to scrutinize her face.

Her freckles stood out in stark contrast to her pale skin. Her lower lip trembled. He needed to make her forget—make himself forget—for just a little while, the threat wasn't over yet.

Cupping her cheek, he captured her mouth in a kiss. Her lips met his hungrily; she slipped her tongue into his mouth. A hint of mint tickled his senses.

He could never get tired of kissing her. Everything about it felt right, from the firm press of her silken lips to the tiny sounds of pleasure escaping from her throat. He wanted to consume it, hold on to every perfect sensation so he could remember it all later and relive the moment again and again.

Without warning she broke away from the kiss. Grasping his hand, she led him wordlessly to her bedroom. "Unzip me."

Fumbling with the tiny clasp, he pulled down the tab, revealing the creamy skin of her back. With a slight shimmy of her shoulders, the simple navy dress fell to the floor and pooled at her feet. She unhooked her white bra and dropped it on the pile of fabric before turning to face him, wearing only a tiny pair of white panties.

He ached to trace her beautiful breasts. They were full and firm and swept up to her small, pink nipples.

"I don't want to wait any more," she said huskily. "I want to feel you against me. Inside me. I need you." Her plea took his breath away.

In a heartbeat, he kicked off his boots, stripped away his T-shirt and jeans. His boxer-briefs joined the growing mountain of clothes on the floor in seconds. His cock stood up against his stomach.

Inch by inch, his eyes tracked those tiny panties slipping down her legs, until his Olivia stood bare before him. And finally, there was no more waiting.

Sweeping her up into his arms, he reveled in the skin-to-skin contact. He kissed her like she was the air he breathed. They moved as one toward her unmade bed, and he lowered her to her back. She was a fucking feast laid out in front of him. Lying on top of her, he ran tender kisses along the column of her neck, then moved down to lave attention on her breasts.

"Touch me," she groaned, her own hands sliding down his back, kneading his skin.

He traced over the hourglass of her figure, from the outside of her ribcage, to her slender waist, down the flare of her hip. Shifting the bulk of his body to the side, his right hand traversed her pelvic bone, ending its journey in the slick warmth between her legs.

"You're so wet," he groaned, his middle finger sliding in and out of her pussy, spreading her moisture across her slit.

"I want you. I've wanted you for so long. More. *Please*."

A second finger joined the first, and her hips rose to meet them. His thumb kept a steady slide over her clit as he fucked her with his fingers.

Without looking, she reached back awkwardly and felt for the drawer of her nightstand. She yanked it open and pulled out a handful of condoms she dropped beside her on the bed.

No words were necessary. He stopped touching her only long enough to slip on his protection, then plunged his aching cock into the heaven between her spread legs. Her wet heat enveloped him.

He should savor something this exquisite, but his body was greedy for the bounty laid out before him. He'd been starving for her too long.

Gripping her shoulder, he thrust with powerful strokes. Her gasping breaths matched his rhythm, and a thin sheen of sweat dotted her forehead. In his fantasies of making love to her, Olivia was always mindless with pleasure. The reality was even better, because her eyes locked on his with laser-like focus.

The magnitude of their connection turned him on even more. He was ready to explode, but one crucial thing had to happen first.

"Come for me, baby," he whispered, slipping his thumb above the spot where their bodies connected. She cried out, and her body tightened around him. The muscles contracting around his cock pushed him beyond his control. Unable to hold back another second, he came with her, roaring her name. The intensity left him light-headed.

Rolling onto his back, he pulled her onto his chest, his dick still buried deep inside her. He felt her hot tears on his skin, and his stomach dropped. "Did I hurt you?" he asked hoarsely.

She lifted her head. Her eyes were still wet, but a soft smile teased her lips as she rubbed her chest. "Only in the very best way."

Her words echoed his own from a week before. God, had it been only a week?

Smiling, he let himself relax into this perfect

moment. Never in his life had he made such a deep connection to another person. He hadn't thought he would ever know how it felt to be in love.

He knew now, without a shadow of a doubt.

He loved Olivia Turner, and there was no way he could ever live without her again.

***

Liv

Even though he played it cool, Liv couldn't miss how Jonathan freaked out over her tears, but she couldn't think of any words big enough to capture how she felt. Sex had never been like this before. She felt him in every muscle, every bone in her body; he was everywhere. Everything.

This is what it meant to feel alive. The high she got jumping out of a plane was a pale imitation.

The clock next to her bed said it was five-forty-three, though it felt much later. Her stomach rumbled in agreement. "What do you like on your pizza?" Reluctantly, she disentangled herself from his arms and broke the physical connection between them.

Just for now, she vowed. There would be more loving later.

Jonathan sat up with her, tying off the condom and dropping it in the small trash can near the nightstand. "Load it up. I like it all." He paused. "Except anchovies." His nose wrinkled. "Or green peppers."

Whipping out her phone, she pulled up the app

for the pizza place around the corner and placed an order. Jonathan disappeared into the bathroom and came out seconds later with a warm, wet washcloth. A tinge of pink stained his cheeks as he held it out awkwardly to her. She accepted the offering and cleaned up quickly.

As she went to drop it in the hamper, she noticed him slipping on his boxer briefs. Quickly, she snatched his T-shirt and pulled it over her head.

When he raised his eyebrow, she gave an exaggerated pout. "I'm not ready for you to get dressed." She twirled, the extra fabric of his big shirt billowing around her. "If I'm wearing this, you can't."

Jonathan folded his arms and gave her a hard look, but he didn't fool her for a second. He had laughter in his eyes. Satisfaction.

Her gaze strayed down to his torso. He was The Rock and Thor rolled into one. Stepping closer, she ran her fingers across his sculpted chest. "I love seeing you this way. Your body is—" She licked her lips and dragged her gaze up to meet his.

"My body is *yours*. My heart. My soul." He made a noise in the back of his throat. "Dirty and broken as it is. It's all yours. I love you."

The tears came back with a vengeance. Like before, they were the happy kind. A mixture of joy and gratitude and…falling from a great height. Carol knew what she was doing when she added this to her list.

Fearful anticipation shadowed his face as he waited for her reply.

Cupping his face, she whispered fiercely. "I love

you too. I have never felt this way about anyone. You say you're mine?" He nodded. "Well, I am *yours*. I don't know how this is going to work. I don't know how we're going to get you free, but we will. I won't lose you. Do you understand? Whatever it takes."

He kissed her, a gentle brushing of the lips. "Whatever it takes."

The pizzaman disrupted the moment with two raps on the door. She grabbed the box with quick thanks, grateful she'd paid online.

Jonathan slapped her ass. "You always answer the door commando?"

Laughing, she set the box on the table and threw open the top. The rich scent of pizza sauce and freshly baked bread was heaven. "Your shirt is longer than some dresses I own." She pulled out a slice of cheesy goodness and bit in to a small piece of nirvana.

He frowned. "Maybe I need to check out some of those dresses."

"What you need to do is eat up. Because when we finish this pizza, the only thing you're gonna see is my bare ass before I climb on top of you for round two."

He finished his first slice in three bites.

Within five minutes, there was no more talk. The pizza was history, and Jonathan's clothes were on the floor, where they belonged.

***

Sucre

"You're sure you saw *Brick*?" Sucre glared at his nervous employee. Quinton was only sixteen, and Sucre used him for light surveillance work. The kid did a good job blending into the background.

Today, he'd sent Quinton to follow Tre. Even though Brick's protégé tried to hide it, he knew Tre was losing his shit over his little brother rising in the ranks. Tre was already a loose cannon. Sucre needed an accounting of what he did every minute until he knew for sure the kid wasn't a threat.

Tre trashing some school teacher's car was of little interest. But Brick playing her knight in shining armor was another story. Perhaps *this* was the mystery person who had received his video clips.

Quinton shifted his weight from one foot to the other. "Not a hundred percent sure, no. I was a ways down the street. After Tre left and I texted you, I stopped at McDonald's for a burger. When I was coming out, I saw Brick–or a big guy who looked like Brick—changing the tires on the car Tre had trashed."

"You didn't try to get a closer look?"

Quinton shook his head emphatically. "No, sir. You texted me to come back."

Irritation rose. "And you didn't think to drive closer to the parking lot first?"

Another shake of the kid's head. "No way. Not my job to think. It's my job to do as I'm told."

For fuck's sake. Those were the words Brick made all of his new recruits memorize. Most of them were too stupid for him to give them leave to think on their own.

"Fine," he growled. "Do some sniffing around. Find out who the teacher is. Then I'll figure out if she's of any use to me."

As Quinton scampered off to do as instructed, Sucre leaned back on his throne. If the woman could be any kind of leverage over Brick, it would be a major boon. The man's grandmother had died a week ago, and Sucre didn't know how much longer he could keep the information quiet. He was almost out of photos to send. Thank fuck he'd thought far enough ahead to keep a few in reserve. With the old lady out of the picture, he needed a new way to control his best soldier.

He'd considered using Kane Hale once he learned Brick had befriended him at his construction job, but he knew better than most, only a fool would trifle with the guy's motorcycle club. After some thought, he decided such a plan would be more trouble than it was worth.

But Brick had no other friends. No other entanglements. Hell, he wasn't even sure the man had a sex drive. Brick never took advantage of all the free pussy roaming around. Most guys considered it one of the best perks of the job.

Maybe he needed to pay him more money. If he couldn't force him to stay, maybe he could entice him.

He discarded the idea as quickly as it occurred to him. Brick had plenty of money. The bastard had been squirreling it away for years.

No. Force was the only way to go.

He grinned as a text from Quinton lit up his phone.

Olivia Turner.

At least now he had a place to start.

CHAPTER TWENTY-SEVEN

Brick

Brick knew something was wrong as soon as he saw the receptionist's face at the nursing home on Saturday. His heart sped up at the resigned look she flashed him. "What's going on? Has she taken a turn?"

Mrs. Beckwith motioned him to follow her toward a private family room. She tried to get him to sit down, but his blood pumped too hard to let him relax.

"I'm sorry, Brick. Your grandma has passed."

The words didn't register. The woman's mouth still moved, but her words didn't matter. Besides, she couldn't be right. He clutched his phone. Sucre had sent him a picture yesterday.

"I want to see her," he said quietly.

"I'm not sure—"

"Now." There was no room for argument in his

tone.

She sighed. "Let me get the doctor."

He paced as she left him alone in the room, his emotions a churning mess. On the one hand, it was a punch in the gut to lose the only family he had. His grandmother had been the single constant in his miserable life. She never baked him cookies or rocked him to sleep, but she cared for him in her own way. For a long time, she was all he'd had. Someone in the world who cared if he lived or died.

He'd done everything in his power to make sure she lived a comfortable life. She had a warm bed to sleep in and food in her belly. It was more than his piece-of-shit father had ever managed for her.

But despite the loss, her death also meant hope. She'd been the only thing keeping him under Sucre's thumb all these years.

He was finally free.

The doctor walked into the room, Mrs. Beckwith nowhere in sight. "I understand you want to see Sylvie. Come this way."

Together, they walked the sterile halls down to what was presumably the man's office. The doctor gestured for him to sit, but he shook his head sharply. "What happened? Where's my grandmother?"

"The renal failure finally got the best of her. She's already been moved to the county morgue."

He stilled. "Renal failure? My grandma didn't have problems with her kidneys."

The doctor shot him a sympathetic look. "I'm afraid she did, for about six months now."

Anger flared. "No one told me about this."

"It's almost over," she'd told him. "I'm dying."

Why didn't he take her seriously? Ask more questions?

"It wasn't our decision to make," the man said calmly. "Your grandmother was mentally fit and did not give us permission to share the details of her condition or treatment with you. It was her choice, Mr. Barlow. She knew, even with the dialysis, it was only a matter of time, since she wasn't a good candidate for transplant."

He shook his head, flexed his hands. "When did this happen? Why didn't you call me?"

The doctor grimaced. "It happened last week. I honestly don't know why no one contacted you. A phone call is protocol. Believe me, I am going to make it my business to find out."

"Don't bother." He already knew the answer. Whoever Sucre had in his pocket here had made sure to keep this a secret as long as possible. It was in Sucre's best interest for Brick to think his boss had power over him. "Did she leave any instructions? What she wanted for her burial?"

"She left you a letter she dictated to one of her friends. There was a copy in her file, but it's missing now. Fortunately, she also gave one to me for safekeeping." He pulled an envelope out of a pocket in his white coat. "I'll give you a moment alone. Come on out when you're done."

He ripped it open before the man made it out of the door.

Dear Brick,
I know you're upset with me for not

telling you the whole story about my kidneys. I knew you didn't take me seriously when I told you I was dying, but there was nothing you could do about it anyway. You've already done enough. More than I deserved. You put yourself in that bastard's hands, so I could live in peace. And I have. This place was exactly what I needed.

But my time is done.

Besides, you've waited long enough to live your life. I know you've done some bad things, but I also know why you had to do them. Forgive yourself. If you can, forgive me, for all the years you've suffered. Then, try to start over. Get as far away from all this as you possibly can.

Don't waste your money on a fancy service for me. I don't need it. Just scatter my ashes at Piedmont Park.

I'll be watching you from wherever my tired old soul goes next.

She didn't sign it, but he had no doubt those were his grandmother's words.

He balled the letter tightly in his fist, then hurled it at the wall only to watch it bounce pitifully to the ground. His blood burned to break something, to swipe everything from the desk onto the ground. Instead, he stomped outside to the gazebo where he sat with her last. Then he vaulted up and wrapped his hands around one of the beams framing the turret.

He didn't count as he pulled his body up and eased it down. His mind was too busy raging. He pulled up…eased down.

It didn't matter whether he could have saved her. She was dead. After everything he'd fucking done to keep her safe, she was dead anyway.

And she knew. She fucking knew what it cost him.

Why wasn't it enough to save her?

His lats and his biceps burned, but he pressed on, pushing himself harder. Until the anger drained away. Until the impotence stopped crushing him. Until he could really focus on the words his grandma had left behind.

She thought he'd done right by her. She was grateful. She was sorry.

Could he forgive himself?

Who knows?

Could he forgive *her*?

Wiping the sweat from his forehead with the back of his hand, he looked up at the blue sky. That one was a no-brainer. Even though his heart weighed heavy, he was ready to start his new life, and in her way, his grandma had given him her blessing.

He wasn't going to waste this chance.

***

Brick's first order of business was to collect his cash from the apartment. He needed money if he had any chance of making a clean break from Sucre.

Everyone seemed to be watching as he parked his truck and strode into his place. He emptied out the hollow leg of his table, stuffing all the bills into a backpack. Gently, he wrapped his tiny, childhood race car into a bandana and added it to the bag, along with the photo of his grandma and the napkin from the Majestic. Those were the only things he wanted to keep. Everything else here could be replaced.

He'd tried calling Olivia on the way back, but the calls went straight to voicemail. The plan was to go to her apartment from here and never look back at his old life again. He'd disappear. If anyone was fool enough to come after him, they wouldn't live to regret it.

He almost didn't recognize the hope—the promise of freedom—fluttering in his chest. It was so foreign, fragile.

Hefting the pack on his shoulder, he didn't even spare a look around as he walked out the door for the last time. Still no answer from Olivia when he tried calling her again, but her car sat in the parking lot when he pulled up to her building.

His hand was poised to knock on the front door

when he caught sight of Tre's little brother, watching him from the sidewalk. A hundred ways to kill the kid shuffled through his head, but if the boy was here, it might already be too late. He turned away from the door and approached the teenager with caution.

The kid, Devon, shook his head before he could say a word. "Sucre's got her."

He swallowed the bile rising in his throat and stared at the boy's face. It was almost expressionless, except for a small twitch in his left eye.

"I wanted to stop them. Miss T was always good to me. She tried to get me out of this hellhole. I was afraid to let anyone see she mattered to me, though, so I kept my mouth shut."

For a moment, he'd forgotten the kid's connection to his girl. "What did they tell you to do?"

Devon's focus flickered around the parking lot, probably looking for a sign of whether the boss had set up spies. "I'm supposed to be watching for you. Sucre's got a suspicion you might be involved with Miss Turner, but he's not sure. I was supposed to stay out of sight and tell him if you showed up. Here." He held out Olivia's cell phone. "They're gonna be searching for this. Your pictures are all over it."

He shoved the phone in his pocket. If Sucre already had Liv, killing the kid would do no good. Cold sweat trickled down his back. Panic gripped his heart like a vice, but he fought to ignore it. He had to use his head if he wanted to save her. "What tipped him off?"

"He didn't tell me. He said he was sure the lady would be of interest to at least one person in the crew, and he needed to know if she'd be of interest to you as well. I don't think he realizes I know her."

"Shit. Tre had a tail."

Devon stood up straighter. "What does my brother have to do with this?"

"Olivia came to your apartment trying to find you." He had no idea if Devon realized what a sociopath his brother was, but now wasn't the time to mince words. "He's been stalking her ever since."

"This is really bad," Devon whispered.

"You don't know the half of it. She only wanted to help you. She didn't understand what your brother is." He clenched his fists as shards of anger broke through his icy fear. "Do you?"

"Yeah." From the expression on his face, Devon understood the situation completely.

"Tre trashed her car at the school yesterday." He gestured to the Corolla, which still showed evidence of the attack. "She called me for help. I made sure your brother was gone, but I should have realized he'd have a tail. Sucre's probably just waiting for him to implode over you getting recruited."

"Tell me what to do. How can I help?"

He considered the boy, thought back to Olivia's steadfast belief he was destined for something better than all this. "Stay here. Don't let them know you've seen me. Don't let them know what I've told you. Wait until they call you, and act like everything is normal. But don't lie about your connection to Olivia. In fact, you need to disclose it as soon as you can. Otherwise, it seems like you're hiding it. You got me?"

"Yeah. What are you gonna do?"

A very good question. "I'm gonna do whatever it takes to make sure she gets out of there alive."

***

Liv

When a strange man grabbed her from her front porch, it didn't even occur to Liv to try and fight back. All her sister's pep talks, all of her training…and still, her brain couldn't process what was happening fast enough for her to react.

So instead of slipping away or twisting the guy's fingers, she was a sack of potatoes when someone shoved her into the trunk of a car. Thirty minutes later, someone pulled her back out and dragged her into a shady bar. Though it was obvious she was there against her will, no one so much as batted an eye.

The man clasping her arm let her go in front of an ornate throne in the back of the room. The thing looked ostentatious and ridiculous, much like the man who sat on top of it. The man in the sick video she could never unsee.

He wore a white suit like the one John Travolta had in *Saturday Night Fever*. Flashy rings adorned his fingers and a familiar thick, braided gold chain circled his neck. The crisscrossed braid made her think of the ring she'd given to Jonathan. The one like her mother's.

She wanted to kill Sucre de la Cruz, but she was outmanned and outgunned. It's why she didn't roll her eyes, why she didn't laugh, and why she didn't scream. She forced herself to breathe as his gaze slid over her like he was assessing a horse to stud.

"Do you know why you're here?" His voice carried a hint of a Spanish accent, and it was as smooth as aged bourbon.

She clenched her hands to her chest as she shook her head.

Sucre smiled, but it didn't reach his eyes. It was a serpent's smile, frightening and cold. "My name is Sucre de la Cruz, and this," he spread his arms wide, "is my domain."

She trembled, not even trying to hide it. Let him think his name alone made her quiver. His reputation had permeated Atlanta like a poisonous fog.

This time his smile showed teeth. "I see you know of me. I wonder how. Perhaps my face looks familiar. Or is it my body? I'm told I look even better without my clothes."

"Everyone knows who you are." Refusing to accept the bait, she kept her voice meek, subservient. No reason to poke the bear.

He picked up a lock of her hair, then let the strands fall from his fingers. "Even a sweet little school teacher such as yourself?"

She swallowed against her dry throat. Nodded. The less she spoke, the less she'd get herself in trouble.

"Tell me, Miss…"

"Turner," she whispered.

"Why do you think you're standing before me right now?"

She would never admit to knowing Jonathan. Never. "I don't know," she whimpered.

"Really?" He cocked his head, then glanced over her shoulder. "This lady look familiar to any of you?"

"I've seen her." An unfamiliar voice rang out from the small crowd surrounding them. "She was with Devon at Burger King the other night."

The information clearly took him off guard. He sat up tall in his seat. "Aren't *you* full of surprises? Tell me, Miss Turner, what do you have to do with my Devon? And how do you know of his association with me?"

She lowered her eyes. "Devon is—was—one of my students. My best student. I had encouraged him to t-try for a scholarship. When he didn't do it, I pushed him, and he said he had obligations in his neighborhood, and he worked for someone important." She fudged the details a little, but it paid off when Sucre puffed up. "I didn't know it was you."

Sneaking a glance at the small crowd around her, she continued. "When he stopped coming to class, I dug up his address and tried to talk to his brother about why he wasn't in school anymore."

Sucre chuckled. "Ah, things are making much more sense now. You're very smart, telling me the truth of things. What did you think of Devon's brother?"

"He scared me." She wrapped her arms around

herself. "Not at first. But at the end. It was like I was a mouse, and he was a cat, toying with me, waiting to pounce."

"I guess you're smarter than you look."

The voice behind her was terrifying and familiar. The hairs on the back of her neck stood up as she felt Tre move in behind her.

"You sensed exactly what was happening, but what I want to know is—how did you get away from me?"

Sucre nodded, waiting for her answer.

"I hid. There was a burned b-building. It was so dark." She shivered at the memory. "There were rats."

Tre stomped his foot. "I *knew* I should have checked in there. I didn't think a sweet little thing like you would have the stones to go inside." He ran his finger up the line of her jaw. "I won't underestimate you again."

She prayed he would. "I-I'm sorry, Mr. De La Cruz, for intruding in your business. Really. I didn't realize you were the important man Devon was talking about. I only wanted to look out for my student. I swear, I won't ever step foot in this neighborhood again."

"My dear." Sucre tutted. "If only it were so simple. I understand now how you've taken Tre's interest, but it solves only half the mystery. What I really want to know is how you're involved with Brick Barlow."

She frowned. "I don't know who that is."

Sucre shook his head sadly. "Dear Miss Turner, I hope you're lying. Because if you're Brick's girl, no one here will touch you. It would be in my best interest to keep you safe." He shrugged. "If not, I'm afraid I won't be able to stop my young tomcat from playing with his new mouse."

He pulled a phone out of his suit pocket and made a call, putting it on speaker. Tears threatened when she heard the answering voice.

"Sir?"

"Devon. Have you seen any sign of Brick?"

"No, sir, but the lady who Quinton grabbed? She's one of my teachers. She's really nice. I can't imagine her anywhere around a guy like Brick."

Sucre cocked his head. "If you recognized her, why didn't you say anything to Quinton?"

"I report to you, sir. Besides, I wouldn't try to talk Quinton out of his orders. It wouldn't be my place."

Sucre seemed to accept the words as his due. "Fair enough. Why don't you come on back? You can keep your teacher company while we sort all this out." As soon he hung up, Sucre shot out a text, then stuck the phone back into his pocket. "I've invited Brick to join our little party. Maybe we can get to the bottom of this once the gang's all here."

CHAPTER TWENTY-EIGHT

Brick

Brick had precious little time to come up with a plan if he wanted to get Olivia out of Sucre's hands. The only chance he had was to reach out for help. Though he dreaded the way he knew it would play out, his first call had to be to Will.

Pulling Olivia's phone out of his pocket, he called up the contact.

It only rang twice before her brother answered. "Hey Liv, we still on for dinner tomorrow night?"

"Sucre's got her," he rasped. "I need your help to get her back."

"Fuck." A crash sounded on the other end of the phone.

"I'm calling Kane. Maybe between the three of us, we can come up with something." Without waiting for a response, he dialed in his friend and merged the calls.

"Liv, is everything okay?"

He filled them in on everything that had happened over the past two days. Well, everything pertinent to the situation at hand. "I have an idea, but I'm gonna need help with the details and the execution. Kane, do you think your club might be interested in making a little extra cash?"

Thankfully, they hashed out the plan quickly, because he'd barely had the chance to drop off the money before Sucre summoned him to the club.

He sent word to Kane and Liv's brother before heeding the call. It would only take about twenty minutes to get there. He could only pray it wasn't too late.

When he walked in, the vibe inside El Cabron was different than he'd ever felt. There was a sense of anticipation, like the dead-eyed girls, the drunks, and the thugs held their breath. Gripping his backpack, he made a beeline straight for his boss.

"Could I steal a minute alone, sir?"

Sucre examined his expression. "Are you worried about something, Brick?"

Of course, he hadn't missed Olivia's stark, white face as she sat miserably on Tre's lap a few feet away. He pretended she wasn't anything special, though, just another girl scratching an itch for Sucre's crew.

"My grandmother passed," he said soberly.

His boss held a hand to his chest. "Did she? I'm sorry to hear it. Sylvie was quite a woman." He stood. "Let's talk in my office."

Dutifully, he followed and closed the door behind him.

Sucre whirled to face him. "I have to say I'm surprised. I thought you might take your stash of money and try to make a run for it."

"Is that what you thought I was saving for?" He pulled the backpack off his shoulder and emptied the contents on the bed. He'd already removed his keepsakes and stashed them in the truck. "I've been saving up to make a proposal."

Eyeing the money, Sucre folded his arms. "What kind of proposal?"

"I want to buy in. Become a partner in your business."

Sucre's eyebrows shot up so high it would have been comical if the stakes weren't so serious. "You *what*?"

"I've got about forty thousand dollars here. Look, I'm tired of knocking heads together. I'm tired of fighting, but really, how far can I make it in the real world? I tinker with building shit, but who am I kidding? This is who I am." He deepened his voice. "I know this is always gonna be your business. I was only hoping my role might change. Grow. I'm not getting any younger."

"Why wait for your grandmother to die to bring me this proposal?" Suspicion laced every word.

He shrugged. "She wouldn't have approved. I waited out of respect to her, but she's gone now. I've got to do what's right for me."

"So, you give me this money. What do you get out of the deal?"

"My cash means you can front more loans. More loans mean more interest. Part of those profits would go to me. Maybe I could help with recruitment." His face hardened. "But you wouldn't treat me like one of your employees anymore. No more tests of loyalty. And you will never touch me again."

Sucre laughed. "What's stopping me from keeping this money and rejecting your proposal?"

"You'd have to kill me, which would be a waste. I could help you."

"You're not understanding me." Sucre rapped twice on the wall.

"I know exactly what you meant. You and I both know my grandmother's health forced me into this life. The only way I'm staying in it is on my terms. You could kill me, but you have nothing to make me stay your bitch."

Tre let himself in, a quivering Olivia, grasped tightly in his hands.

"You sure?" Sucre taunted.

Intentionally oblivious, he scoffed. "You're trying to throw pussy at me again? Come on, boss."

"You're telling me you don't know this woman?"

He stared at the love of his life with dead eyes. "I've never seen her before in my life."

"You're saying you wouldn't care if I left her to Tre's tender mercies?"

He barked out a laugh. "I wouldn't wish that sick fuck's tender mercies on anyone, but I'm not selling my life away for some stranger." It was a gamble, but he had few cards left to play. "Let him take her home. Maybe he can get some of his perversions out of his system. He won't be much good to you otherwise."

Liv let out an involuntary cry as Tre grabbed her crotch roughly through her jeans. "Does this mean I can have her, boss?"

Sucre stared at the ceiling like a parent would, dealing with an unruly child. "You know it's not truly a hunt when someone hands you the prize on a silver platter, but fine, take her. Go."

He wouldn't let himself watch Tre pulling her away. Instead, he gathered his money and returned it to his pack. "I guess you need time to consider my proposal."

"No. I accept." Sucre held out his hand for the backpack, and he handed it over right away. "I think you're holding out on me a little, though. I thought you had closer to fifty thousand dollars in your old table. What are you doing with the rest of the money?"

"I thought I would put together a special service for my grandma, you know? Even if I'm the only one there, she deserves to have something nice."

Sucre looked at him with a hint of pity. "You really are a sentimental fool."

"I thought maybe we could call the whole crew together. Make an announcement. It would mean a lot to me."

"Sure, Brick, call everybody in. Tell them to get here in the next thirty minutes."

A half an hour would be perfect.

***

Liv

Liv didn't expect Jonathan to do anything to tip off Sucre to their relationship. Still, when he acted like she meant nothing to him, it was a knife in her heart. When he'd looked at her, she saw nothing of the man she knew in his eyes. He was empty.

She had no choice but to save herself. *You can't win the prize if you stop running the race.* Of course, she couldn't do it from the trunk, where someone had shoved her yet again. It would have to happen when they got to Tre's apartment.

Keeping her breathing as even as possible, she worked to stay calm so she could think this through. It would only excite him more if she gave in to her fear.

The knowledge helped her manage a blank look of acceptance when he finally opened the trunk to let her out. His disappointment was evident. Snarling, he yanked her by the arm to the pavement beside him. "Don't even bother trying to scream. No one here will help you."

"I believe you," she murmured. The street was deserted, and she had no illusions someone would come outside if she cried out.

"You don't seem very scared, Miss Turner. I think I might have some ideas about how to change that. I can be very…inventive." His gold tooth flashed when he smiled.

"Oh, I'm scared. But it's different than before. Last time, I was running for my life. I was so sure you would catch me. It was the most terrified I've ever been." She hung her head. "Now I know I'm going to die. I have no choice but to accept it. There's no chance for escape."

He slapped her across the face, and tears sprang to her eyes. She allowed them to fall, keeping a look of utter defeat on her face. It had the desired effect.

"You're ruining it." He hit her again, and she tasted blood on her lip.

"Go ahead. Get it over with."

He'd already pulled back his hand for another strike when he froze, then dropped it to his side. "You know what we need here? A little drama. A little…anticipation." He tipped up her chin with a crooked forefinger. "Nobody likes when a party ends too soon. How about we make it a little more interesting? Build in a little foreplay, heh?"

Her eyes widened. Oh God, was he talking about sex? Her arm ached as he curled his fingers around her bicep again and dragged her toward his apartment. She cursed herself for the hundredth time for ever coming here in the first place. Tre pushed her inside, then leaned against the front door. She stood frozen in front of him.

"We're gonna do exactly like we did last time. I'm gonna give you a head start to run. Then I'm gonna chase you. And when I catch you," he laughed low. "Well, there won't be a single part of your body that doesn't know it's been conquered."

He stepped away from the door. "Last time, I gave you three minutes, and you escaped me, but this time I know you better. It won't happen again." He stroked his hardening dick through his pants with the heel of his hand. "You ready, baby? Three minutes. On your mark. Get set. Go."

Unwilling to waste a second, she ran out of the door like a shot, making a beeline to the burned-out building. It was probably the first place he'd check, but she'd be a sitting duck if she stayed out in the open.

She went in through the same blackened doorframe as last time. At least she knew some of the terrain. Her heart beat in her ears as she hoisted herself through the hole in the ceiling of the back bathroom. Thanks to Eduardo's punishing calisthenics, this time, she could climb up on her own.

There was no source of light except for the few places illuminated by the setting sun's rays trickling in from the charred patches in the structure. She'd lost her phone around the time someone snatched her from her apartment. Her eyes were slowly adjusting, but she saw little more than large shadows. It would have to be enough.

She stepped carefully, all too aware the floor beneath her could be unsound. Digging deep in her memory, she searched for Jonathan's warning.

The third floor, he'd told her. The center of the hallway was bad.

She needed a way up there.

Her eyes picked up more of her surroundings. Now she could make out the location of the doors and the scurrying movement of the rodents at her feet. She had no time to be squeamish.

The ceiling above her appeared to be intact, so she left the room behind, searching for a way up. She found it in the fourth room she tried, climbing up from a countertop still covered with dishes and trash, which crunched under her feet.

Part of the wood broke away in her hands as she tried to hoist herself up, but eventually she found a beam solid enough to support her weight. Finally, she made it to the third floor. And now she could hear Tre moving below her, whistling the same slow melody as before. If she ever made it out of here, she'd never listen to the Rolling Stones again.

Squinting down the long hallway, she could see a few holes in the flooring, maybe two doors away; she needed to get Tre to walk on the bad stretch. But how? The only way he would charge through would be if he was chasing her, but that would put her in the danger zone first. Unless...

She eyed the ceiling speculatively.

If she could get to the fourth floor, she could come back down on the other side of the hallway. Use herself as bait. She had to move quickly. It would only work if she made it into place by the time Tre got to the third floor.

She needed a place to climb.

Praying for a miracle, she hurried into the apartment directly across from her.

***

Tre

Tre congratulated himself on the idea to let the pretty teacher run. It was so much more fun when they ran. He could imagine how quickly her heart beat, how the fear overwhelmed her.

He was hard as a rock right now; his cocked

throbbed in his pants. The first thing he would do when he caught her was fuck her senseless. No doubt he'd fuck her again when he got through with her. Anticipation zipped through his veins.

He had no doubt Miss Turner returned to the same hiding place as last time. He could hear her movements echoing in the walls. She scurried above him.

He used his phone as a flashlight, trying to find a way up. There. In the bathroom.

Goddamn this place was nasty. It smelled like an old campfire and a sewer combined. There was shit in the toilet, most likely from squatters. Probably the same idiots who left their needles on the floor.

This girlie would to pay extra for making him get his hands dirty. The only mess he liked was the kind he made himself. He wiped his palms on his pants once he was firmly on the second floor, then ran the beam of his flashlight across the room. No sign of her, except an unmistakable trail left behind on the sooty floor.

She'd been here.

He cringed when he got to the kitchen where she'd hiked herself up to the third floor. Roaches covered the old dishes on the counter, and he refused to look any closer at what else was there.

The wood broke apart in his hands when he started to climb. It took longer than he wanted to make it to the next level, but he wouldn't give up on his prey. He'd punish her for making him do all this work.

Going still, he listened for a sign of her location, but he heard only silence. Maybe she was hiding.

No, the trail was still there, moving out the door.

A thump jerked his attention away from the floor to the end of the hall, where the teacher cowered. She dashed into the open door next to her, and he picked up speed in pursuit.

It only took three long strides before his boots broke through the fragile floor. His body hit the ground before he had a chance to scream.

CHAPTER TWENTY-NINE

Brick

The thirty minutes after Liv and Tre left were the longest of Brick's life. He focused on his breathing as he waited for Sucre's entire crew to arrive. Every fiber of his body strained to go after his woman, but he had to trust his failsafe would come through, or all of this would be for nothing.

There were dozens of guys in the organization, from the dealers to the pimps to the bookies, and the muscle, like himself. By the time Sucre set, about forty guys had gathered in the bar, all loyal to the boss, all curious about why he called them.

They gathered around Sucre at his throne and Brick in his chair beside him.

"My friends. I've brought you here for a very special announcement." All eyes followed Sucre as he rose to his feet. No one noticed the extra men, all clad in leather, creeping in around them.

"Brick has been an important part of this organization for the past fifteen years. He's worked by my side, earning my trust, following the rules. Starting tonight, he is becoming something more. He's not merely a collector or a punisher for wrongdoing. Tonight, he takes his place at my side as a partner."

Sucre clapped, and the crowd followed suit.

Brick cracked a half-smile and waited for the noise to die down. Then, he stood next to the man who'd made his life a living hell. "Thank you. Sucre is right. I've done this job for many years. All this time, it's been about what I can do with my fists and what I can do with this gun." He pulled his Glock out of his waistband and waved it carelessly in the air. "I'm ready for a new challenge."

Still smiling, he turned the gun on his longtime boss and slammed it into the side of his head. Before the bastard's body even hit the floor, he opened fire, picking off the shell-shocked men around him.

They were still reaching for their own weapons when the brothers of The Skulls M.C. ambushed them from behind.

Kane trained his gun on Sucre, allowing him to watch his empire crumble in front of his eyes.

The massacre took less than a minute to play out, and not even the bartender was left alive when it was all said and done. Bodies littered the floor.

He turned to Sucre, who rose to his knees and lifted his chin defiantly, despite the inevitability of what was to come.

"Go ahead and kill me if you want, but you'll

never be free of me, Brick. You'll never be anything more than the monster I made you." The boss laughed darkly. "I'll be with you for the rest of your life."

He cocked his head. It was strange to see Sucre on his knees. Strange, but satisfying. "The only thing you'll be…is a stain on the linoleum."

A single shot to the head ended the reign of Sucre de la Cruz.

It was a cleaner death than he deserved.

Kane stepped forward. Blood dotted his face and matted his beard. "Where's your girl?"

He grimaced. "Tre took her to the apartment. Will should be there already, but I've got to go." He surveyed the blood, brains, and other nasty shit around him. "You sure your guys can take care of all this?"

"For ten thousand dollars paid in advance? Yeah, brother. We've got this."

"Thanks, man. I'll never forget it." He leaned down and put one more slug in Sucre's head, one last *fuck you*, before wading through the bodies out the front door.

Half of his plan had been a success, but none of it mattered if Will couldn't get to his sister in time.

***

Liv

A loud crash verified Tre had stepped into Liv's trap, but even with such a hard fall, there were no guarantees. In every horror movie she'd ever seen,

328

the bad guy always got up again.

Her heart thundered in her chest. She held her breath, straining to catch a hint her stalker had resumed his hunt.

Before her lungs gave out, a familiar voice cut through the silence. "Liv!" It was her brother. "Liv, where are you?"

It sounded like he was right outside. Having him so close mobilized her to break out of her frozen fear. "Will, I'm coming out." She sent up a prayer of thanks he was here. Now she just had to find a way out of this damn building. This side of the structure was unfamiliar.

She tested each step before she took it, making sure the floor could support her weight. Within a couple of minutes, she found the stairwell and made her way to the bottom floor.

Relief washed over her when she finally pushed her way out and saw her brother's face. She should have known he'd be here. He'd always promised he'd be there when she needed him.

But why was he raising a gun?

Suddenly, an arm clamped around her neck. A shot thundered past her, and her brother fell to the ground.

A voice she knew would haunt her for the rest of her life, whispered in her ear. "You think you're so smart," Tre hissed. "I'm going to fuck your dead skull, you bitch."

She didn't think about it. Her body took over.

Tuck. Push. Step. Duck.

She tucked her chin beneath his arm, pushed back with her shoulder, stepped out, and ducked under his arm. Then she did exactly as her sister had instructed…She ran like hell.

***

Brick

Brick stopped breathing when Tre put Will on the ground and grabbed Olivia from behind. No way he could get a clean shot from here, and he wouldn't take the chance of hitting her with a stray bullet.

His only hope was the element of surprise. He stalked forward.

But suddenly, his girl took off running. Twisting and turning, she'd escaped Tre's hold and fled his way. He knew instantly the moment she recognized him. Her face transformed from terror to hope.

He fired as she scurried behind him. The bullet clipped Tre in the shoulder, and the bastard's gun clattered to the ground. Not good enough. He pulled the trigger again, but nothing came out. He reached in his pocket for another clip, but there was nothing there.

Fine. He'd kill the sick fuck with his bare hands.

Roaring, he ran full tilt toward the man who tried to take away his girl. Tre was already reaching for his gun. A shot went off, and fire tore through his bicep, but he didn't slow down. He couldn't. He smashed into Tre at top speed. A hard right-hook to the jaw dropped the kid to the ground.

The calm detachment he wore like a second skin burned away with the fire of his wrath. He kicked

Tre in the ribs, the steel toe of his boot crunching bones beneath it.

He reached down and clamped his big hand over the front of Tre's face, lifting him back to his feet. Then locking his fingers around Tre's forearms, he shook the bastard violently.

"You wanted the thug life, you dumb fuck? You think you're all badass trying to destroy something perfect?" he bellowed in his rage and began slamming his fist into Tre's face. "You. Will. Never. Touch. Her. Again." He accentuated each word with another hit.

Tre had long stopped struggling beneath him. The only sound was the slapping of his knuckles against wet, meaty flesh...until Olivia whimpered behind him.

Grasping his enemy's head, he twisted until he heard the familiar crack of a broken neck.

Tre had asked him once what his favorite way to kill someone was. Now he had an answer.

He released his opponent, dropping him gracelessly to the ground.

Sobs wracked Liv's small body as she ran to her brother. "Will," she cried. "Oh my God, Will."

He closed the distance between them in a few long strides. "Let me check him."

She dropped down beside him as he knelt next to her brother and took his pulse. It was faint, but unmistakable. "He's still alive." He handed Liv his phone. "Call 911."

A quick inventory of Will's body revealed the bullet had hit him in the chest. It was on the right side, though, so it didn't hit the heart. The lung might be another story. Distantly, he heard Olivia begging for an ambulance.

Shivering against the chill in the air, he pulled off his dark flannel shirt and put pressure against Will's wound. He couldn't do anything to help the man breathe, but he would do his damnedest to make sure the guy didn't bleed to death.

Olivia crawled to the other side of her brother, whispering nonsensical words of love, her tears dripping down into his blonde hair. Soon, the plaintive wail of a siren grew close, and the running footsteps of paramedics moved in behind them.

Gratefully, he stepped out of the way, into the beam of a police flashlight. "Put your hands in the air," the young cop shouted.

He did as the officer commanded. Olivia stood next to him, her hands up as well. "He's been shot too. Please. Look, he's bleeding." Keeping one arm up, she gestured to Tre with the other. "He's the one who did this. It was him."

Cops were always wary of him because of his size, and it didn't help he'd been hovering over Will's body when they arrived. But Olivia's pleas were difficult to ignore.

One of the EMTs checked him out, while the other loaded Will into the ambulance. "It's a through-and-through," she barked out to her partner, her attention trained on Brick. "Come on, you can ride in the ambulance with us."

"No." His voice was implacable. "I'm not leaving Olivia here alone."

The woman's hard face softened. "One of the officers will follow with her right behind us. Right,

Jude?"

The young officer nodded grudgingly.

"I'll be right there," Olivia assured him. "I'm safe now. I promise." She wrapped her arms around his waist.

How could she want to touch him when he just showed her the kind of thing he was capable of? He murdered a man with his bare hands, and he did it right in front of her eyes. Yet here she was, seeking comfort in his embrace.

He allowed himself a moment to soak in her touch before he stepped back. Holding her by the shoulders, he scanned her from head to toe. A bruise was forming on her left cheek. Cuts and scratches peppered her arms. She was filthy, but he could find no signs of any substantial injury.

Still, he needed to keep her close. "I'll ride with Olivia and the cop."

Jude shook his head emphatically. "No way. You ride in the rig, sir. The lady will be okay with us."

"Jonathan, *please*. I'll be fine. Let them take care of you."

Her plea did what the EMT's demand couldn't. He could deny her nothing.

Shooting the cop a dark look, he warned the man. "She'd better be okay." He hadn't come this far to lose her now.

It was his first time riding in an ambulance. The siren blared in his ears. He was mesmerized, though, watching the paramedics work.

Will struggled to breathe. The EMT said something about a pneumo-hemothorax. The monitors went crazy. He tried to stay out of the way.

The woman did something to help. He couldn't really see what with her back to him, but the frantic beeping of the heart monitor returned to a normal rhythm. When she leaned to the side, he could see she held a big needle in Will's chest.

He shuddered. Liv would be devastated if Will didn't make it.

"Are you all right, sir?" the petite brunette asked. It took a moment to realize the paramedic was talking to him.

"Yeah." He gripped the bandage wrapped around his arm. "I'm just worried about my friend."

"I think he's going to be okay. Rest. You've lost a lot of blood."

He closed his eyes, intending for it to be only a moment, but the second he relaxed, he passed out.

***

Liv

"We need another gurney." The paramedic was already calling for help the moment the ambulance doors opened. Liv stood only a few feet away thanks to Officer Jude's ability to keep up with the rig.

A swarm of doctors stood at the back of the ambulance and whisked Will's gurney away the moment the wheels hit the ground. She stood on her tip-toes, trying to see Jonathan. She couldn't so much as catch a glimpse until the doctors unloaded his limp body in front of her. It took three men to lift him.

"What's happening?" She chased behind them.

The EMT she'd seen examine Jonathan's arm grasped her hand. "He lost consciousness. Probably from blood loss. Are you family?"

She nodded, her neck still craning to follow Brick and the doctors, but they were now out of sight. "Will is my brother."

"The blond man with the chest wound?"

She nodded miserably.

"And the big guy?" the woman prompted.

"He's—he's my everything." Tears poured from her eyes. "I need to be with him. Please."

"Do you have anyone you can call?" The paramedic guided her to a chair in the waiting room.

"My sister," she whispered. "But I don't have my phone."

"We'll get her here," the woman assured her. "And I'll wait with you until she arrives."

Once she sat down, and the adrenaline began to fade, her surroundings sank in. The green walls, the cacophony of crying, whispers, and the hums and beeps of various machines. The smell: antiseptic and mop water.

Hospital.

Her stomach threatened to rebel with the barrage of sensory information, every sound and scent reminding her of the poison the doctors pumped in her veins to keep her alive. Reminding her of the warrior woman who inspired her to live, even as she lost her own fight for survival.

Minutes clicked slowly into an hour.

The paramedic, Lara, kept her word and stayed

at her side until Iz ran frantically into the room. "Any word?" Izzy's eyes moved wildly. "Will. Do you know anything?"

She shook her head. "I'm still waiting."

The wait was interminable. Police detectives filtered in and out, asking questions. She filled out paperwork, though she had precious little information she could give about Jonathan. She vowed to herself she would learn everything about him after this, from his middle name to his blood type. Every fucking thing.

It was one o'clock in the morning before one of the doctors came out with news. "Are you the family of Jonathan Barlow?"

She jumped to her feet. "Yes."

"He's stable. We've moved him into a semi-private room if you want to see him."

"And Will? William Turner?"

The doctor shook his head. "I'm sorry. He's not my patient, but I'll see what I can find out." He led them to Jonathan's room.

Her chest hurt to see him so vulnerable. Had she looked this fragile when she was a patient here?

A thin hospital gown covered his thick torso. The doctors had taped an IV to his hand. "Is he going to be okay?"

The doctor smiled. "Yes. He just needed blood and some fluids to help fight the dehydration. We cleaned and stitched his wound. Now, the best thing for him is rest." The man turned for the door, then glanced back. "I'll go check on your—"

"Brother," Iz whispered.

She pulled a chair up to the bed and wrapped her

fingers around Jonathan's free hand. Feeling the warmth and vitality of his skin soothed her instantly. She rested her head on his chest, feeling even more comfort from the steady beat of his heart. She closed her eyes and concentrated on the rhythm. In moments, the exhaustion of the day hit hard, and she drifted to sleep.

She startled awake at the sound of voices.

"—really very lucky he got here so quickly. We've repaired the damage to his lung, and he's recovering in the ICU."

"Can I see him?" Izzy spoke before Liv could even finish processing the doctor's words.

"Only one visitor at a time."

Izzy glanced over, and she nodded tiredly. It's not as though she could be in two places at once anyway.

She watched her sister disappear out of the door and jumped in her seat when Jonathan squeezed her hand.

"I'm sorry." His voice was raspy, but it was the sweetest sound she'd ever heard. Her eyes brimmed with tears, and she pulled his hand to her lips for a kiss.

"Sorry?"

"You went through so much because of me. And then—then you really had to see who I am. What I am. Not in some video on your phone, but right there in your face. I killed the crazy fucker with my bare hands right in front of you, and I would do it again. I'm not sorry I did it, but that's the whole point. You deserve better than a fucking thug like me."

"I would have killed him myself if I could have. You saved me. Don't you dare judge yourself for not regretting it." Her voice shook. She rubbed the back of his hand over her cheek. "I was so scared leaving you in the bar. I didn't think you'd be able to get away."

"I would die before I'd turn my back on you. Never doubt it. I am a lot of things, but above and beyond all of them, I am the man who loves you more than life itself."

"What about Sucre?" she whispered. "Won't he come after us?"

He shook his head, his features grim. "He's dead. They're all dead. I killed them." He sat up, his eyes blazing. "They will never hurt you again."

"But your grandmother…" She could never live with herself if she paid for her freedom with an old woman's life.

Jonathan rubbed at his eyes and rested against the pillows. "She passed last week. The doctor only told me this morning. I was on my way to tell you when I found out you'd been taken."

"I'm so sorry," she murmured.

"Don't be. She died of natural causes, and she was ready to go. I did my duty by her, but now I'm free. For the first time in my life, I can do what I want. Be what I want. And all I want is you." He paused. "If you'll have me."

"If I—? Oh baby, wild horses couldn't drag me away."

CHAPTER THIRTY

Brick

Brick only spent one night at the hospital, but it was enough to make him glad he'd ponied up the money for healthcare coverage this year. It really did pay to have insurance. He was surely the only guy on Sucre's crew with a PPO. Of course, there was no crew left anymore.

Olivia hadn't left his side the entire time he was there, and she desperately needed some real sleep. They shared a car to her place, while her sister stayed with Will. Olivia had peeked in on her brother before they left, but he was still heavily medicated and unconscious. She'd return later to give Izzy a break. In the meantime, he'd make sure she got some rest herself.

They stumbled into her shower, and he barely got a chance to enjoy the warm press of her skin before they got out again. The baser part of him wanted to make love to her now, to prove to himself she was whole and his, but her wan face and the circles under her eyes convinced him to take the high road.

They tumbled into her bed without a stitch on, but they both fell asleep in minutes.

He woke up with Olivia's back to his chest, her breast in his hand, and her round ass cozied up next to his cock. His very hard cock. The last time he'd woken up this way, he couldn't have her. This time, it was a different story.

Without jostling his girl, he leaned back to the nightstand and grabbed one of her condoms. After sliding it on, he returned to his position at her back. His hand crept back to her breast.

He trapped her nipple between his middle and index fingers, plucking it gently. Moaning, she arched her back, thrusting her ass against his dick. His hand traveled leisurely down her flat stomach, over her mound to her bare, sweet pussy. She was slick, wet, and ready to take him.

Without prompting, Olivia lifted her leg, sliding it up, over his thigh, clearing the way for him to push himself inside. He'd meant to go slow, to glide his thickness over the sweet valley between her thighs, but his cock drove home on the first thrust.

A groan escaped his throat. Making love to this woman was like nothing he'd ever felt before. It was more than his dick, more than his body; his soul connected with hers. His heart beat for her. If anyone had ever described sex to him that way before, he would have never believed it.

It seemed love made all the difference.

His fingers rubbed at her clit as his cock filled her up. "You feel so good, baby. I'm not gonna last."

She turned her head, giving him her profile. "It's okay," she whispered. "We have all the time in the world."

Her words lit a match to the lust ready to ignite in his veins. Still, he was determined to get her there with him. He rubbed harder, faster, his fingers flying over the center of her pleasure. It wasn't until she cried out, he allowed himself to come with her, her contracting walls heightening his pleasure.

He kept her in his arms when they finished. "I wish I could always wake up this way."

"You can," she sighed sleepily. "All you have to do is ask."

Though Olivia fell back asleep, her words kept him awake far longer.

***

Liv

Will looked so young and fragile lying in his hospital bed, hooked up to IVs and machines. A four-year age difference had seemed so much when Liv was growing up, and when both their parents died, he was the protector and provider all rolled into one.

She could have lost him last night.

Izzy sat vigil in the chair next to his bed. The doctors had moved him to a private room while Liv was home sleeping the day away. She'd bet all the money in her bank account Iz hadn't slept a wink.

"You need to go home and get some dinner and

sleep," she said gently, resting her hand on her sister's shoulder. "It's already six o'clock."

"What if he wakes up?" Izzy rubbed her eyes. "What if he doesn't? What if he needs me and I'm not here?"

As much as she loved both her siblings, there was a special bond between the two of them she didn't always understand. It had been even stronger since Will had gotten out of jail. She didn't begrudge them; she knew there was enough love in their family to go around.

"*I'll* be here, Iz. I know you want to stay, but you're no good to him this way." Deep circles ringed beneath Izzy's eyes, and her hands trembled. "Grab a few hours of shut-eye. Take a shower. Come back in the morning. I promise I'll call you if anything happens during the night."

With one last mournful look at their brother, Izzy stood and trudged out of the room, leaving Liv alone to watch over him.

The wait lasted only a few hours. Around nine, Will's hand twitched. A few minutes later, his eyelids crept open. It took a little while for him to process his surroundings, but once he did, he tugged on the tube taped to his mouth.

"Will, no. The tube's helping you breathe."

His eyes bulged, and he thrashed on the bed, making gagging sounds. She hit the button for the nurse, then laid across her brother's arms and torso, to keep him from hurting himself.

The nurse joined her quickly and pushed what Liv imagined was a sedative into his IV. His thrashing stopped. "It's a normal reaction to waking up with a tube," the nurse assured her. "We've been lowering the ventilator support in the past few hours. We'll be ready to take it out first thing in the morning."

Despite her promise, she didn't bother her sister with an update, though she did call Jonathan, and they talked for a while. He was home in her bed, taking it easy. He still had his own healing left to do.

Part of her wished she could be there with him, but her family needed her now. The only reason Will was even in this condition was because of her. The least she could do was be here for him, no matter what kind of dread this hospital dragged up.

She watched TV and played on her phone before dozing off around midnight. She woke at dawn to the sound of her brother snapping his fingers. He appeared irritated and impatient, but at least he wasn't losing his shit.

"I'm awake," she mumbled, searching for the call button. "Let me call the nurse."

She stepped out as the medical team removed her brother's tube. His hacking cough echoed down the hall. Izzy should've had a fair amount of sleep overnight, so she texted her to return.

She considered taking a seat in the waiting room, but her feet passed the row of chairs and continued toward the elevator. Up to the sixth floor. To oncology.

The space was achingly familiar and worlds apart at the same time. Her cancer treatment felt like a lifetime ago, but if she closed her eyes, she could imagine Carol standing next to her. Laughing with her. Crying with her.

"Tell me it didn't come back."

Liv didn't need to open her eyes to recognize Donna's gravelly voice. The fifty-something nurse had been here with her through it all.

"No. The doc says I'm in complete remission. I'm only here as a visitor." She turned to stare into the woman's warm brown eyes. "Being here takes me back."

Donna tsk'd. "There's no going back, sweetheart. Only forward."

She rubbed at her chest, trying to soothe the growing ache. "Carol used to say the same thing."

"Where do you think she heard it in the first place?"

A smile tugged at her cheeks, but it disappeared as quickly as it came. "I miss her," she whispered.

Donna nodded and grasped Liv's shaking hand in her dark, steady one. "Of course, you do. But you know she wouldn't want you to keep mourning. She'd want you to—"

"Live. I know."

The nurse led her to a cluster of chairs and waited while Liv worked out what she wanted to say.

"Ever since I lost her, I keep thinking of her advice. For a long time, I tried to live the way she would've wanted me to, but I was missing the point, huh?"

Donna held her gaze.

"I'm not supposed to live how she wanted me to. I'm just supposed to—live."

"You were like family to her. You were there

when she needed someone in her life the most." Donna's smile was encouragement, sympathy, and a little bit of pride. "She told me once there's all kinds of ways to love. When it's right, the more you give, the more it fills you up. She loved you like that. You filled her up."

"She did the same for me."

"Then part of her is still here." Donna tapped Liv's chest. "Thanks to you, she lives on."

The ride back down the elevator passed in a bit of a fog, but by the time she returned to the third floor, she felt a clarity she didn't even know she'd been missing. She was about to sit with a cup of vending machine coffee when the nurse waved her in.

Will still appeared miserable, but without the tube, at least he looked like he was going to recover. He wore an oxygen mask, but it comforted her to know every breath he took was his own.

She returned to her seat beside him. "How can I ever thank you?"

Her brother lifted the mask. "I didn't save you." His voice sounded like sandpaper, and he winced, putting the mask back in place.

What the hell difference did it make? "You almost died for me. It all happened so fast. Maybe if you hadn't been there, the bullet would have been meant for me. It was when he was focused on you, I got away."

He breathed heavily but didn't try to talk. She could tell he didn't agree.

"There was nothing else you could have done. Nothing else *anyone* could have done." She squeezed his shoulder. "You were there when I needed you most. I'll never forget that. Neither should you."

Iz slipped in the room and offered her a sympathetic look. Her sister understood Will as well as she did. He would never see himself as the hero he was. He'd always feel like he should have done more.

It was her brother's way. He tried to slay dragons, protect the people he loved. He blamed himself for things he couldn't control, and if his sisters needed it, he wouldn't hesitate to drop himself in a hole so deep, he'd never see the sun.

It never made sense he'd committed a crime and risked a separation from his family. It not only cost him ten years of his life, it cost her and Izzy their big brother. It was a decade he should have spent having fun and building a life. Instead he spent all of his twenties trapped in a nightmare.

Clearing her throat, Izzy joined her family. "You scared me, big brother. Let's never let it happen again."

He lifted the hand with the IV attached and flipped her off. It made her smile, which was probably the entire reason he did it.

Izzy caught the ball and ran with it. "Silent communication? Does this mean you're a captive audience?"

Pulling up a chair, Iz laughed. "You know this means he can't argue, right?"

She met her sister's grin with one of her own. "This is our opportunity to say anything we want, and he can't talk back." She hoped her light tone hid the tremor in her voice as she turned back to Will. "Actually, I was telling him thank you."

She ruffled his hair. "You're the best brother a girl could ask for. On a totally different note, though, maybe now is the best time to tell you...I'm in love with Jonathan."

Will's eyes narrowed, but he didn't try to speak.

"He's starting his life over without all the crazy shit he was mixed up in before, and I'm going to be there with him every step of the way." She hesitated before going on. "You've always supported me in everything. I hope you can support me in this too."

He nodded soberly.

"Okay," Iz said briskly. "Out with you. Go spend some time with your man while I hang out with Mr. Target Practice here."

It was supposed to be funny, but she didn't know if she'd ever be able to laugh about this. "I will. But I need a few more minutes to make sure my big brother is okay."

A man cleared his throat from the doorway. She'd never seen him before.

He had wavy, black hair. It had a few wisps of silver in it, which made it more striking. Just like his face. He possessed Greek heritage, with olive skin, a proud nose and full, dark, eyebrows to complement what appeared to be hazel eyes.

Izzy squirmed in her seat, scanning the man appreciatively, and Liv almost groaned aloud at her reaction. The man was certainly attractive, but her brother was in the hospital for Chrissakes. This was hardly the time to be twitterpated.

"—don't need to worry about rushing back to

work," the man was saying to Will. "Your job is safe. I want you to focus on getting better, okay?"

Will pulled down his mask. "Thanks, Xander."

The gravel in his voice propelled Izzy forward. Handsome or not, Will's visitor needed to let him get his rest. "Stop trying to talk and let your throat heal." She held her hand out to the man her brother had called Xander. "I'm Isobel, Will's sister."

He accepted the handshake. "Xander Karras. I'm the foreman on Will's construction crew."

Izzy hummed in acknowledgement but didn't release her grasp.

Liv cleared her throat, and her sister dropped his hand like a hot potato. "It's really nice of you to come check on Will, but the doctor says he needs some rest."

"Yes, of course." He glanced first at Izzy, then turned back to Will. "I won't keep you any longer. Don't even call me for a few weeks, Will. We're all pulling for you to get better."

He didn't look at Izzy again as he walked out the door, but she never took her eyes off him.

When Will made an exasperated noise, she finally stopped staring at the empty doorframe. A blush crept over her cheeks, as she returned to his bedside and picked up the crossword puzzle on the table beside him as if nothing had happened.

It wasn't often Izzy Turner showed interest in a man, but her reaction to Will's boss was hard to ignore. Liv decided to file the knowledge away and think about it again…if her life ever got back to normal.

***

Brick

It was weird for Brick to hang out with Kane in his apartment. He'd never invited anyone here before, but the things they had to discuss required discretion. Liv was visiting her brother, and this was as good a time as any to wrap up loose ends from their takedown of Sucre's operation.

He couldn't breathe for a second when his friend dropped his old black backpack on the table in front of him.

"You forgot something at the bar the other night, brother."

Honestly, he hadn't thought about the money except as an element in his plan to destroy Sucre. Having it here now opened up a world of possibilities. "I'll never be able to thank you for what you've done for me."

Kane rubbed his beard. "You can start by coming back to work soon. Matt won't say shit, and I hate working in silence."

He barked out a laugh. "Give me another day or two. I *did* get shot. That should buy me a little time off."

"How's Will?"

"Liv says he's awake. Mad as a hornet's nest she got kidnapped, but he's gonna be all right."

"You think he'll ever accept you in his sister's life?"

"I hope so, but he doesn't have a choice. I'm in this for the long haul. I love her, man."

"I've been in love once." Kane's face was stark. "The best and the worst thing that ever happened to me."

One day, he would ask his friend to tell the story, but not today. "The best, yeah. The worst is all behind us."

Now Kane cracked a smile. "Because you fucking killed everybody, brother."

He shrugged. "How's the house on Burgundy Street coming along?"

"It's practically done, but Xander is freaking out because there still isn't a buyer. With all the trouble at the Decatur house, he's really feeling the heat."

"Still no buyer? The house is perfect." He thought about the family he'd pictured building a life there.

"If you like it so much, why don't you buy it yourself?"

"I ca—"

Kane picked up the backpack and threw it at him. "You've got the down payment. You've got the girl." He smirked. "You know it was built by the best. What are you waiting for? The only thing standing in your way is you."

***

Liv

Liv felt like a different person as she walked through the halls of her school Tuesday morning. So much had happened since the end of last week, but everything here somehow stayed the same.

Funny it surprised her.

The doctors were supposed to release Will from the hospital tomorrow. He needed to take the next few weeks off work, but otherwise, his life would be going back to normal too.

The police accepted her version of events from Sunday night. She told them she'd been there to check on her student when some crazy guy with a gun started shooting. Thank God, her brother and her boyfriend had accompanied her to such a terrible neighborhood, or who knows what might have happened.

She'd feared the state of Tre's body would cause a stink, but it looked like the cops had their hands full. When they investigated further, they discovered a macabre cage under Tre's bed. They ordered tests to identify the hair and skin residue they'd scraped out of the hinges. Other sets of DNA analysis might identify the dozen fingers found in a velvet lined box on his nightstand.

In the face of all that, she figured the police were just glad Tre was finally off the streets.

As far as she knew, no one had asked any questions about Sucre or his crew. The police had found no bodies. They all simply disappeared. Including his infamous bruiser Brick Barlow.

Brick was a thing of the past. Now only Jonathan remained.

She floated through the day on autopilot. Ate lunch in the cafeteria. Then froze on the way back to her classroom, when Devon Lowry approached her in the hall.

Books clutched to his chest, he kept a respectable

distance. "Can I talk to you a second, Miss T?"

Her mouth moved, but no sound came out.

"We can talk on the quad," he offered. "Lots of witnesses."

She nodded and followed him to an empty bench outside. His buddy, Justin, grinned and waved like a fool from a strip of grass a few yards away.

"I'm so sorry about what happened to you."

Jonathan had told her how Devon helped him hide their relationship. If it wasn't for Devon's loyalty, things would have played out very differently. It was why he was nowhere near the bar when Jonathan cleaned house. Still, she had never really expected to see the young man again.

"It's not your fault. You tried to warn me to leave it alone."

He nodded gravely. "I did, and I know what happened to you was horrible, but you saved me. If you and Brick hadn't done what you did, I would be working for Sucre the rest of my life. Because of you, I have a chance to get out of here. And if I can take it, I will."

She still wanted a future for him. He'd been out of school for a while, but with some help, he could easily catch up. "I'll help you any way I can."

"You've already helped me more than I can say. I'm just glad I could help you a little too."

***

Jonathan was already at her apartment when Liv got home from school. He swept her into a kiss but pulled away quickly. "Come out to dinner with me tonight."

She took in his jeans and button-down shirt. "Dinner, huh? What should I wear?"

"You look beautiful in anything. It's casual. Wear whatever you like."

Warmed by his words, she took a quick shower and changed into her favorite jeans and a blue pullover top that matched her eyes.

They rode in his truck in comfortable silence, until she recognized their destination.

"Majestic!"

He smiled at her enthusiasm and parked the truck. They walked in hand-in-hand, straight to the booth where they'd sat so months before, making a memory. They didn't even need to check the menu, both ordering the same thing: a Deluxe Burger for Liv and a Majestic Special for her man.

As they ate, she told him about her day and filled him in on what happened with Devon. Being with him here felt so natural. So right.

"I'm going back to work in a few days," he said, dipping a French fry in some ketchup. "The Burgundy Street house is almost finished." Chewing his food, he pulled out his phone and opened his photos. "Take a look."

She flipped through the pictures, slowing down to appreciate the shots of the kitchen. "Those cabinets are beautiful. You guys have really outdone yourselves."

"I want it to be ours."

Her jaw dropped.

"I love you, Olivia Turner. I want to marry you and have kids with you. And I want to live in this

beautiful house with you and grow old together."
He dropped to his knee, and the restaurant went
silent. "Make me the happiest man on this earth.
Marry me."

His broad face was so earnest; his brown eyes,
big and clear. There was nothing she wanted more
than to see his face, kiss his lips, every day for the
rest of her life. "Yes. Yes to the house. Yes to the
kids. Yes to growing old and wrinkly together. I
would love to marry you." As one, they rose to their
feet, and he spun her in a quick circle next to the
booth.

The restaurant broke out in cheers.

"Only one condition," she whispered in his ear.
He froze. "You've got to give me a preview of our
wedding night as soon as we get home."

He relaxed and nipped at her shoulder. "Then
we'd better get out of here right now. You're in for
a long night."

CHAPTER THIRTY-ONE

Brick

He didn't understand at first why his grandmother had wanted her ashes scattered at Piedmont Park. Not until he picked up her urn at Magnolia Green, and an elderly woman with a walker stopped him in the residents' hall. He didn't know her name, but he recognized her from the music room where he often found his grandmother.

"You're Sylvie's boy, right?"

He nodded. "Yes ma'am. I'm Br—Jonathan, her grandson."

The woman gestured for him to follow her toward the day room. "She talked about you, you know? All the time. Told everybody about your construction job and bragged on the flowers you brought her…and the treats."

When they arrived in the common area, he held out his arm to help her settle in a chair. He took the seat next to her and waited for her to continue.

"Sylvie was my best friend. She had a lot of regrets. She talked about them too, dictated the letter to me for you." That solved one mystery. "One thing she was really worried about was whether you'd understand why she wanted you to take her to Piedmont Park."

"I'm sorry, ma'am. Maybe I should, but I don't."

The woman nodded knowingly. "You were only a boy. It was before your father died, one day he wasn't too far gone with the drugs. Sylvie said the three of you went out to the lake and had a picnic. She said your mama had bought you this little pocket racer the week before, and you ran all around with it."

He wracked his brain for some trace of the memory as the lady continued. "It wasn't really an extraordinary day by most people's standards. Sylvie cherished the memory because it was the closest she says y'all ever came to something normal. Your mom couldn't go with you because she was working, but she packed the picnic with whatever she could find. Cheese sandwiches. Dill pickles. And a big bowl of Jell-O."

"With three spoons," he whispered. The memory still wasn't entirely clear, but he had flashes now of the day at the parl. "I think there was a kite."

"That's right. Someone who had been there before you left it on the ground because it was torn. You spent hours with it, though, determined to make it fly. The afternoon she died, she was still thinking about that day, wishing she could've given you more like it."

356

"It helps to know she wanted to. I wish she would've told me."

"In the end, I think she wished she had too."

***

Olivia came with him to set Grandma's ashes free at the park. After he told her the story from the nursing home, she insisted on packing them a picnic with grilled cheese sandwiches, dill pickles, and Jell-O. She even packed three spoons.

One for Grandma, she'd said.

He didn't remember any more of that day, but the snippets he recalled at Magnolia Green gave him some comfort.

It was Liv's idea to bring a kite with them. Together, they flew it beside the water, after they released Grandma's ashes into the wind.

"Maybe we'll bring our children here one day," she mused.

For a moment, he allowed himself to fantasize about building a family with her. A beautiful, blond pixie of a little girl. A son with his dark hair and her sparkling eyes.

He would teach them how to play ball. He'd go to their school plays. He would make them feel safe.

They'd never have to fly someone else's discarded kite. Or cling to shards of broken memories to know someone loved them.

"I'd rather bring them to the Majestic," he whispered. "All the best memories are built there."

EPILOGUE

Liv

"I'm sorry the entire crew couldn't make it." Liv surveyed her dining room table now bursting with family and friends helping them celebrate the holiday. "We might have had to be creative with seating, but I hope they know they're welcome."

Jonathan lifted her hand and kissed the back. "Cy has a thing with the guys in his old Ranger unit, and Matt is with his kid. They're with people who care about them, don't worry."

He knew her so well.

She had never been so happy in her life. Now she wanted to spread her joy to everyone around her.

She and Jonathan had only been in the new house for two weeks, but it already felt like home. Carol's framed Dare to Dream list hung on the wall in their bedroom, now with red checkmarks made next to the last two entries.

They'd had a quiet Thanksgiving at Izzy's and it was lovely, even though Will was still recovering from his gunshot. Now he was almost back to his normal self, she was determined to do Christmas the way she remembered it from her childhood: loud, crowded, and filled with laughter.

Izzy helped her cook a huge turkey with a sweet and savory cornbread stuffing. They argued over how much celery to use, the same as when they were kids. Beth, a new friend she'd made at the gym, brought macaroni and cheese.

Kane brought corn on the cob still in the packaging from KFC. He shrugged as he handed it over. "Hey, sweetheart, corn is corn." He was right. It tasted fine.

Jonathan's boss, Xander, brought a huge Greek salad topped with red onions and feta cheese. His young assistant Robby came with him, carrying two big pitchers of iced tea.

It was perfect.

She stood to clear the table, but Jonathan blocked her path and pushed her back down to her seat. "What are you doing?" she giggled. "Does this mean you're in charge of the clean-up?"

His smile was soft. "I'm a little late. I should have had this ready when I asked you to marry me." He held up a black velvet ring box. "But you don't think I'm gonna miss giving you a way to let the whole world know you're mine."

Tears filled her eyes as he opened the box to reveal a familiar braided gold band and a solitaire diamond engagement ring. "It's perfect, but how—"

"It was your mom's." He spoke quietly. "Your sister's been saving it for you since she died."

A short nod from Iz confirmed his words. Tears

tracked down her face as her future husband slid the sparkling ring on her finger. The braided gold ring she'd given him months ago—the one modeled after the wedding band—never left his pinkie.

"I love it." She rose, tugging him to his feet, and buried herself in his arms. The table erupted in cheers and catcalls, but she kept her focus on the man in front of her. "And I love you. Now, we'd better get on with planning this wedding if it's going to happen before the baby is born."

Jonathan stopped breathing and grabbed the back of a chair for support. "You're—"

"Pregnant? Not yet." She wrapped her fingers around the front of his shirt and whispered. "But once all these people get out of here, we can get working to change that." The doctor had given her a clean bill of health at her check-up last week and the green light to start a family if she wanted.

A whoop went up from Kane at the end of the table. "Sounds like a good thing no one brought dessert."

"Oh, I'm having dessert," Jonathan growled. He lifted her into his arms and started for the stairs. "Merry Christmas. You guys can all let yourselves out."

Want to read the next installment of the
Cooper Construction Series

SNEAK PEEK

CHAPTER ONE

Amanda

Nathan's fingers dug into the tender skin of Amanda's inner arm. "How many times do I have to tell you? Fundraisers for my office are not opportunities for you to run your mouth."

She clenched her jaw against the urge to tell him to fuck himself.

"Do you have any idea how many women would give their eye-teeth to be in your shoes?" he hissed, tightening the pressure of his grip.

More than she could count, most likely. In his late thirties, society considered Nathan Shaw one of Atlanta's most eligible bachelors—handsome, rich, and from a political powerhouse family as old as time. His perfectly styled blond hair framed an aristocratic pale face with blue eyes and expertly arched brows. He never left his penthouse dressed in anything less than befit his station. The man was practically Georgia royalty.

He was also an arrogant, entitled bastard.

"Actually, Abe," he mocked her voice in a high falsetto, "I think the money would be better spent on a domestic abuse shelter." He shook her so hard her teeth clacked together. "We might as well flush it down the toilet."

"He asked my opinion," she gritted, her head beginning to ache.

Nathan slammed her against the wall, the back of her skull bouncing off the plaster. "*My* opinion is *your* opinion, and you damn well know it."

He let go of her, and she slid to the floor. Hanging his tuxedo jacket on the back of one of the tall chairs he kept tucked under the island in his high-end kitchen, he appeared to be done punishing her.

Her instincts screamed otherwise. She curled herself into a ball, protecting her head, as a vicious kick landed to her lower back.

"If you are going to be at my side, you will behave as your breeding should dictate." His voice no longer betrayed his anger. He locked it down, replacing it with a honeyed cadence of practiced ease. Measured. Controlled. "Do I make myself clear?"

Only one answer would allow her an escape from this. She lifted her head. "Yes," she murmured.

He graced her with a serpent's smile. "Excellent. Now get off the floor. You'll ruin your dress."

Her hindbrain shouted to scoot away from his outstretched hand, but the rejection might set his blood boiling all over again. She fought her instincts and wrapped her fingers around his.

He pulled her to unsteady feet, then released her hand. His fingers tugged on the strands of dark red hair escaping the simple chignon her stylist had created. "Your hair looks all tumbled, pet."

Fuck.

Slowly, he unpinned the rest of her locks, the look on his face growing heated. By the time all her hair rested thick on her shoulders, she could make out the tent in his pants.

She swallowed back the bile burning her throat.

"Gorgeous," he said huskily. "I want to unwrap you."

Before she could move away, he yanked down the side-zipper on her shimmering strapless silver gown. It pooled on the floor at her feet.

So much for his concern about it getting ruined.

The cool kiss of air against her exposed skin made her shiver. All she wore now were her high heels and the tiny scrap of black lace masquerading as underwear.

Getting naked with him was never part of the deal. She bent quickly to grasp the expensive fabric and pull it up. It got as high as her waist before he locked his hand around her wrist.

"I think you need to be reminded who wears the pants in this relationship." His voice dipped lower. "Perhaps what you really need is for me to take what I want and fuck your sweet ass. Maybe *that* will teach you your place."

Gritting her teeth, she shook off the embarrassment of standing there half naked. "No."

He probably could have forced her. Obviously,

too many highballs had him crossing lines he'd only skirted in the past. There had been times he'd squeezed her arm too hard or pushed her away with a little too much force, but he'd never hurt her the way he had tonight.

Still, she'd been firm in the past declining any invitations into his bed. Her resolve wouldn't change now. Or ever.

"Let me go." She squared her jaw. "Unless you're willing to do this against my will."

A snarl twisted his face, and he clenched her wrist tighter. She stopped breathing, a cold sweat dotting the curve of her back.

Maybe she'd miscalculated. A dozen worst-case scenarios shuffled through her head. Nathan breaking her wrist. Breaking her arm. Forcing himself inside her.

Should she scream? Run?

Before she could even form a plan in her head, he blanked his expression, then let her go. "You know me better than that." He gave her his back and moved languidly toward his bedroom. "I'm headed to bed. Don't forget to leave the dress."

She didn't breathe until he left the room. Shaking all over, she kicked off the heels still binding her feet, then slid the dress off completely and draped it over Nathan's jacket. It wasn't hers to take home, just a rental he'd made for the night.

Gulping in lungfuls of air, she unzipped the small duffel bag on the counter. She shoved her head into the soft T-shirt, her arms getting caught for a moment before she could cover herself completely. She couldn't get her sweatpants and shoes on fast enough. The idea of being naked and vulnerable with him so nearby made her stomach turn.

God, she hated this place. Hated the man who lived here.

And hated her father for putting her in this fucking mess to begin with.

Closing the door gently behind her, she speed-walked the hall to the elevator from Nathan's penthouse. Her tennis shoes squeaked on the marble floor.

The doorman nodded politely and called the valet for her car. If he noticed the moisture in her eyes or the darkening skin at her wrists, he studiously ignored it.

Nathan had only tried to get her in bed once before, and at the time, he'd accepted her demure rejection with a profession of old fashion values. It fit with his image, even if his southern charm was nothing more than lip service.

Her own condo beckoned from just a few miles away, and though the traffic in Atlanta was usually insufferable, it would be an easy drive this late at night.

She caught sight of a shooting star as she slipped into the driver's seat, and misery thumped harder against her chest.

Her life hadn't always been like this.

There was a time she knew what it was to be loved.

It was a mistake thinking about it. Knowing how much better it could be, knowing she'd never have it again, only made a bad situation worse.

***

13 years ago

July

"Deny it all you want, Mandy, but I know you're only wearing that tiny little dress to drive me crazy."

Kane's dark eyes gleamed as he dragged his gaze over her body. Stalking toward her in long strides, he approached from the parking lot where his brother had dropped him off. His fingers flexed, as though he wanted to touch her, but he held back.

Her blood heated with his regard, and giddy laughter bubbled with the nickname he'd given her. "I'm not denying anything." Tilting her head, she fluttered her lashes. "What other reason could there be?"

She gestured for him to step closer to the grass next to the fountain. She'd arrived at Grant Park a full fifteen minutes ahead of their date so she'd have time to set the scene, though the lush clearing and the water feature provided almost ready-made romance. Her heart beat double-time as he closed the remaining distance between them.

Hello, gorgeous.

Kane Hale had nothing in common with the buttoned-up snobs her father always picked out for her, which was probably part of the attraction. Frays peeked from the hem of his worn jeans, and his Green Day T-shirt hugged his wiry frame.

He wrapped his arms around her waist and lifted

her off the ground before fitting his mouth against hers. Even after three months together, his kisses heated her blood.

Butterflies danced a riot in her stomach as she ran her hand over his damp close-cropped brown hair, then gripped his broad shoulders. He smelled faintly of shaving cream, and her fingertips fluttered over the smooth skin of his cheek.

His tongue swept the seam of her mouth, and she opened eagerly with a small sigh.

She could have forgotten they were in the middle of a popular park if a small dog hadn't started yapping at her feet. Her eyes flew open as a gray-haired woman pulled on the animal's leash and harrumphed, presumably at their very enthusiastic, very public display of affection.

Kane chuckled and took a step back. "See what you did? That old lady was practically scandalized." Laughter danced in his eyes, and her heart swelled fuller than ever.

She ran her fingers over her tingling bottom lip. "At least I know I won't be the only one staying up tonight reliving our kiss."

He stroked her hair and tipped his forehead to hers. "You were never going to be the only one. I'll be thinking about it all night."

It would be so easy to fall into his arms again, but too much distraction would torpedo all her careful planning. Squeezing her eyes shut for fortitude, she broke contact and knelt on the blanket with the picnic basket. Shadows edged the nearby trees, signaling the transition from dusk to dark. The park would be closing soon, but she'd timed their meal to avoid as much of the Georgia summer heat as possible. Even at seven-thirty, though, the thin cotton of her dress stuck to her skin, and she knew her forehead probably glistened with perspiration.

At least she didn't have any makeup to melt off. Kane always made it a point to tell her she was beautiful without it.

"Sit with me. Eat one of these damn hot dogs." She patted the ground beside her. "You know I only packed them for you."

Kane settled on the blanket, but they didn't eat right away. They held hands and watched lightning bugs flit around the trees and laughed at the mom chasing a toddler making a bee-line to the water.

Eventually, Kane fished his foil-wrapped treasure out of the basket. "One day I'm going to get you to try one. It's positively un-American you won't eat a hot dog."

Shaking her head emphatically, she swallowed the bite she'd taken from her PB&J. All the food she'd packed had been simple fare; cooking wasn't one of her strengths. "I may be crazy about you, but I'm not crazy. Do you have any idea what's in those things?" She shuddered.

"You're crazy about me?" He waggled his eyebrows and finished the second half of his hot dog in one bite.

Her face heated. A smartass quip hovered on her lips, but she swallowed it down and went with the simple truth. "Yeah."

His smile widened with her quiet admission, and he ran his hand up the side of her arm. "How crazy are we talking about?" he teased gently.

"Somewhere between Nick Nolte's mugshot and Tom Cruise jumping on the sofa with Oprah."

He pursed his lips in mock concern. "Pretty crazy, then." His fingers snaked around the column of her neck, and he pulled her closer, his breath hot on her skin. "It's a good thing I'm every bit as crazy about you."

She leaned forward and brushed his lips with hers. The desire shooting deep into her core felt positively audacious in public. When she pulled away, his stare locked on her face.

"Let's get out of here," he whispered. "I need to be alone with you."

Great minds think alike.

A make-out session in her backseat would not only scratch her itch, but it would provide the perfect inspiration for some toe-curling dreams in the nights to come.

Nodding, she grabbed the picnic basket while Kane snatched the blanket from the ground. Together, they speed-walked to her car.

She stopped short when he grabbed her shoulder.

"Look. A shooting star. Make a wish."

Glancing up, she caught the tail end of the light blazing across the sky.

I wish Kane Hale would be my first. She blinked. *And my last.*

"What did you wish for, baby?" He tucked her hair behind her ear. "I wished nothing will ever come between us."

She slapped his shoulder. "No. If you say it out loud, it won't come true."

Taking the picnic basket from her hand, Kane

put it in the trunk, then laced his fingers with hers. "Hush. We control our fate. Not luck. Not the stars. So, you'd better get used to this face, because it's never going to change, and there is nothing in this world that's going to take me away from your side."

She hesitated. "What about the club?"

His father wouldn't stop pushing for Kane to join the MC where he was a founding member. Not only were his parents deep in the life, his brother, Scott, was too.

As much as she adored Kane, she wanted no part of his world. Those guys treated women like crap. Even the "old ladies" like Kane's mom were second-class citizens, considered barely a step above talking blow-up dolls.

The guys she'd met from the crew? Rude, crass, and violent. Probably criminals. And they were Kane's family.

"I'm not going to join. I told you. I've never wanted that kind of life." He kissed her hand. "I want a real relationship. I want a home and a job and kids who aren't embarrassed by their dad when he comes to their school to pick them up."

He said all the things she wanted to hear, but based on everything he'd told her before, she knew rejecting the club could drive a wedge between him and his family he may never overcome.

"I don't want you to lose your parents or your brother and resent me one day for it."

"It's never going to happen. With you or without you, I'm never going to join." His voice hardened with resolve. "I promise, Mandy. As long as I live, I will never be part of my family's MC."

***

Kane

Present Day

Blood and gore stuck to Kane's boots as he tromped through what was once the city's most notorious drug den. Now it bore the hallmarks of a slaughterhouse. Bodies littered the floor, all members of the crew once run by Sucre de la Cruz.

All dead at the hands of the Skulls MC.

His gaze met his brother's across the dimly lit room. Scott's tongue peeked out of his toothy grin. No doubt, he reveled in the carnage.

Kane only came for his friend, Brick. Well, Brick and the ten thousand dollars the man had promised the MC to help him take out his drug dealer boss and the bastard's crew. The violence didn't excite Kane like it did Scott. He considered it a necessary evil to protect his club.

They were his family.

When everyone else had started killing, his job had been to hold a weapon at the drug lord's head, so the piece of shit could watch his empire crumble before his eyes.

He found it immensely satisfying. De la Cruz and his organization had been a stain on Atlanta for years. The guy ruled through violence, fear, and death. Now his reign was over. Not only did Kane have a hand in the takedown, he did his part without taking a single life.

His brothers were another story. They ripped

through Sucre's men like they were made of tissue paper, and they loved every second of it. All the crazed smiles and laughter would have given it away even before they'd raided the bar and started toasting with tequila shots.

In his years with the club, Kane had seen plenty of violence up close and personal, but he'd never had to kill anyone. Maybe it was a cop-out, but he didn't want to start a body count now.

He swiped one of the tarps piled right inside the front door and dropped it next to a body. Nobody could skip clean-up.

Holding his breath against the stench of viscera and human waste, he grabbed the dead man's arm and slid him onto the black sheet of plastic. He had to plant one foot on the tarp to keep it in place. Stealing a quick gulp of air through his mouth, he knelt and rolled the man up like a burrito. Blood coated his hands and speckled up his arms over his sleeves of tattoos.

He climbed to his feet to repeat the process with the next body. There were about forty to dispose of and only fourteen brothers to get the job done.

Cue Ball lugged each drug-dealer-burrito to the pickup parked out front. Once they were all loaded up, the brothers would take them to Sucre's own dump-spot, the one Brick had told them about, ready-made with barrels of sulfuric acid. Not only was it convenient, but he could appreciate the poetic justice in it.

A playful slap landed on his shoulder as he finished wrapping his third body. "Fuckin-A, man. You really came through with this job tonight. We needed this money in a major fucking way."

Scott didn't exaggerate. Ten thousand bucks was less than a lot of crews would demand for a job like this, but right now they needed it like water in the desert. The club hadn't been making the same kind of cash it once had. Sure, they brought in enough to get by, but the profits from running guns declined more every year. The demand was still there, but the weapons were easier to come by these days. Buyers weren't willing to pay as much for a middleman anymore.

Most of the guys made ends meet with a second job. Scott worked on cars. Kane did construction.

He didn't mind his day job. In fact, he preferred it. He never had to wash blood off his hands after a day nailing up sheetrock.

"I'm glad to do it." The old scar on Kane's cheek tugged when he smiled. Even at thirty-two years old, it felt good to have Scott's approval. He loved his brother, even though they didn't always see eye to eye.

He gripped the backpack Brick had left behind after the massacre was done. No telling what Scott would do if he suspected there was another forty thousand dollars in arm's reach. "Are you heading out with Cue Ball or staying here to bleach the place down?"

"Are you serious?" Scott barked out a laugh. "You think I'd miss a chance to drop bodies in vats of acid, so I could stay here and play housemaid? Fuck you, man." He chuckled as he walked toward the front door.

Kane pulled the elastic from his hair and

gathered all the stray pieces back into a ponytail at the back of his neck, then surveyed the bar. All the bodies were gone, but it would take hours to mop up all this blood. Half a dozen members of the crew had left with Scott to dispose of the bodies, while the other half of the team stayed behind to manage the mess.

It was after midnight by the time they'd erased the evidence of the massacre. As much as he wanted to go home, he had to head back to the clubhouse to meet up with the disposal team and divvy up the money they'd made tonight.

He gave his hands a final wash in the sink behind the bar before he strapped on his helmet and settled on his bike. A Harley Davidson Dyna Super Glide Sport. Black, it was only a few years old with a matte finish.

The engine purred to life, and the rides around him did the same, creating a humming chorus. Kane pulled onto the dark street, and the others followed in a single file line before sliding into a staggered riding formation.

Anemic yellow light shone through the windows of the wood-framed clubhouse when they arrived. Without the sun to illuminate the outside, shadows hid the fading paint and sagging shutters, which both betrayed its age.

All curves in a nearly indecent little black dress, Charlene greeted him at the door the minute he walked in. She wrapped herself around him like a cheap suit, all itchy and ill-fitting. The smell of nicotine wafted off her skin. It even overpowered the bleach and stink of the night still clinging to him from the job.

"I was starting to worry about you, baby." She stuck out her painted bottom lip in an exaggerated pout and twirled a strand of bleached blond hair around her finger. "I've been here all night."

"I had a job." The words came out gruffly, but he didn't have it in him to pretend he cared.

Unfazed, she cupped his jaw with her hand. "It's cool, you—" Her nose wrinkled as she peered at his beard. Using her middle finger and thumb, she pulled something from the unruly coarse hair on his face.

Oh, Christ. Was that a bone shard?

His stomach roiled, and he pushed her away. "Go home, Char."

"But—"

"Go. Home."

He didn't bother to watch her long enough to see if she listened. In truth, he didn't care where she went, as long as he didn't have to deal with her. Rubbing the back of his neck, he trudged to the back room where they held all club business, the room they called the chapel. He was the last to arrive. All but two of the other fifteen chairs were taken. They were situated along an oblong table, the seat at the far end noticeably vacant.

The guys cheered at his arrival. Some clapped; others knocked on the worn wooden table.

Forcing his burning eyes to acknowledge his brothers, he dropped heavily into his chair to the left of the president's position. "C'mon now, y'all did the work too. We all earned it."

"But you brought in the business." The booming

voice from the door prompted every man in the room to scramble to his feet, even Kane, who wobbled a little when the blood rushed from his head. "I'm proud of you, son."

Despite his sixty years and decades of hard living, Malcolm Hale still cut an impressive figure. He matched Kane's six feet, one inch, and probably came close to his two hundred pounds of muscle. Even though he didn't ride often with the MC, he started the club with his brother, Wes, and as president demanded the respect he considered his due. He also demanded his sons call him Malcolm, just like everyone else did.

Stepping to the head of the table, the man lifted the stack of hundred-dollar bills already waiting in the center. "Ten thousand?"

It wasn't really a question, so Kane stood silent.

Malcolm cracked a wicked smile, a lot like the one Scott flashed in the middle of the bloody bar. "To take down Sucre de la Cruz, it would have almost been worth doing it for free. We helped make that fucker a king. I'll bet he never thought we could break him just as easily." Amid catcalls and cheers, he dropped the money back to the table. "Five hundred dollars a man. Twenty-five hundred for the club. Now, get the fuck out of here so I can get myself a blow job."

Biting back a sigh, Kane swiped his share and made his exit quickly. There was no telling if Malcolm's dick would be getting sucked by Kane's mom or some piece of club property tonight. Neither possibility was one he wanted to think about.

He only had to drag himself a few blocks to his apartment, and he couldn't wait to get inside to close the door on this long and nasty day.

Too bad he couldn't close the door on this life. As deeply as he loved his brothers, the way they lived turned his stomach sometimes.

Closing the distance to his private space on his Harley, he kicked off his boots on the porch before heading inside. No need to track DNA evidence through his home. The blood had dried, but it could still mark up his carpet.

He stopped in the bathroom first, hiding Brick's bag of cash under the sink. Then, leaving his filthy clothes in a pile on the floor, he climbed into the shower and tipped his head forward into the spray. The hot stream sluiced through his hair, and the water at his feet threaded with the rust-colored remnants of his violent night. Once it ran clear, he grabbed the soap and made quick work of his body.

He'd shower again in the morning—right after he bagged up his clothes to burn them—but he wouldn't be able to sleep covered in death. Satisfied he was clean enough, he squeezed the water from his hair and toweled off, then padded naked to his bedroom.

Charlene was spread out nude on his king-sized bed. When he'd told her to go home, he meant for her to go to *her* home, not his. He didn't invite any women into his private space. Ever.

She had some fucking nerve.

Thank fuck she was asleep. He'd lay next to Charles Manson if it meant getting some rest. Sliding beneath the sheets, he gave the woman his back.

How the hell did she get in here?

He sure as fuck never gave her a key. Charlene was not his old lady, and he'd never pretended otherwise. He wasn't interested in calling any woman his own. He'd tried it once and had never regretted anything more.

A flash of dark red hair and sea-green eyes scratched at the back of his brain, but like he'd done hundreds of times before, he shoved the memories down, squeezed his eyes shut, and fell into dreamless sleep.

KANE

COOPER CONSTRUCTION SERIES
BOOK 2

BY JEN DAVIS

https://www.amazon.com/Kane-Cooper-Construction-Book-2-ebook/dp/B07MY7BZZ2

Acknowledgements

So many people helped make this book possible with their amazing feedback and support. Thank you, Joanna, my first reader and friend for encouraging me, even as you worked on your own stories. Thanks to my reviewing crew, Shelly, Ronelle, Elle, and Debz for giving me input—as well as my Twitter author pals, Allison and Luna…and everyone who beta read for me.

Big love to Sara and Brighton for seeing something worthwhile in this book, even though it's a bit off the beaten path. And thank you, Christina and Lydia, for your enthusiasm and unflagging belief in my words.

I couldn't have done it without you guys.

About the Author

Jen started her love affair with romance novels, first as a reader, then as a reviewer and blogger. She launched the Red Hot Books blog in 2010 and jumped into Book Twitter shortly after.

She wrote her first books, a YA/NA trilogy under another name back in 2016. But Brick is her first foray into Adult Contemporary Romance.

Jen is happily married to her high school sweetheart. Together, they're raising two kids, a cat, and a dog who is afraid of his own shadow.

She spends her days working as television journalist and her nights curled up with a good book.

Facebook:
https://www.facebook.com/jen.davis.author

Twitter:
http://twitter.com/redhotbooks

Website:
http://jendavis.net/

Join our Reader Group on Facebook and don't miss out on meeting our authors and entering epic giveaways!

Limitless Reading

Where reading a book
is your first step to becoming
limitless...

LIMITLESS PUBLISHING *Reader Group*

Join today! *"Where reading a book is your first step to becoming limitless..."*

https://www.facebook.com/groups/Limitless Reading/